DARK SIGNAL

FORGE BOOKS BY SHANNON BAKER

Stripped Bare

Dark Signal

DARK SIGNAL

SHANNON BAKER

A TOM DOHERTY ASSOCIATES BOOK

NEW YORK

This is a work of fiction. All of the characters, organizations, and events portrayed in this novel are either products of the author's imagination or are used fictitiously.

DARK SIGNAL

A Forge Book
Published by Tom Doherty Associates
175 Fifth Avenue
New York, NY 10010

www.tor-forge.com

Forge® is a registered trademark of Macmillan Publishing Group, LLC.

ISBN 978-0-7653-8547-5 (hardcover)
ISBN 978-0-7653-8627-4 (ebook)

The Library of Congress Cataloging-in-Publication Data is available upon request.

Our books may be purchased in bulk for promotional, educational, or business use. Please contact your local bookseller or the Macmillan Corporate and Premium Sales Department at 1-800-221-7945, extension 5442, or by email at MacmillanSpecialMarkets@macmillan.com.

First Edition: October 2017

Printed in the United States of America

0 9 8 7 6 5 4 3 2 1

To the Furmanator
And all the crews riding the BNSF rails

And to Walt Leser
Who has been there from before the beginning

ACKNOWLEDGMENTS

I'm grateful to everyone who makes it possible for me to keep hanging out in Kate's world. First and foremost, to the readers who found Kate, and Nora Abbott, before that. You'll never know how much I love you for letting me tell my stories.

Dave Pier and Mike Webb drank beer and brainstormed with me about how and why someone would be murdered on the railroad. Thank you for the fun, if somewhat disturbing, afternoon.

Thank you to Smith, who provided sanctuary and helped me stave off insanity. I couldn't, and actually never have, written a book without the brainstorming of Janet Fogg, and that's a debt I can never repay. Hats off to Alan Larson, for the Writers' Book Club and ongoing education. I owe big thanks to Dru Ann Love for encouragement, and Terri Bischoff for talking me off the ledge, over and over and over.

To Jess Lourey, in deep gratitude, for your example of courage and daring, and who kept me giggling on the Lourey/Baker Double Booked Blog Tour. Road trips are always more fun with friends!

To Samantha Jo Lien at Roger Charlie, for helping get the word out about Kate. A special thank-you to Jessica Morrell, for her expertise and guidance.

Thank you to my agent, Marlene Stringer, who knows everything.

Kristin Sevick, editor extraordinaire, thanks for shepherding Kate and me to the greenest pastures. And to Bess Cozby, Carrie Watterson, and all the gang at Forge, a hearty thank-you for making me look better than I really am!

A big hug to Sheriff Shawn Hebbert, who doesn't seem to mind my questions about cops and criminals, cars and guns, and the workings of a one-man county sheriff's office.

Thank you to Sharon Connealy, not only for reminding me about life in the Nebraska Sandhills and providing breathtaking photos for my website, but for sharing more than thirty years of friendship. We've lived some life in all that time, haven't we?

To Joslyn and Erin, the best friends a mother can have, thanks for being so remarkable.

And to Dave, who had so many ideas about how to kill someone on a train it was a shame I could use only one, you make everything possible.

DARK SIGNAL

1

Sometimes, you've got no choice in life but to jump off the cliff. I'd jumped and landed on a crumbling ledge, clutching a root to keep from falling.

That's why I stood sandwiched between Betty Paxton and Ethel Bender in the drafty commissioner's meeting room at the Grand County courthouse. I raised my right hand and swore away my next four years.

The whiny strains of country music jangled from the radio in the treasurer's office, one door down. Clete Rasmussen, commissioner since the days of Moses, continued addressing us in his booming, if pained, voice. "I will not advocate nor become a member of any political party or organization that advocates the overthrow of the government of the United States or of this state by force or violence. So help me God."

My mumbled "I do" mixed with that of Betty and Ethel.

Betty's spiked hair was probably cutting edge when she first sported the do twenty years ago. Now it reminded me of Bart Simpson. She tossed off a smile. "Good to have you aboard."

With her scowl and thin lips that looked like someone drew them with a pencil, blue-haired Ethel let out a sigh like a deflating tire.

Betty and Ethel exited the room, leaving me and Clete alone.

This was my first, and hopefully only, pledge to protect and serve the good people of Hodgekiss, Nebraska, and the four widely spread communities that populate the sprawling ranch country of Grand County, where cattle outnumber people by more than fifty to one.

I adjusted the stiff brown shirt I'd washed several times to soften and smoothed my hands down my hips, knowing the twill uniform pants didn't flatter my figure. Who cares?

Clete clapped his hands. "That about does it."

The bruising purple of evening showed outside the two-foot-high windows that ran along the top of the meeting room. A clear night like this wouldn't temper January's knife-cold. It's the kind of night the cows huddle in the corner of the pasture, pressed close together to share warmth.

I didn't need to worry about cows anymore. Later tonight, with wool socks keeping my toes toasty, flannel pajama pants, and long-sleeve T-shirt, I'd snuggle under a down comforter. Alone.

Clete cleared his throat, a sound like thunder in a box canyon. He lifted a cardboard carton from the hulking desk in the corner. "Here's the sheriff stuff. Ted dropped it off this afternoon."

For Ted—the previous sheriff and my husband of eight years and ex-husband of nine months—giving up the tools of the office would have been a knife in his heart. Too bad.

Clete rested the box in my open arms. "There's the inventory sheet you need to fill out and sign, along with the phone and, uh . . ."

"The gun." I finished for him. Taking that gun off his hip must have felt to Ted like disrobing in public. In truth, I probably hated that exchange more than he did. Guns and I didn't have a love relationship.

"In for a penny, in for a pound," Dad always said, so I'd better open my heart to the .40 caliber Smith and Wesson. Tomorrow.

The phone in the box let out a chirp so familiar to me, yet one I hadn't heard in nine months. It took a moment to convince myself it wasn't Ted's phone, but the sheriff's phone. And I was the sheriff.

I set the box on the conference table and pulled the phone out, punching it on. "Sheriff's phone." I winced. That's how I used to answer it when I was Ted's wife and he was sheriff.

"Whew."

"Sarah?" I recognized the voice of my best friend and sister-in-law.

She let out a breath of relief. "You didn't answer your phone, so I took a chance you'd already got this one. I didn't want to talk to Ted."

I glanced at Clete, who eyed me with irritation. Or indigestion. With Clete, it was hard to tell. Sarah wasn't likely to call me to chat, so I stepped into the hall. "What's up?"

She huffed into the phone. "Damn, it's freakin' freezing! Why did you have to be born in January?"

Oh no. My stomach sank. "Tell me it's not."

She gave an irritated sigh. "It is. Louise planned a surprise party at your parents' house. We're pulling up now."

My brother Robert hollered in the background, "Surprise!"

I hated that my older sister Louise was using my birthday as an excuse to get a goodly portion of the eight Fox kids together. I groaned. "Dad and Louise are the only ones who like these things."

Sarah groaned along with me. "I feel ya. Looks like your dad is late. His pickup isn't here, but according to Louise, he was supposed to be back an hour ago."

You couldn't count on the railroad. Dad had worked for BNSF for close to forty years. We were all used to his unpredictable schedule. "Thanks for the heads up."

"Consider it my birthday present to you. Now get your butt over here. Don't leave me alone with these crazy people."

I laughed. "You had a choice whether to join this family and I warned you."

"We love them, though." Her voice quavered as if she ran. "Just hurry, because, you know, sometimes love isn't enough."

I pocketed the phone and went back to the commissioner's room. Some kind of Cinderella midnight magic happened at the Grand County courthouse at the stroke of five. By the time I got off the phone, every sign of life had vanished. Even my breathing seemed to echo in the now-empty building. I didn't spare more than a single thought for hundred-year-old ghosts before grabbing my new brown sheriff's coat, complete with patch featuring a windmill in a pasture.

I hesitated and gave myself a big mental push to settle my gun into my holster. Like a puppy with his first collar. Eventually I'd get used to it.

I clattered down the wide steps that led to the back door of the courthouse, not wanting to head home to a house filled with well-meaning but boisterous family. My breath retreated down my throat at the first intake of the frigid night air. The cold made me cough, and my nose hair stuck together. I retrieved Thinsulate ski gloves from my pocket one split second before my fingers froze and shattered.

I climbed into the cruiser and jammed the keys in the ignition to fire her up. The key turned, and headlights blasted, the radio blared, wipers lashed across the windshield, and I yelped. With a flash of adrenaline, I slapped at switches, frantic to turn off the chaos, and in the confusion hit the toggles near my right elbow, and the siren screamed and light bar sprang to life.

Smack, whap, punch. The noise and lights died and I spent a second slowing my heart rate. Eight brothers and sisters meant I was no novice with practical jokes, but I hadn't expected this petty mischief from Ted. In the official cop car.

Wincing in anticipation of some other prank, I slipped the gear shift into drive. The Charger's heat blasted on before my headlights brushed the street. I caught a whiff of Irish Spring overlaid with a musky, man scent. Ted. He was all over this car. Tomorrow I'd buy one of those pine tree deodorizers.

The phone rang again. I considered not answering it, assuming if Sarah thought to call me on the sheriff's number, other brothers or sisters would figure it out, too. But it was the official number, and I'd best get used to responding.

This time, though, I was ready with a firm "Grand County sheriff."

"Kate?" The familiar voice sounded surprised. "Oh. Didn't know you'd already been sworn in."

"How're you doing, Marybeth?" I knew the dispatcher in Ogallala from my years as the sheriff's wife. With way more prairie than people and several counties boasting the sheriff as the only law enforcement officer, all 911 calls routed to Ogallala, a town of not quite five thousand souls. Marybeth had been dispatching down there for a long time.

Marybeth's serious voice struck me. "Highway 2, mile marker 146. BNSF tracks. Possible death. Ambulance called."

A call. Not traffic, not a kitten in a tree. Something big. Something bad.

What had I sworn in for? My mouth dry, I said, "On my way."

Marybeth hung up and left me with a terrible thought.

Possible death. Just east of town a few miles. Dad was coming from the east. He was late. An icy chill that had nothing to do with the winter ran over my skin.

2

I calculated the accident happened seven miles east of Hodgekiss, just past where County Road 67 crossed above the tracks. A half moon cast dull light across the frozen prairie, the blue illuminating like the fake night of TV shows. The pulsing from the light bar atop the cruiser reflected off the hood and the surrounding black highway.

Please be okay, Dad. Please be okay. The litany looped through my brain as I raced toward the scene. The overpass caught the strobe of my roof lights. County Road 67 rises in an arc across the tracks and forms a right angle with the highway. A train was stopped under the underpass with about twenty cars on the western side and maybe a mile of train to the east. Even though this train headed east and Dad worked the westbound, I couldn't let up on the worry. Maybe the two trains hit head-on, or Dad's train derailed, stranding the eastbound. All I could see in the dark was one train stopped on the tracks.

I neared the overpass and slowed enough to steer the cruiser off the road, across the weeds, and down an embankment to the graveled railroad right of way. I strained to see ahead, along the double track, searching for the train engine.

The red and blue flashes throbbed against my brain. *Please be okay.*

Even though I kept the gas pedal down and I bounced along the rough access with the speedometer registering thirty-five to forty, it felt like slow motion. I clenched my teeth against the thought of two engines head to head, their steel mangled, Dad's body crushed in the cab on the westbound. I flew past a few more cars and drew in a relieved breath. The high beam of the eastbound's headlight shone on empty track.

A figure huddled close to the engine. His head ducked into his shoulders and his arms wrapped around himself. The orange safety jacket reflected the headlights of the cruiser, and the man lifted his head as I pulled up.

Bobby Jenkins. He'd graduated from Grand County Consolidated High School the same year as my youngest brother Jeremy. I knew Bobby was a conductor, like Dad.

BNSF crews consist of an engineer, who drives the train, and a conductor, who is responsible for the physical train. It's the conductor who sets hand brakes and throws switches, and the engineer who stops and goes and manages the speed. There was always talk of downsizing to a one-man crew, but conductors and engineers know two people are as important for keeping each other awake as they are for running the train safely.

I reached for the flashlight. This steel monster must carry eight D batteries and could serve as a club if needed. I dubbed it Big Dick and flipped it on, relieved it shone brightly since I wouldn't put it past Ted to remove the batteries.

I grabbed a ski cap Ted kept in the cruiser, slid my hands into my gloves and climbed out. I angled Big Dick toward the ground so the beam wouldn't blind Bobby. Even in the dim glow I saw dark splotches on his skin. I brought the light up, still avoiding a full-on blaze into his face. My first shocked thought was right. Blood smeared his face and drops covered his jacket as if he'd been in a macabre rain storm. He rocked back and forth emitting a high-pitched wail.

This was going to be bad.

Three engines rumbled as they idled, their pop-off valves pssht-ing into the night.

I approached slowly. "Bobby. What happened?"

His lips trembled and he shook his head from side to side.

He wasn't making me feel any better. I stepped closer to him. I peered into his face and compelled him to make eye contact. "What's the problem?"

He looked at me with an unfocused gaze. Squeezing his lids shut and shaking his head, he shivered and his teeth started to chatter. The train idled behind us, so it had been thrown into emergency, which stopped it. Bobby must have done that. He'd been alert enough to report his engineer's injury, but whatever rational mind he'd had then had busted out of the barn now.

I touched his orange-clad arm, trying to bring him around. "Why are you out here in the cold?"

He whimpered.

Blood splattered from his face down. "Are you hurt? Where's your engineer?"

He howled.

Okay. This was getting me nowhere. Bobby didn't seem to be too badly injured, and I needed to get him out of the cold so I could find the engineer, who might be in worse shape. I pulled Bobby by the arm and led him to the cruiser. I opened the back door. "Why don't you sit here and warm up?"

Like limp linguini he allowed me to guide him into the back seat and shut the door. I ducked into the driver's-side door, started the engine, and slapped the heat control on high. "You okay?"

He definitely was not okay. But the ambulance would be here soon.

Ogallala dispatch autodialed all the members of the volunteer Hodgekiss fire and rescue squad. The unit would take off the second enough crew members showed up to man the team. Sometimes, if there was a high school ball game or play or some other meeting in town, enough trained personnel might be around to reach the fire hall within minutes. If there was a wedding and most of the members had been drinking or an away game and too many people out of town, or haying season when the majority were out in remote fields on tractors, it could take much longer or they may not be able to help at all.

I prayed suppertime on a Thursday night meant enough people could be mustered in a hurry and were zooming our way. I coughed at the cold in my lungs and turned back to the train. The constant low roar of the three engines and the blue and red lights from my cruiser kept me jumpy.

Bobby smeared in blood and the engineer nowhere in sight. Possible death.

I ran toward the train, Big Dick's beam bobbing in front of me. The orange of the BNSF logo throbbed in the flashing lights from my cruiser. "Hello. Anyone here? Engineer?" My voice rang sharp in the frigid air, shrill against the bellowing engines. I hadn't expected an answer, and silence is what I got.

Big Dick in one hand, I gripped the metal handrail running up the side of the cab. My boots rang on the cold steel steps. Dad racked up forty years on the BNSF, and yet I'd never been in a train engine. Trains had run up and down the tracks, whistles blowing every few hours my whole life. My eyes had scanned over a train engine a million times but had never really seen it. The engine was so much bigger than it seemed while I waited with impatience in my car at the flashing crossing arms.

Even as they idled, the chugging engines felt powerful, like thoroughbreds at the starting gate. They vibrated and the air compressors hissed.

The steps were steep, and my footsteps clunked on the meshed metal. I reached to the grab irons and pulled myself to the next step and one more. The stairs led to a narrow platform centered in the nose of the hulking steel engine. The door to the cab where the engineer and conductor rode opened off the platform.

I hoisted myself to the platform of the engine. The cab door hung open. Bobby would have exited there, probably hurtling himself from the cab out of the engine. He'd been desperate to leave. My gloved hands braced on either side of the opening to hold me back, as if in solidarity with my thudding heart. The only thing that convinced me to continue was the knowledge that this was my job.

I left the platform at the nose of the train and entered a narrow passage. Three steps led up to the engineer's seat on the right of the cab, and the conductor's, Bobby's, seat on the left. "Hey, are you there?" I called, breathless with the climb.

I'd expected the cab to feel warmer than the outside, but there was no change in temperature. I had to purposefully place my foot on the first step. "Hello."

The smell hit me. So much like Stranahan's Meat Processing kill floor. My raised foot missed the next step.

With Dad's long tenure and Grand County's population of only five thousand, the odds of me knowing the engineer were pretty good. I braced for something terrible.

The blue and red light pulsing through the windows and the constant rumble of the engines made me wonder whether the tremors I felt were from the train's vibrations or my fear.

I made it up the last step and swung the flashlight to the engineer's side. The high-powered beam slashed across the night, adding a smaller version of the train's headlight, and it seemed wrong, somehow. The realization hit me. The flashlight's beam didn't reflect back to me. There was no windshield.

Shattered glass would account for the blood on Bobby. What force could explode the thick safety glass used for train windshields?

I pointed Big Dick behind me. The back glass on the right side was also shattered.

One more shuffling step brought me directly behind the engineer's chair. My light swung from the empty windshield downward and I swept the beam over the cab. Tiny glass shrapnel covered every surface. A pile of something filled the engineer's seat. It obviously wasn't a person. A lump of dark fabric with points of reflective material catching the light like stars in the night sky.

I stared at the jumble and tried to make sense of it.

No. Oh God. No. Ice dropped to the bottom of my gut, and I gasped.

I squeezed my eyes closed and fell backward a step. My vision showed me one thing but my brain wouldn't acknowledge it. I opened my eyes and tried to focus Big Dick's beam. The light vibrated on the steam rising in the subzero night as my hand shook. I understood why Bobby couldn't talk. I couldn't stop staring. The awful image burned into my brain.

I lurched backward and scrambled down the steps, stumbling and catching myself as I hurtled through the door, probably like Bobby had.

I'm not Bobby. I'm the sheriff.

I gripped the grab irons, and suddenly I was blinded by a spotlight. The oncoming train's whistle blasted, the sound snatching my soul from my chest. The train, likely the one Dad rode, roared around the curve directly in front of me. It couldn't be moving more than twenty miles an hour as the headlight swung away from my face to point down the track.

The hulking train caused a gust of diesel fumes and the squeal of steel on steel, the couplers clacking and chirping as each car thundered past me. I gasped for air, feeling the passing train suck my breath with it. It trumpeted like a herd of elephants and I gripped the grab bars. After an endless time, the train retreated, the *tshk-tshk-tshk* of the wheels on the last car disappearing with the blinking red lights at the rear of the train, leaving the heaving and rumbling engines of the train on which I stood. The train with what was left of the engineer in the cab.

I leaned over the rail and puked.

3

I staggered to the cruiser and threw myself inside, slamming the door and ripping off a glove with my teeth. The rumble of the passing train faded. My shaking hand reached for the radio, and my mind blanked. I dropped the radio and pulled out the sheriff's phone.

Marybeth answered, "Dispatch."

My voice wavered, and I cleared my throat, willed myself to be steady, and said, "I'm going to need help."

Marybeth spoke with authority. "What's the situation?"

I cleared my throat again. "There's a . . . The engineer is. . . ." I bit down to gain control. "Fatality. Subject in train cab, presumably the engineer, identity unknown."

"COD?"

I blanked.

Marybeth came back on. "Cause of death."

"De-de-decapitated." I inhaled. "Bobby Jenkins, conductor, minor injuries, sitting in the cop car."

"Okay. State patrol is on the way. He'll be at your location in thirty minutes. BNSF authorities are en route."

"10-4."

Marybeth shifted from professional to concern. "Maybe you should call Ted as backup. Just to help out until the statey gets there."

I pushed my numb feet against the floor and straightened my spine. *I don't need no stinkin' Ted.* The quiver vanished from my voice. "What's the ETA of the rescue unit from Hodgekiss?"

"They just left the fire hall."

I swiped at my nose, which had started to run in the heat of the car. "I'll stay with Bobby until they get here."

I dropped the phone back into my pocket and twisted in the seat to face Bobby. The Plexiglas divider was open between the front and back, and I smelled the familiar odor of diesel and engine that clung to Dad's clothes when he came home from work. "We're going to get you out of here soon. Can you tell me what happened?"

Thawing out and the few minutes away from the carnage had helped him considerably. He still trembled but his eyes looked clearer. He sounded like cold pea soup. "I don't know."

I held his gaze and spoke slowly. "What do you remember?"

His intake of breath bounced in his throat like a rock down a cliff. "We were r-r-riding along, and Chad looked over to his h-h-house."

Chad. Oh man. Chad Mills. The engineer. He was a few years older than me in high school, but he'd gone to Danbury High. Danbury was the town east of Hodgekiss on the edge of Grand County. I knew Chad only to say hi. I was on a barely nodding acquaintance with his wife, Meredith.

I kept my voice gentle. "Chad lives around here, doesn't he?"

Bobby nodded and swiped an arm across his face, smearing the blood. "Yeah. Just up County Road 67. You can see his yard light from the tracks."

"So he was looking for his house. . . ." I left it dangling so Bobby would finish.

Bobby's voice grew stronger as he focused. "His wife always flashes the yard light when he goes past. We all tease him about being pussy-whipped, but most of us think it's sort of cool they are, like, they seem to really l-l-l- . . ." Suddenly he broke into tears. I felt like crying myself.

I pulled off the ski cap and my other glove and unzipped my coat. The heater in the cruiser was doing a fine job. I let Bobby recover, and when he seemed ready, I continued. "So you were both watching the yard light flash, and what happened?"

He shook his head. "That's why we were looking so long that way and not at the tracks. The light was off. Chad was all worried, and I was telling him it was probably burned out."

A faint glow of red behind us announced the rescue unit turning from the highway.

Bobby's voice lost the gained strength, and it flickered with panic. "Then it all . . . the whole thing. I mean, I don't know what happened, but everything exploded. There was this crash and glass. I screamed at Chad, but he didn't answer, and it was dark and loud, and the wind rushing. I plugged it. I didn't know what else to do. The brakes set up, and we finally stopped. The train stopped."

From listening to Dad, I knew that "plugged it" meant the airbrakes were fully applied and the engines switched to idle. They never kill the engines since engines have no antifreeze. They are always left to idle when the temperatures are below forty degrees, even in the yard when they don't plan to use them for days. "You did exactly the right thing."

He started to cry again. "When it stopped I saw Chad. I mean. I saw the part of him." He covered his face. "His head was gone and there was all this blood."

"And that's when you called it in on the radio?"

His dropped his hands. "I did?"

I nodded. The rescue unit made its way down the access road toward us.

"I don't remember anything after that. I don't even remember how I got into the car."

"That's okay," I said. "You did fine. The ambulance is here, and they'll probably take you to the hospital in Broken Butte."

Tears streaked through his gruesome mask. "What about Chad?"

I tried to sound like an experienced sheriff, calm and comforting. "We'll take care of him."

I pulled on the ski cap and yanked up my coat zipper, grabbed my gloves, and ventured out again. After the overheated car, the cold squeezed my lungs, and I had a coughing fit. Harold Graham and Eunice Fleenor, the best EMTs on the squad, ran toward me.

Eunice, an all-business, middle-aged mom with close-cropped gray hair, popped off questions, and I answered them as quickly and with as little drama as possible. It took less than two minutes to relay all I knew. By that time, Harold was helping Bobby from the back of the car.

Bobby leaned on Harold, and they lumbered toward the ambulance while Harold peppered him with questions. Harold's curiosity and mild voyeuristic bent were well known.

"You say it's Chad Mills?" Eunice asked, tilting her head toward the train.

"I haven't made a positive ID." Because I didn't look for his wallet, and he doesn't have a head. "But I'm fairly certain."

"I'll just take a look to make sure there's nothing we can do for him."

I stepped out of her way, not anxious to check out the ghastly sight again. I'd see plenty of it when the state patrol and the railroad investigators showed up. I knew enough from Ted's time as sheriff and from sheriff's training. They'd set up lights, and I'd need to take photos of the scene.

It didn't take Eunice but a quick glance to understand Chad was beyond her help. With a grim face, she marched past me toward the rescue unit. "Rough first night, huh?"

So bad I'd rather be celebrating my birthday with my crazy family.

I flapped my arms across myself to get the blood flowing and warm myself up. The rescue unit flipped the lights to frantic flashing and gained speed after turning onto the highway.

I stood in the flickering of my car's light bar, alone with the hissing and growling of the idling train. A coyote let out a long yip, answered several hills away, followed by a slew of barking from a nearby ranch. The nearest ranch would be Monen's Horseshoe Lake place, about six miles north. On a still, cold night in the Sandhills, sound had a way of going walkabout for unexpected miles.

Just me, the 'yotes, and poor headless Chad out here on the prairie. It wasn't even six o'clock but it felt like midnight. The half moon had worked its way a few degrees across the sky, still high enough to shed a blue glow on the frozen land.

I set a quick pace to the front of the train and examined the nose of the engine cab. Standing on the tracks, the train rose above me like a moveable steel building. A metal skirt, a modern version of the old cow-catcher, would clear the tracks of critters, debris, and snow and keep the train moving. My eyes were level with the platform that led to the cab. The steps to the gory scene drew my gaze. The shattered engineer's window would be another ten feet above the platform. I shivered at the thought of Chad up there and continued to the far side of the train. The annoying grind of the idling train couldn't be stopped until someone from BNSF showed up. Ignorant of exact safety procedures for trains, at least I knew hand brakes would need to be tied to secure the train from moving.

I wandered back and forth like a hound, with my flashlight on the ground instead of my nose. I didn't venture more than ten yards in any direction, knowing I had to stay with the body until someone else arrived. The temperature had to have dipped at least ten below zero, and after about twenty minutes, I retreated to my car to warm up.

Not long after that, headlights turned off the highway, and I watched in my rearview mirror as they approached. I recognized the light bar and figured it for the state patrol Marybeth had sent my way. I shrugged back into my coat and pulled Ted's cap low, grabbed my gloves, and met the trooper between our vehicles.

He was bundled up in a heavy coat with a ski mask hiding his face. "Trey Ridnoir," he said by way of introduction.

"Kate Fox."

"Oh yeah. Kate Fox." His breath puffed from the mask. "Sorry. I'd forgotten the election."

I'd no doubt there'd been some insider gossip within the western Nebraska law enforcement community about me and Ted running against each other. It wasn't so much about me beating an incumbent as about the two-timed wife ousting her cheating husband. It must have given idle tongues lots of wagging opportunity.

I sounded breathless, not really knowing how to begin. "Hodgekiss rescue took one crew member, Bobby Jenkins, to Broken Butte. Minor injuries if any. Looks like maybe some cuts on his face and neck from broken glass. I took an initial statement. He's shaken up, of course, but I don't think he knows what happened."

Trey nodded. "And the other crew member?"

I swallowed hard and pointed at the idling engine. "In the cab. The windshield exploded at the overpass. I'd guess he was killed on impact."

Trey strode toward the engine, and I followed, stopping beside the tracks and watching as he pulled himself by the grab bars and hopped up the stairs. He disappeared into the door. The light from his flashlight swung around, through the open window and down, where it stopped for several moments.

His descent was much slower, and he lowered himself to the ground next to me. "Sorry you had to be first on the scene. The train cab is pretty messy." Sounded like he wanted to add, "little lady," onto the end of that.

"I searched the ground for clues to the accident but didn't spot anything out of the ordinary. I hadn't expected to, though. According to Bobby, everything had been normal until they reached County Road 67."

"Good work, Kate." More than a smidge patronizing, but he was probably tying to be nice to a rookie.

Since he looked more bandit than cop, I couldn't tell whether I'd recognize his face from meetings or conferences I'd attended with Ted, but county and state didn't mingle that often. "I haven't had much experience with crime scene investigations."

He had nice lips. Probably something I wouldn't notice if I had access to a whole face. But they weren't flabby or too thin and looked like maybe they'd form into an easy grin. This line of thinking was an obvious ploy to sidetrack my brain from the grisly scene in the cab.

"Well," he exhaled and steam chugged into the sky. "The NTSB and BNSF investigators will be here soon." He paused. "NTSB. That's National Transportation and Safety Board."

Really? And here I thought it stood for Never Trust State-Patrol Boys. At least he didn't see fit to explain BNSF, a subject I knew a bit about because Dad had been a conductor since before I'd been born. I could speak knowledgeably about the union negotiations for the merger of Burlington Northern with the Santa Fe in 1986 and the benefits to the conductors of staying in their district from conversations around our kitchen table.

I'd had about enough of hanging around the chugging engine and craved some silence before having to venture back into the cab. "If you'll stay here with the body, I'm going to walk the train. See if I can spot anything unusual, especially at the overpass."

I hopscotched across the other tracks and trained Big Dick toward the west. The rumble of the train faded as I trekked away from the engines, sweeping the light back and forth, inspecting the gravel of the track bed and the knee-high yellow and brown weeds trembling in the slight breeze. Walking on my numb toes hurt while blood pushed down to warm them. By the time I'd made it the mile back to the overpass at County Road 67, everything but my face felt functional. My lips had lost all feeling, though, and frost clung to the tiny hairs under my nose.

I approached the overpass, slowing my steps to allow time to swing the flashlight more slowly and thoroughly. What would cause the windshield to explode at this site?

The farther I walked from the engines, the quieter the night grew around me. Another coyote's cry brought an answering yip from the north. Headlights peeked between the railcars as a car eased off the paved road to the railroad access. The crush of gravel and the chug of the car's engine passed me on its way to the front of the train. The vehicle crept toward my cruiser. A few more vehicles turned from the highway and drove to the engine. I guessed the rigs belonged to the road foreman and probably the trainmaster, maybe railroad officials.

I strode west, the flashlight sweeping from the train, across the prairie and back to the train. About fifty yards west of the overpass I spotted it. I walked a few more railcars down before I'd seen enough and started back the way I'd come.

Flashlights and headlamps slashed arrows of light through the darkness. I'd made it about halfway along the train before strained men's voices cut the air. They must have seen Chad, and some strong soul had sent someone to tie the hand brakes. I wished they could kill the engines. Somehow the dull roar and vibrations increased the full horror.

One figure broke away from the front engine and started my way. I assumed it was Trey. The light from his high-powered flashlight marked his path. Gravel from the track bed crunched under his footsteps.

I kept moving, each step bringing me closer to the flashlight beam traveling in my direction, sweeping back and forth, as I'd done. I heard his boots crunch and even his heavy breathing, as I'm sure he heard me.

He started talking before he reached me. "Come on back and warm up. The trainmen are here, and the officials are on the way. They'll figure out what malfunctioned on the unit or the tracks and get their reports together."

I stopped and waited for him. "The NTSB isn't here?"

He shook his head. "I'll call Ben Wolford in Broken Butte. He's the coroner for Grand County, right?"

I nodded. "It's more than an hour's drive, so we should notify him immediately."

Trey, a substantial presence at least six feet tall and bulky beneath his thick coat, shifted his weight and took a step backward, readying to return to the headend of the train. "Usually, unless we suspect foul play, he'll have us act as coroner and fill out the reports. He won't want to get out in this hellacious cold."

I didn't follow Trey. "We'd better get him out here."

He rocked between his feet, as if impatient to get me moving. "I appreciate you wanting to do everything by the book on your first major incident, but really, forcing an old man to drive sixty miles in this weather might cause a heart attack."

I held my ground. "I'll call Ben."

His shoulders dropped, and his head tilted slightly in his snuggly ski mask, as if in reluctant indulgence. "Seriously, the railroad investigators will figure out what broke and create a safety report to fix the issue and make sure it doesn't happen again."

I sniffed at what felt like a runny nose, but since snot would freeze, was probably just the sensation of my relatively warm breath. "It's not a safety issue."

"What is it then?" This time, there was no patience in his voice. It was plain irritated.

"Murder."

4

After the slightest pause, Trey's voice betrayed amusement. "Murder, huh? In my experience in fifteen years of law enforcement, accidents are far more likely than murder."

"I understand that." I turned around and started walking away. A quick glance down assured me I actually had feet, not solid blocks of ice.

After a moment, he fell in with me. "Then what makes you think this is murder and not an accident?" Trey didn't need to check out his feet. He wore Sorels, probably lined with Thinsulate and maybe even boot warmers. Sure, I was reaching on that, but I couldn't stop the fantasy of warm feet.

I didn't answer until we'd made it back to the overpass. I pointed Big Dick to the underside of the bridge. Two wires dangled in the air, like no. 9 wire used for fencing. They were attached to a metal shaft bolted along the braces of the overpass. "That."

Trey stepped closer to me and trained his flashlight on the same area. He studied it. "What am I seeing here?"

"That's where a railroad tie was hanging. See how the wires are positioned exactly to the side where the engineer would sit?" I sniffed again. I couldn't feel my nose, and enunciating my words was complicated by my frozen cheeks and mouth.

A huff of disbelief escaped from his nice lips. "That's some wild imagination you've got. I know you want to solve big cases and have all this excitement as sheriff. But the truth is, the crime-fighting world out here is routine. Dull stuff for the most part. You'd be better off not wasting your time looking for the obscure murders and whatnot."

If I were Sarah, I'd have a sharp retort to his patronizing tone. But I'd learned to swallow the quick jab, since it rarely helped my situation.

He sounded like he held back a chuckle. "Why would you even think about a railroad tie? Why not a steel rail or a tree branch?"

I lowered the beam to shine thirty yards down the tracks and out toward the barbed wire fence defining the right of way.

Trey followed the light. His neck jutted slightly, and I imagined he squinted behind his toasty mask. "What's that?"

"The railroad tie that went through the windshield."

A second ticked by and one of the coyotes howled. Trey's response came out slow and quiet. "The . . . um . . . those lumps out there. They're . . . ?"

I clicked off Big Dick, letting the blue of the moonlight settle. "Not sure, but my guess is that's what's left of Chad's brain."

5

Trey didn't have much to say while we double-timed it back to the front of the train. He finally spoke. "I'll drive back and take pictures."

I pulled off my glove, immediately feeling the burn of the frigid air, and found Ben Wolford's number stored in the sheriff's favorites. Even after I explained the details, he happily signed over authority to me as acting coroner. I couldn't blame him for not wanting to venture out on a night like this, but damn, that meant I'd have to inspect what was left of Chad's body, smell that awful slaughterhouse odor again.

Even an emergency C-section on an old cow during a blizzard would be better than this. With each step toward the engine and the bustling road crew, I reminded myself of my job. Grandma Ardith always said, "You do what you have to do."

As trainmaster for the Broken Butte subdivision, as well as county commissioner, Clete Rasmussen didn't get to enjoy a cozy night tucked in at home. He'd probably just kicked his boots off from the swearing in when he got the call to head out here. Since he lived in Hodgekiss, it hadn't taken him long to get here. He stood in insulated coveralls, cell phone pressed against his head, issuing orders. He motioned us over, and I rocked back and forth while we waited for him to hang up. "Lead engine's trashed. We need a new unit."

He lowered the phone, looking wrecked. He covered his face with a thick-gloved hand and paused, dropping his head for a second. He blinked and found his normal scowl. "We've got a crew ordered. It'll take some time to switch out engines. But there's a siding up a ways and we'll drop it there and tie it down."

Trey nodded. "NTSB will need to look it over."

"What about Ch-Ch-Ch- . . ." It was like the words stopped up in his throat. He coughed. "The body?"

My jaw tightened. "I need to process the scene. Once I finish that I'll release him to Eunice and Harold when they're back from Broken Butte."

Clete stared at the engine, the blue and red lights mingling with the workers' flashlights and headlamps. He cleared his throat and managed to say, "Right. Okay."

Trey and I headed to his cruiser and climbed in. He started it up and punched the heat, let out a breath and pulled off the ski mask, blonde hair sparking and standing on end.

I slid my hands from my gloves but kept my cap on to conserve maximum body heat. I reached into my pocket for my phone, relieved the battery hadn't dwindled in the frosty air. I ignored the herd of missed calls from my brothers and sisters and called the rescue unit. Eunice assured me they were on their way back.

After disconnecting, I held my hands to the heating vents, gritting my teeth as they thawed. I kept my toes wiggling to encourage circulation, but I really wanted to cry and moan and bang the dash to wait for the pain to work its way out.

"Damn, it's colder than a witch's tit." Trey lodged his hands under his armpits like heat-seeking missiles. "Sorry."

He insulted my intelligence, discounted my observations, and the only thing he apologized for was using colorful language. "What's the next step?"

Trey seemed younger than I'd suspected, maybe inching toward forty. Fair haired, his skin flushed from the cold. Without his ski mask, his chin had a strong set. If that was an indicator of character, this man was a regular George Washington. "We need to work the scene so they can clear the track as soon as they get the new crew and engine."

I hoped Ted hadn't moved the camera from the trunk of the sheriff car. "I'll need to inspect the cab so I can release the body."

Trey pursed his lips. "I'll do that."

"Dead body would be a county issue." I sounded more certain than I felt. Heck, I didn't want to take one more look at the pile of flesh that used to be a man. I'm sure Trey didn't crave the sight any more than I did.

Trey pulled his hands free and flexed them. "The investigators won't get here for a couple of hours. I'll brief them and walk them over the scene. It'll take at least that long to get all the pictures and secure the engine. The general protocol on murders, unless it's something cut and dried, is for local sheriffs to let the state patrol handle the investigation."

I wasn't so sure about that, but I welcomed his experience. "I'll be glad for your help."

I don't think he liked my response. Didn't matter. We fought the cold for the next few hours. The railroad crew had bright shop lights so Trey and I were able to get the photos we needed. We inspected the busted windshield and even got some relatively good pictures of the apparatus under the bridge, though we'd have to get better photos in daylight.

We kept watch while the EMTs gathered up what was left of Chad. I managed not to puke again when Eunice Fleenor and Harold Graham pried the frozen bits of the body from the walls and floor.

We eventually retreated to Trey's car while the relief crew switched out engines and the train chugged away. The heater blasted and still I shivered. Clete and the road foreman took their leave.

Trey leaned back and closed his eyes. "I'll wait here for the inspectors. You might as well head out."

I stared out at the black prairie. The moon had retreated long ago, leaving the night dark and cold. "Someone went to a lot of trouble to rig that up. Do you think it was set for any train or this one specifically?"

Trey didn't open his eyes. "No one could know what the tie would do or who would get hurt. It's got to be some sicko's idea of a prank."

Maybe. "But why would he hang the tie so it hit the engineer's side? Why not center it, maybe take out both the crew at one time?"

Trey let out an irritated exhale. "Let's just wait until daylight before we round up suspects."

I tapped the dash. "It was dark so a black creosote tie hanging on the underpass would be hard to see, but if the engineer wasn't even looking down the track, it would be impossible."

Trey opened his eyes and sat up. "You've got an excess of energy, and I know what you can do. We need to notify next of kin. Probably ought to do that a.s.a.p. before the conductor—"

"Bobby Jenkins."

"Right. Before he gets on the phone and spreads it around. These railroaders are worse than a gaggle of hens when it comes to gossip. I swear they've got everyone on speed dial, like my mother's prayer tree at church."

He might not have the best delivery, but he was right. Dad fielded calls and texts from his fellow conductors and engineers almost constantly. He also watched the train lineups on his phone and computer and knew who crewed which trains. Gossip circulated with the speed of lightning and sometimes the accuracy of a ten-day weather forecast.

Ted had occasion to inform family of deaths, mostly from car accidents or farm implement catastrophes. It hung heavy on him for days, and he wasn't a particularly empathetic soul. Before I ran for sheriff, I considered that sad aspect of the job and knew I'd be called on to perform it. I just didn't think it would be on the first day.

It would only take a few minutes to drive to Chad's house. He lived a half mile north of the County Road 67 junction. Meredith, now his widow, could probably see the flash of the emergency vehicles blinking between the rail cars.

After nearly freezing all my parts earlier, I didn't welcome the nervous sweat breaking out under my coat on the drive to the Mills's ranch house. I practiced my opening phrase out loud, trying for the right mix to show sympathy and strength. If someone knocked at my door to tell me about my husband's death, how would I need them to act?

An old, dented Ford pickup was parked under the yard light as I pulled up. Snow had been spitting for the last hour or so, but not enough to stick. I stepped out, my boots crunching on the dirt drive. The coyote's call didn't offer any advice.

As much as I didn't want to tell Meredith about Chad's death, she'd want to hear it even less. I wove through the white vinyl front gate that separated a carpet of thick, dead lawn from the drive. Flagstones sunk deep and nearly buried led me to the processed wood porch.

Though not large, their house was only a few years old. A two-story arts and crafts like you'd find in the newer suburbs. It didn't look too bad out here on the prairie, just not authentically old and run down like most houses. I made it up the first step when the front door flew open.

Meredith rushed onto the porch. She wore black yoga pants and a fleece tunic, her feet burrowed into down slippers. "What's happened? Is Chad okay? Should we go to the hospital?"

A tall figure appeared behind her in the doorway, silhouetted by muted light from the living room. He stepped onto the porch and rested a hand lightly on Meredith's upper arm. He had a voice like hot chocolate, comforting and gentle. "Let her get inside."

She backed up, her eyes never leaving my face. She stopped in the middle of a small living room, tasteful in decor. A riveted leather couch and loveseat faced a fireplace with a crackling flame. The aroma of burning pine filled the room. Western art hung on the walls, cowboys and Indians, from my brief glance. The hardwood floors reflected the fire's glow. A cozy nest for the childless couple that, if Bobby Jenkins was right, were devoted to each other.

"Tell me." Her voice leaked out as if she wished she didn't have to ask. "Is Chad okay?"

I didn't remember what I'd planned to say. "I'm sorry."

She squeaked, her eyes wide and wet. A hand flew to her lips.

"There was an accident on the train, and Chad was killed." I could have told her I suspected someone murdered her husband, but there would be time for details later. Right now, she had to hear the news.

Her knees melted, and in slow motion she started to sink.

The tall man behind her moved gracefully to latch onto her arms and keep her from hitting the floor. He directed her to the leather sofa and folded her down. She wrapped her arms around her body and rocked. I didn't think anyone could be that pale and not pass out, but she kept rocking while fat tears streaked down her face.

"No. Oh no." She threw back her head and screamed. The sound pierced my skin and vibrated to my bones.

I stood helpless as the man knelt in front of her. "It's going to be okay." His words were meaningless, yet so true. Yes, in the grand scheme of Meredith's life, it would eventually be okay if she let it.

But for this moment and for many more to come, it would probably feel as though her life were over. She might even wish she'd been the one to die, feeling that maybe Chad was the lucky one not to have to fight through all this pain. Right now, "it's going to be okay" might sound like the biggest lie ever told.

She covered her face with shaking hands and doubled over. The deep sobs shook her whole body, and soon she howled, as forlorn as the coyotes in the hills.

The man's jaw tightened, and he winced as if Meredith's wails stabbed him. He placed a long-fingered hand on her back and rubbed a small circle across her shoulders. This time, he didn't say anything.

I felt like a stupid lump in the middle of the room. I'd faced the death of my sister, Glenda, so I had some idea of her loss. I'd loved and depended on Glenda and knew the hole makes a deafening sucking noise as your world collapses.

The man straightened and exhaled deeply. He backed away from Meredith and joined me. "I'm Josh Stevens." He cast a sad gaze at Meredith. "She's got family in Omaha. I'll call them."

Josh Stevens. The name tickled some memory, but I didn't bother to dredge it up. Including the shock of shaggy dark hair and his lanky build, he reminded me a bit of Abraham Lincoln. A much more handsome version, not quite so drawn, but with a quiet dignity I'd imagined of the legend.

"Thanks." I might be a cynic, but something seemed strange. A married woman whose husband had just climbed on a train bound three hundred miles to Lincoln and wouldn't be home for another twenty-four to thirty-six hours, late night, a man in the house. “What are you doing here?” I might have found a less confrontational way of asking, but I blurted it out.

He blinked. He spared a look at Meredith then back to me. “Mere called me. She knew Chad was on a train heading east from the depot. She could see when the train stopped. She saw the flashing lights, probably the ambulance or you or whatever. She tried to call BNSF but couldn’t get through to anyone, and even if she had, they wouldn’t tell her anything. That’s when she called me.”

The train had stopped a mile away. “Why didn’t she go check it out herself?”

Meredith had resumed her rocking and brought her volume down to a sob.

“She wanted to, but I told her to stay put. If there’s an accident, she couldn’t do anything but get in the way of people trying to help. If it was a train malfunction, she wouldn’t be able to help. It’s dangerously cold out there.”

“So you came over after she called?”

He shifted and his eyes flicked away. “I’ve known Meredith a long time. She can be . . .” He trailed off as if reluctant to talk about her. “My ranch is just a few minutes away down that road.” He pointed toward a south window, I supposed indicating the single-lane gravel road. “So I thought maybe I ought to drive over and calm her down.”

I’d been at the scene for several hours. “You’ve been here since?”

He nodded.

“Was the yard light on when you got here?”

Josh seemed taken aback by that. “As a matter of fact, no. Meredith seemed pretty upset about that, insisted I get the ladder and change that, even though it was dark and Chad’s train had already passed.”

Interesting.

Meredith dropped her hands to her lap. “Josh?”

He swiveled away from me and hurried to her. "I'm here." He spoke with great gentleness and caring.

She reached up and clutched his hand, drawing him down to her. She threw her arms around him, burying her face in his chest. "Josh, Josh, Josh." The words deteriorated into a jumbled mass of syllables and sobs.

Not Chad, Chad, Chad.

6

Weak winter sunlight struggled through the sheers. I unfurled from the burrito I'd wound myself into during the night. I yanked my feet back up. The bottom of the bed felt like an ice rink. The two wool Pendleton blankets and down comforter had held in my body heat, but emerging from my cocoon would be painful.

After leaving Meredith Mills, I'd stopped to see that the tracks where the incident happened were clear and the area as empty as any at 3 A.M. in the middle of winter. I'd gone home to find a stack of birthday cards on the kitchen counter and a homemade banner crayoned by my nieces and nephews taped to the kitchen wall. Relief at missing the party mingled with dread of how Louise would make me pay.

I was surprised Dad hadn't returned from work by then. I supposed there was a hullabaloo at the depot in Broken Butte. They probably didn't have details, but they'd know about Chad's death. I'm sure there had been some heavy coffee drinking going on in the crew room at the depot.

I would have liked to sleep later, but the minute I came to, I saw the gruesome details of last night. I blinked against the memory of the engine cab with Chad's remains splattered and bloody. I snorted, trying to get the smell out of my nose. The butcher's kill floor smell was probably my imagination, but it lingered.

I squinted at the doorway and the steep stairs beyond and wondered if I'd die of exposure before I jumped from the covers and catapulted myself downstairs. I burrowed deeper, building my courage for the undertaking.

One, two . . . THREE.

I threw back the covers, leapt from the bed, jumped to the stairs, and took them two at a time. Two leaps from the bottom I miscalculated, hit the step with half of my foot. My knee buckled and I tumbled. I might have yelped. I know I cursed. I bounced against the wall, hit my hip on the last stair, and landed in a heap in the dark living room.

I lay there for a second to make sure I hadn't broken anything. It's not like I hadn't crashed down these stairs before. I remembered more than one instance when a good percentage of Foxes rushed down the stairs for warmth and one would trip, dominoing the rest of us in a tangle of limbs and tears, usually ending with someone throwing a fist.

I rolled over, pushed myself to my knees and, using the stair rail, levered myself to stand. The adrenaline of the fall stirred my blood enough I no longer risked freezing. Still, it wouldn't take long for the floor to chill my feet. Dad's grip lay by the front door with his steel-toe work boots in a heap. A pair of wool socks dribbled out the top where they'd fallen when he flicked them off. Since I needed to shower this morning anyway to wash away the odor of Chad's death, I grabbed the socks and yanked them on.

With no hope of smoothing my bedhead and really not caring

much, I followed the smell of fresh-brewed coffee. Along the way, I grabbed an old crocheted afghan from the couch and wrapped it around myself as I shuffled into the kitchen.

Dad stood at the stove in his canvas Dickies and flannel shirt. He stirred oatmeal, the smell flashing me back to countless chilly school mornings. With the herd of Foxes jockeying for bathroom time, parents' signatures, fights about who owned what shirt, and last-minute homework help, oatmeal was the easiest and most affordable way to send us all out of the house with at least an attempt at a full belly. If you add to that mix a father who spent half the time away from home on a train and an artist mother who might forget she had children when in the throes of creation, it wasn't unusual for oatmeal to be on the supper menu, as well.

I hate oatmeal.

I zeroed in on the healing potion dripping into the carafe on the counter under the window. Two inches of new snow ricocheted the sun into my eyes. I squinted to the blue sky, happy the early morning storm had dissipated and thankful there were no clouds to drop more snow. Three months until winter eased up.

Just last winter I'd had my own bedroom. In seven more months would I be standing in this same spot, grumpy because it was too hot to sleep upstairs and still missing my privacy?

"Have a nice trip?" Dad asked.

"Very funny." With the afghan draped over my shoulders, I reached for a mug. "I might have broken bones, and you'd still be in here stirring your oatmeal."

He turned off the gas flame and put a lid on the pot. "From the level of cursing, I figured you weren't hurt too bad."

The cheery red decor of the kitchen clashed with my mood. Meredith Mills's morning would start bleak and cold, if she'd even slept at all last night. The first day of a lifetime without her husband. A sheriff had to learn how to absorb the unimaginable bits of other peoples' lives and still keep going. Maybe running for sheriff hadn't been a smart move.

This kind of introspection called for a shot of cream for my coffee. I stepped back and reached out for the refrigerator door handle and nearly jumped out of my highly attractive socks.

Josh Stevens sat on the bench of the picnic table that served as the Fox family meeting place, resting his head against the wall. He watched me without expression.

"Oh." That's always a great conversation starter. "I didn't know you were here." Now I figured out how I knew Josh Stevens's name. He worked on the BNSF with Dad.

Not that I wanted to impress a stranger, or an almost stranger, sitting unannounced in my father's kitchen, but I don't think I could have appeared more unimpressive if I'd worked at it.

Dad opened a cabinet and rattled dishes to pull out two thick ceramic bowls. One benefit of a sculptress mother is having useful artwork. Despite nine kids who broke anything breakable and some things that weren't, the cupboards were full of Mom's unique pieces.

"Chad's accident has everyone upset," Dad said. He dished oatmeal into bowls. "Josh came by to, you know, talk about it."

I poured a dollop of cream into my cup and didn't offer my opinion about the accuracy of the term "accident."

Dad walked the oatmeal to the table and placed one bowl in front of Josh and the other on the opposite side of the table. He reached for the cream I'd set on the counter. "I guess we'd like to know any details you might have." He made a circuit by the butcher block and wrenched open a drawer for spoons and closed it with his hip.

Josh lifted his head from the wall. His face and neck seemed more stone than flesh. "What happened to him?"

I avoided his question. “How’s Meredith?”

He winced as if I’d shot an arrow at him. “She’s not doing too good. Her sister got here a bit ago, and she had some pills. Maybe she’ll be better after she rests some.”

I poured my coffee and wrapped the afghan tighter around me, leaving my hands free. Like a T. rex, I reached for my cup and leaned my butt on the counter, wrapping my fingers around the mug and drawing it close. “You and Chad were good friends?”

Josh’s eyes traveled to the corner of the ceiling, and his jaw tightened while I waited a beat. He nodded. “We used to be. Since fourth grade.”

Trooper Trey Ridnoir would probably squawk at me for asking questions, but it wasn’t a formal interview. And I’d be sure and share the information with him. “Why ‘used to be’?”

Dad deposited his loot on the table, pushed the sugar bowl shaped like a giant strawberry toward Josh, and lowered himself into a chair.

A muffled telephone ring perked my ears. I clacked my cup onto the butcher block and leapt for my sheriff’s coat on the hook by the door. By the second ring I held it to my ear.

“Kate? Vicki. What can you tell me about the train wreck and Chad Mills? Make it fast. I’ve got to send the copy to the printer in an hour for this week’s edition.” Vicki Snyder, *Grand County Tribune*’s proprietor, reporter, sales force, editor in chief, and all-around annoying person.

“You’ll have to talk to BNSF for any information.”

Dad raised an amused eyebrow at me. We all know the road foreman or Clete, the trainmaster, are instructed to turn the media over to the official BNSF spokesperson, who, if you can find one, won’t pass along anything meaningful. Asset protection. No comment.

“Come on, Kate. A quote from the sheriff—” I punched off.

Dad looked serious. "What's going on?"

I picked up my cup and lowered my face to my mug to let the steam defrost my cheeks. "I'm not too involved in it. Trey Ridnoir, the state trooper, is handling it."

My phone rang again. "Morning, Kate." It was Aileen Carson. "Jack and me just heard about Chad, and Jack wanted me to ask you what happened."

Before I could tell Aileen that I didn't have any information, another call came in. I hung up and saw three missed calls, all going to the official voice mail, which would direct them if they had an emergency to hang up and call 911. It rang again, and I punched the call off, turned the ringer to vibrate, and monitored the caller ID.

Josh sprinkled sugar on his oatmeal. "There must be some reason for you not to have turned it over to NTSB and the BNSF safety board."

I considered him. "Do you know of anyone who would want to hurt Chad?" Really, I should be letting Trey question Josh.

Dad dumped in two heaping spoonfuls of sugar and flooded it all with cream. He scooped the sloppy mixture into his mouth and watched me with interest.

Josh left the sugar to melt on top of the cooling lump. He placed his spoon into his oatmeal, not disturbing the rubbery surface except where the edge of the spoon cut through. His brown eyes looked so deep that only a major disruption could cause a ripple, like an isolated lake surrounded by the protection of towering mountains. "Everyone liked Chad."

Might as well jump into it. "Why did you come by here this morning?"

Dad swallowed. "Katie. That's not hospitable. Our house is open to everyone, you know that."

"Everyone" usually meant the Fox kids, spouses, offspring, all their friends and relations. And although it might include a railroader from time to time, I'd never seen Josh Stevens, a man closer to my age than Dad's, eating oatmeal here first thing in the morning.

Dad swallowed another sloppy bite. "Josh is helping Meredith out. He's trying to find out answers to the tragedy. I'd like you to tell him what you know."

At some point I might be called to choose between being a daughter and serving as sheriff when it came to confidential information, but not this time. I pulled the afghan around me and sipped my coffee. "I don't know much more than Vicki Snyder at this point. The state patrol wants to take the lead, and I'm playing border collie and trying to get everyone heading the same direction."

Josh studied his oatmeal but didn't touch it.

Dad whipped his spoon around his mush and might as well have been stirring my stomach. "So you suspect Chad was murdered."

"I didn't say that."

Dad didn't look up from his bowl. "And neither will we."

When I considered running for sheriff I drew a *t* graph and listed pros and cons. On the pro side, I needed a paying gig, and sheriffing was mostly a light work assignment. I'd have time to moonlight with day labor on ranches. More importantly, I'd have time to scout out full-time hired man positions.

But there were cons to the job. Among them, being on call and being forced to get tough with my friends and relatives in the event they wandered close to legal lines. Even good people get in trouble. I didn't relish serving papers to any of my kin.

I'd gone back and forth and finally decided I could deal with the cons. But in all my planning I'd never imagined conducting a murder investigation.

That was pure undersight on my part, since last spring Eldon Edwards was murdered and Ted was shot. That's the night my niece Carly went missing. You'd think I'd learned the sheriff job could be trouble.

I refilled my cup, even though I'd only downed a few sips. I'd leave Dad and Josh to their gossip concerning their fallen comrade. "I need to call Robert and Sarah. I was supposed to help them preg check today."

Dad swallowed another bite. "They'll figure it out without you."

Probably. But I'd rather be out with the cows, even in this cold, than trying to track a killer.

Josh hadn't moved and looked like he didn't intend to eat his oatmeal. Good call.

The kitchen door opened, and Louise burst in, as only my always-righteous older sister can. Like all of us, she was named for the Academy Award Best Actor or Actress for the year of her birth. In her case, it was Louise Fletcher who won for Nurse Ratched in *One Flew Over the Cuckoos' Nest.* Did she grow into the character, or was it an unfortunate coincidence she had some of the same traits?

Her commanding voice filled the kitchen before she fully entered and closed the door in a whoosh of frigid air. The smell of warm bread and savory meat beat out the cold. "You get a free pass for last night, I guess, but we'll have to reschedule your party. They're saying Chad Mills was killed last night. What happened?"

Man, I got off easy on that one. "Party?" I sounded overly surprised and delighted. "What party?"

"Oh don't give me that. I know Sarah—" She glanced up and her eyes stopped on Josh. Her mouth dropped open. Silent for one of the only times I could remember.

Fascinated by Louise's reaction to Josh, I continued to hold up the kitchen counter.

Color drained from her face, and her mouth stayed slack as her gaze flicked from Josh to Dad to me and back.

Silence grew so that I started to feel bad for Louise. "Josh, this is my sister, Louise Merrihew. Louise, this is Josh Stevens. He works with Dad."

Louise found the ability to shut her mouth, but her eyes stayed wide, like a cornered skunk.

Josh dipped his head. "Morning, Louise."

Dad watched them with the same expression as when he supervised our family football games, like he knew something would break, just not when or what. He was both curious and ready to make repairs, or rush one of us to the ER.

Louise dropped her eyes and swallowed. She seemed to remember she held something and set a foil-wrapped plate on the counter. Her voice sounded like hooves on rough sand. "I brought you runzas."

She reached behind her and felt for the doorknob. The door squeaked open and she eased out as if reluctant to turn her back on us. The door clicked closed, and I watched through the window above the sink. Scuttling like a beetle, Louise rushed across the thin layer of snow and jettisoned herself into her faded maroon Suburban.

When I turned back to the kitchen, Dad scraped his spoon on the bottom of his oatmeal bowl, and Josh was back to staring at his as if it contained the meaning of life.

The tail of the black kitty-clock ticked back and forth. Why was Josh Stevens here this early to question me? Because he suspected Chad's death wasn't an accident. Did he know something?

I glanced at a new vibration on my phone, and my heart jumped to my throat. "Excuse me." I shuffled toward the living room and answered. "Ted."

I pictured him in the sunlit kitchen at Frog Creek. "Hi, Kate."

Weird to be talking to my ex-husband as if we were friends. "Shouldn't you be feeding cows?"

He hesitated, and I figured I'd irritated him. Good. "I'm on my way. Hey, I heard about the train wreck last night."

Roxy said something in the background in her hysterical voice, and I waited.

"This is a major situation, and I think you ought to let Trey handle it."

Right. "It's a Grand County matter."

"Ted!" Roxy sounded alarmed. But then, high drama being her calling, it probably was nothing important.

"Wait." Ted pulled the phone from his face and said something I couldn't make out, then to me, "Kate, I'm worried about you."

Worrying about me was no more his job than being sheriff. "How did you even know about the wreck?"

He sounded distracted. "Trey called. He asked me if I knew Chad."

Instant indignation. "Really."

"I have to go," he said. "Just turn it over to the state patrol."

Not likely, Teddy.

7

Damn Ted and his Irish Spring. I needed that pine tree air freshener. At least the cruiser had a good heater, and in less time than it took me to drive across the tracks and through Hodgekiss, she'd toasted up the inside.

I watched the low clouds on my way east and pulled off at the intersection of County Road 67. I bumped off the road to stop at the underpass. I zipped my old barn coat and pulled on my unflattering but warm ski hat. It draped low over my forehead and covered my ears with flaps that ended in bright red wool braids. Because I imagined my uniform smelled like the bloody train cab, I'd thrown it in the washer and asked Dad to transfer it to the dryer. I wore a flannel shirt and Wranglers.

When the good citizens of Grand County elected me, I'm sure no one expected me to conduct a murder investigation. I may not have eight years of experience, like Ted did, and I may be way out of my depth, but there was nothing to do for it. Except back down and turn it over to Trey. And a Fox just didn't do that.

I hauled myself from the heated Charger into the raw midday winter and trotted to the underpass for daylight photos. Because of the below-zero temps, the snow had little moisture and was easily tossed by the slight breeze. Most of the ground was now bare, with the only accumulation in small drifts.

A pulley with a severed cable dangled from the I-beams underneath the bridge. The killer had attached another pulley to the tie. A simple block and tackle. It looked like he'd attached wires to the tie and then pulled the tie back with a rope so it would be suspended out of sight. When he wanted to release it, he'd cut the rope that held it back and let it hang at just the right height to slam lengthwise through the windshield. A complicated, well-engineered get-up.

Was Chad the target, or would any train, any engineer, do?

I climbed back into the cruiser and started her up. While the heat blasted, I dialed Trey. He picked up after a couple of rings.

After his mumbled greeting I started in. "Whoever did this is smart or has construction experience. It took some doing to rig this up and precise measuring to get it just right."

He hesitated. "Where are you?"

"I'm at the underpass. The rigging looks old, like maybe it's used." The winter blue sky faded to a colorless ceiling, not so much clouds as a dead sky.

"Right." He grunted, as if sitting up. "I'm not really awake. By the time the BNSF investigators left and I drove back home, the sun was coming up."

I hadn't been in bed much longer than that and had been up a while. My eyes burned, and the need for sleep pressed in the middle of my forehead. "I thought maybe I'd head over to Meredith Mills's this afternoon. Maybe get some idea if Chad had any enemies."

He sounded alert now. "Wait. No. You . . . you are assisting in this, not . . . I'll do that."

"I'm sheriff." I pushed it out with authority.

"Yes. But you only took office—"

I didn't let him finish. "When will you be here?"

It sounded like he was moving around. "I'm going to talk to NTSB and the BNSF guys in North Platte at noon. I'm sure they're going to sign off that it's a criminal issue and turn the investigation over. Then I planned on going to Broken Butte to the depot and talking to the trainmaster."

I put the car in drive and headed back toward the highway. "Clete won't—"

He didn't wait to hear the rest. "I'll swing back through Hodgekiss on my way home and brief you on what I find out."

I idled before turning onto the highway. "Meantime, I'll go talk to Meredith."

"No." He gave me a firm order. "You've never interviewed a suspect. You don't know what you're doing."

"Suspect?"

"The spouse is always under suspicion. Don't get overexcited on your first investigation. I'll be there later on, and I'll let you know the plan." He hung up.

His order rankled, but my thoughts shifted before I could work up a froth.

What was Josh doing at Meredith's in the middle of the night when her husband wasn't home? They'd explained his presence, but if I'd been worried about Ted, would I have called another man to hold my hand? That comparison didn't work because, for the first thing, I wasn't given to worry. The second thing is that if I'd been concerned about Ted, I'd have gone to find him. And the third thing, if I had to stay at home and wring my hands, I'd call a sister or brother to come over and annoy me so much I'd be distracted.

A gust tossed a handful of ice crystals scuttling across the highway. The milky sky showed no signs of sun or even a hint of blue.

Black cows bunched at the base of hills, staying close to the hay that ranchers had strung along the colorless prairie.

My phone rang, and I dreaded some curious citizen quizzing me about Chad's death. I eased the gear shift into park and pulled my phone out. When I saw the ID, my heart jumped.

I shot out, "What's the news?"

Impatience tapped at my forehead while I waited for Glenn Baxter to cough softly and wheeze in a long breath. "My investigator caught a whiff of Carly in Chicago. She's tracking all of our Kilner brothers."

Glenn Baxter might be my unlikeliest partner. When I met the cable news mogul last spring, I accused him of murdering Carly's granddad. Thankfully, he'd forgiven me and, because he was a steadfast friend of my late brother-in-law in military school, was helping me to find my niece Carly, who was on a mission to discover the cause of a heap of cash her father acquired before he died. The world may see Baxter as a mysterious billionaire, but I knew him as a friend.

My heart dropped. "Just a whiff?"

Baxter's breath whistled before he answered. "I'm afraid the investigator was several days behind Carly."

"Still, it's proof she's okay." Keeping the faith, as Dad would say.

A pause. "She'd talked to Marshall Dugan's administrative assistant."

I searched for the name, brushed away a few clouds and came up with nothing.

Baxter hadn't been expecting a response, he'd been getting breath to continue. "He's CEO of First American Credit Union. The assistant thought Carly seemed interested in offshore accounts."

"Offshore is pretty broad." I waited for him to speak.

"Yes. But it's something."

Not much of anything, really. "You don't sound so great." Subtlety didn't come naturally to me, and with Baxter, we never bothered trying for the polite.

He sucked in a shallow inhale. "I had a treatment this morning. It usually makes it worse before it gets better."

Baxter kept the particulars of his lung ailment to himself. I hoped with all his money and power he'd find someone to cure whatever plagued him. Not only because he was helping me find Carly.

"Thanks for the update," I said. We waited. I didn't know what trotted through his mind, but for me, I liked our connection. Probably because he was the one person in my life I hadn't known forever, who couldn't list all eight of my siblings or the color of the dog we had when I was six. Except Baxter probably did know all that about me and more. He had investigators on his payroll, after all.

"You were sworn in yesterday." That's what I meant about knowing things. "How is it going?"

Aside from a murder? "Fine."

Wheeze in, huff out. "Good."

Riveting conversation, and yet we didn't ring off. The blip of an incoming call made me blink and sit up. "Call coming in."

Baxter sounded as startled as I was. "Oh, sure. I'll let you know if I hear anything about Carly."

I punched the new call to hear Marybeth's dispatch. "Auto accident reported CR 67, seven miles north of Highway 2. No serious injuries indicated. Two vehicles remain at the scene. Called in by local citizen, who names the parties involved as Newt and Earl Johnson."

Great. The Johnson brothers went to school with dad. Bachelors, they lived on their family's homestead in the same house. When they got along, which was about two-thirds of the time, they were the best of friends. When they were on the outs, no telling what might happen. One of their altercations in the Long Branch resulted in the bullet holes still decorating the ceiling.

Marybeth laughed. "Best get used to these guys. I swear I sent Ted after Newt and Earl about once a week."

Huh. Ted never said much about the Johnson brothers. I thought I knew most everything he did as sheriff.

I probably didn't need to check it out since there weren't injuries, but it was close, only seven miles from where I sat in my cruiser.

White, cold sky spewed shards of snow into my windshield. Not enough to amount to anything but reminding me how damned cold January in the Sandhills could be. I shed my gloves. Sometimes, the winter produces a stunning landscape. The morning sky dazzles with blue to rival any sapphire. Hoarfrost shimmers on branches, and the air is so crisp it crackles. With no light pollution to distract, the night sky sings with the brilliance of millions of stars.

That's all true, but it also feels like January nights fall in the middle of the day. The sun slips low at four o'clock, and by five, it's full-on night. Maybe, if you lived in Antarctica, the cold around here wouldn't faze you, but for me, someone who loves the ninety-degree summers, the winters last much too long.

It didn't take long to find them. I slowed down and pulled over to Earl Johnson's gold Monte Carlo, manufactured about the time my parents were thrilling to *Charlie's Angels* on TV, half on, half off the pavement. Facing it, at the same whacky angle to the road, was Newt Johnson's aqua Monte Carlo, same model and year.

It looked like the cars had swiveled on the road and careened partially into the barrow ditch, as if they'd hit a patch of black ice, though the road remained dry. Since neither car looked any more wrecked than normal, I figured the auto ballet was harmless and would have been fun to watch.

Newt and Earl stared at me where they stood between the two cars.

I pulled on my gloves, zipped up the coat and snatched a ski cap. Damn, it was covered in that Irish Spring Ted scent.

I pushed myself into the icy air and crunched across the frozen grass, my feet immediately chilled in my ropers. I approached the boys.

Since they'd gone to school with Dad, I placed Earl and Newt somewhere around sixty years old. The camo shirts they wore hung loose and nearly to their knees. The pants, also camo, looked like they housed sticks for legs. Thick-soled work boots completed their matching ensembles, and I wondered if they bothered keeping track of whose was whose on the rare occasions when they did laundry.

"Howdy, Newt. Hi, Earl." I waved at them both. "What's going on?"

"It all went to hell when the ladder flew off Newt's rig." That was from Earl. They weren't twins, but they weren't more than a year apart. Because their five-foot-seven frames were identical, and they always wore grease-stained caps they got for free from the feed store, and their faces were often covered in grime, the best way to tell them apart was to check the right earlobe. Earl, the older of the two, had bit off the end of Newt's ear when they were toddlers. I doubt that was their first fight. I know it wasn't the last.

I needed a little more to go on. "You had the ladder tied to the roof? What made it come off?"

Earl threw a thumb in Newt's direction. "Noodle nuts can't tie a knot to save his life. I was doin' fine until the ladder flew off like a whirly bird. I hit my brakes."

"And you started to honk like a drunk goose," Newt added. "That's what scared me."

"It wasn't my fault you ran off the road." Earl grunted.

Newt put his hands on his hips. "'Cause I had to turn around and see what your problem was."

Earl's lips pursed like a snippy old lady. "I was tryin' not to hit you."

They looked ready to tear into each other. “Anyone hurt?” I swung away from them to view the surrounding area.

Newt answered. “Naw.”

“You been to the sale in Gordon?” I asked.

The Johnson brothers were known to collect trash. If you’d cleaned out that shed or barn where your grandparents, then parents, then you and your kids had been tossing items you didn’t want to throw away or maybe didn’t have time to drag to the dump, and you finally decided it all needed to go, you called up the Johnsons and they’d take it off your hands for a small fee. I never understood how they made a living collecting trash, unless they occasionally came across something valuable. But then, I never understood cigarette smoking or drug abuse or even Ted’s attraction to Roxy. Some addictions had no logic.

“Nmge fungle sig,” Earl said.

Newt wacked him on the arm. “She can’t understand you.” To me, he said, “Naw. We cleaned out some sheds today.”

Earl stood up and stretched his back. “Out north Sunflower way. Rasmussen’s, Stevens’s, Kellers’.”

“You boys can do a lot in one morning.”

“Weren’t big jobs on any one place.” Earl smiled in a flirty way.

I tested the rope on the ladder they’d reattached to Newt’s roof, wondering why anyone would paint a ladder black. It seemed secure enough now. “You gonna be good to get home?”

“Yes, ma’am,” Earl said.

Newt looked me up and down. “You’re sheriff now?”

Earl shoved at Newt’s arm. “Don’t be an igit.” To me, he said, “I don’t know what Ted was thinking. Most folks, when they trade in, they want something better. The man made a mistake if you ask me.”

I can’t deny it was nice to hear, even coming from Earl Johnson. “I want you boys to be good, now. No more fighting.”

They agreed. And like Mose and Zeke, my seven-year-old nephews, might even have meant it. But like my nephews, it was only a matter of time before they went at it again. I waited while they climbed into their Monte Carlos and drove toward the highway.

I threw myself into the cruiser and leaned into the heat.

Before I put the cruiser in gear my phone rang. I pulled it out to answer Milo Ferguson, Choker County sheriff.

I pictured him leaning against his desk, his legs splayed and his belly hanging low. "Making sure you're clear on the co-op traffic stop tomorrow."

Grand County sheriff joined the three adjoining county sheriffs every few weeks to conduct random traffic stops on Highway 2 or 61 or 97. Once or twice they'd intercepted drug runners. Mostly they caught speeders or issued fix-it tickets. I infused my words with gentle sarcasm. "Wouldn't miss hanging with you boys for the world."

"Always a good time," Milo said. He paused, then in a lower voice, like a kid whose mother makes him say something nice, he added, "Just want you to know I think a woman can do this job like any man. Welcome aboard."

I doubt he'd felt that way nine months ago, before I solved the murder Milo had been ready to pin on Ted. "Thanks."

I hung up and started down the county road. To the west, Chad and Meredith Mills's house caught a slice of sunshine. Trey had told me to wait for him.

My job. My county.

I didn't need Trey Ridnoir's permission to do my job.

I slapped on my blinker. Let's see what Meredith Mills had to say.

8

A gravel road wound from the paved County Road 67 a quarter mile to the house. The two-story house looked newer in daylight, all clean with no chips or wear. The sage green siding resembled wood slats but would never peel and buckle like my parents' house. A broad porch opened to the yard with wide steps, the railing matching the vinyl fence surrounding the yard. A modern steel barn that probably housed their car and pickup and maybe a garden tractor to plow the way to the county road loomed about thirty yards to the south of the house.

The cruiser's tires crunched to a stop. A spiffy silver Audi A4 and a black Lexus LS without a scratch, both with Omaha plates, parked next to Meredith's red Volvo. The metallic paint of Meredith's SUV sparkled in the sun. I'd heard grumbling about this fancy rig, mostly that it was too sporty and not American made. I knew it was US manufactured, but since it wasn't a Ford or Chevy, it made some people suspect Meredith might be a Democrat.

The Smith and Wesson was a lump on my hip. I rested my hand

on it, decided I wouldn't need it in the house and unbuckled the belt. I left it in the car and locked the door.

In the Sandhills' way, I knew more about Chad than our lack of social contact would merit. People talk and facts accumulate, whether I thought about it or not. I knew that Meredith and Chad had bought a few acres from Enoch Stevens, Josh's father. Chad's parents taught at Danbury High School for a few years. That's where Chad had graduated. But his parents had moved on shortly afterward, and he didn't have any other family around here. I didn't know what drove Meredith and Chad to settle here.

But they weren't ranchers, so they'd needed a plot of land only big enough for their house and barn.

I hopped up the steps onto the wide porch. Not the weathered wood of most Sandhills porches; the Mills's was manufactured wood. The kind they'd never need to paint. Material that couldn't be purchased until twenty years ago. As a rule, we Sandhillers didn't splurge on fancy porches. We put that kind of cash into barn improvements, a new tractor, or that snaffle bit we'd been eyeing for a couple of years.

I knocked on the door, praying someone stood close enough to let me in before my lips turned blue. A younger version of Meredith opened the door and reached out to pull me inside. She was all blonde hair and graciousness. "Oh my. Come inside. The cold is killer."

She wore skinny jeans and a sleek black tunic—a get-up not common out here. The tunic flirted around her thin curves, the long sleeves soft against her arms. A delicate silver chain circled her neck with a glinting diamond adding to her elegance. She held out a pale, thin hand. "I'm Emily, Meredith's sister."

Meredith's house smelled of manufactured flowers, as if an army of fashionistas had showered and shampooed and all the scents mingled in a garden of cosmetics. A small entry area opened into the living room, where I'd told Meredith the bad news. From there, the flowing floor plan made room for an oak dining table at the far end, with windows along the south and west sides. A counter bar was visible to the right of the dining room, and the kitchen must be around the corner from the bar.

Feeling dowdy in my jeans and flannel shirt, all covered with my classy barn coat, I introduced myself as a friend of Chad's. "How is Meredith?"

Emily held out her arm to take my coat. "She's not in the best shape right now."

"I understand." She'd probably be feeling surrounded by dense blackness, maybe shrouded in sweats and huddled in a blanket, unable to do anything but stare into space and wait for the worst of it to pass.

A ruckus drew my attention to the stairs. *Thump, thump, thump.* Pristine running shoes, then leggings, then a stylish long-sleeved athletic shirt backed down the stairs pulling a heavy plastic container box that banged on each step. Meredith's blonde hair was scrunched into a bun at the back of her head. She made it to the ground floor. "There's four more boxes upstairs. I think they'll all fit in the back of the Volvo."

"Mere." Emily's voice carried just enough emphasis to sound a warning.

Meredith spun around. Her eyes flew open when she spotted me. "Oh. I didn't know you were here." She sounded breathless and startled. Despite her grief, she wore a full face of makeup, even lipstick. Her eyes weren't red rimmed, though they held a frantic gleam.

I eyed the container box, clearly labeled Summer Clothes in black Sharpie. "Moving?"

Meredith's gaze jumped from the box to me. "Oh. Well. Sitting around was making me crazy. I'd been planning on cleaning out my closets and sending clothes to the women's shelter in Omaha. Emily can take them back with her."

Except Meredith had just said to put them in her own car.

Emily's right eyebrow twitched, and then she smiled. "Why don't I make some coffee?" She backed out of the room.

A distinguished man with salt-and-pepper hair, beige twill pants, and what might be a cashmere sweater stepped out of a room to the right of the stairs. "Damn it, Meredith. My cell keeps going in and out."

Meredith closed her eyes briefly and inhaled, as if asking for patience. "Daddy, this is Kate Fox."

His eyes brushed me, and a polite, uninterested expression landed on his face. "Good of you to stop by." He turned to Meredith. "Can I use your phone?"

"It's on the desk." She directed the last word to his back. To me, she said, "Daddy is in the middle of settlement negotiations. He's an attorney."

An older, and every bit as elegant, version of Emily rounded the corner from the kitchen. She hurried to me in her three-inch black boots and designer jeans. Her blue sweater looked so soft I wanted to stroke it. She held her hand out. "I'm Meredith's mother, Mrs. Sterling. You're the first to bring condolences, and I'm afraid we're not organized, but Emily is brewing coffee so we can at least offer that."

I shook her hand. "Thank you. I won't stay long."

Although she spoke welcomingly, Mrs. Sterling didn't seem thrilled to have me. "Please excuse me." To Meredith she said, "So far I've been able to arrange my caterer to deliver the platters to Aunt Francis, and she'll bring them before the service."

Meredith's jaw tightened for a split second, then she smiled. "Perfect. Thank you."

Mrs. Sterling clicked toward the kitchen. "I can only find the stemware. Do you have the old-fashioned glasses from Grandmother? Oh, and the pastor can only do a morning service."

Again, Meredith blinked. "That's fine, Mother. Thank you."

Every family, every individual, deals with grief in their own way. But the whole atmosphere felt wonky. Meredith's family must have been roused from their beds and hit the road before daylight. Meredith herself couldn't have slept more than a couple of hours at best. Yet everyone acted like this was a normal day, scurrying around. Keeping busy dealing with death.

Meredith hesitated a second as if casting around for polite options and not finding any good way to get rid of me. She indicated we go to the living room. Still a comfortable space, it felt chilly without the crackling fire.

I sat in a leather chair, and she settled herself on a wooden pew next to the cold fireplace, perching on the edge to give me a clear signal she didn't intend our visit to last long.

One big inhale to get me started, and I said, "We suspect Chad's death wasn't an accident."

If the news blindsided her, I couldn't tell. She didn't even blink. "Why is that?"

"Someone hung a railroad tie from the overpass, and it smashed through the windshield." I was thankful she couldn't see the image that ran through my mind. Chad's body a lump of gore. She didn't twitch or even seem to breathe. We sat in silence for several minutes, and whatever went on in her head stayed hidden from me.

"Have you found out anything more?" she asked, a quick glance to the kitchen as if hoping we'd get our conversation over before Emily returned.

"We're really just gathering information right now." I leaned forward and lowered my voice, leaving the decision to inform her family of Chad's suspicious death up to her. "Right now we don't know if the killer intended it for Chad or for any railroad crew that happened to be running that train."

No one knows how they'd react to shocking and tragic news. But I'd have expected a catch of breath, clutch of fingers, at least tears or confusion. Meredith did none of that.

She jiggled her leg, hands stuffed into her lap. "No one has a grudge against Chad, and there just isn't anyone. He was the sort of guy everyone liked."

That popped out as if she'd been thinking about it for a while, not as if she'd just learned our suspicions. I waited for her to continue, figuring her nerves would win out.

They did. "I mean, you can ask his boss at BNSF. Clete Rasmussen will tell you. Chad always helped out, and the work he did for the union was well known."

She glanced at the kitchen again, clearly not wanting anyone to overhear us. "I think it was a random thing, you know. Like some kids causing mischief. They probably didn't think it would amount to much."

That sounded pretty close to what Clete said. "What about Josh Stevens?"

Her eyes opened wider still. "Josh? He's a good friend. He and Chad were roommates at UNL."

"Are you and Josh friends?"

She nodded. "Of course. He's the only person I knew when we moved here." She fidgeted. "I don't want to disparage the Sandhills, but you've got to know it's difficult to make friends when you haven't lived here all your life."

She waved a hand at me. "I mean, you've been to college, seen a little bit of the world. But so many of these people are so, so . . ." She exhaled and shook her head. "It's hard, you know? It might have been different if Chad had family around here or if he'd lived here his whole life."

We tended toward cliquishness, for sure. But plenty of people had come from other places and fit in just fine. Mom didn't fit in because she didn't want to. I suspect she wouldn't fit in anywhere, and she didn't care.

It could be Meredith didn't make friends because she thought she was too sophisticated for the likes of us.

Or maybe we did hold her off some. With her rigid social standards, some Sandhillers might feel uncomfortable and judged, where she never intended any such thing.

"So, you and Josh are good friends?" I asked again.

Emily's appearance with a tray holding three tea cups and saucers, a creamer and sugar bowl in white china made Meredith tense even more. "Really, Chad and Josh were friends. I was sort of the third wheel."

Emily's eyebrow twitched again.

My phone rang, I answered it. "Sheriff's . . . Sheriff."

Betty Paxton gave me a gushing hello, the tinny sound of Jennifer Nettles complaining about lost love whining from her radio in the background. "Can you come to the courthouse today? Bill Hardy's got a pickup he bought in Spearfish. Needs inspection before I can give him plates."

"Give me a half hour." I signed off. "I've got to go."

Emily set the tray down. "Oh please, you must stay for one cup."

She didn't leave me an option short of being rude, and Dad would know. He was like God that way. Even though she filled the cups with coffee, none had sloshed to the saucers. That might be an admirable feat in some circles. Emily handed me a saucer with the cup balanced. "Cream and sugar?"

While I preferred the fixins, I didn't want to try to manage more. The rattling cup on the saucer was enough of a challenge for me. I studied a painting over the fireplace. A herd of mustangs raced through a dusty arroyo. I squinted and looked at Meredith. "Is that an original Jack Sorenson?"

Emily poured a splash of cream into another cup and deftly handed it to Meredith. She added cream and a smidgeon of sugar to her own cup, a tiny spoon stirring soundlessly.

A drip of coffee sloshed over the rim of Meredith's cup and dribbled onto the saucer. "Oh, no." She laughed. "I couldn't afford an original. It's a giclée. A print, you know, with texture so it looks like an oil painting."

Yeah. I was raised by an artist. I knew what giclée was.

Emily twitched an eyebrow at the painting. "Are you interested in Western art?" she asked me.

I started to shrug, remembered the delicate balancing cup and sat still. "I'm no expert but, yeah, I like paintings of the West."

Meredith's eyes darted to a large canvas between the kitchen and living room. It looked like a Frank McCarthy. That most definitely was a giclée, and even then, would cost in the tens of thousands.

I knocked back a swig of coffee, grateful it wasn't too hot and I could lower the level so I wouldn't spill. How the hell could they afford that art on Chad's railroad salary?

Meredith set her cup on the coffee table. The polished wood surface was inlaid with streaks of turquoise. She must have read the question in my face. "We were lucky to grow up around nice things. Mother's tastes run more toward seascapes and impressionists."

Emily giggled. "All those heavy gilt frames and the lights aimed just right."

A ghost smile acknowledged Emily's disdain. "I thought this house needed something more appropriate. I feel blessed that Daddy is generous in our inheritance."

Emily's eyebrows did a tango. I loved Emily and her lie-detecting twitch.

9

On my way back to town I called Sarah. "When I talked to Robert earlier he said you're sick."

She sounded chipper. "I'm feeling better. But you're in deep shit with Louise."

Not the first time and definitely not the last. "She's outright forgiven me."

"That's good because she was in a state last night. She made us eat in a hurry, banged spoons and Tupperware around while she divided up the leftovers. She punished you by not leaving any food for you."

I laughed. "I hadn't noticed. The banner was nice."

"Oh that! She had the kids make that while we cleaned up the kitchen. She wanted you to feel guilty."

I did, but only a little.

That out of the way, I plunged in. "What do you know about Meredith and Chad Mills?"

One thing I love about Sarah is her willingness to cross pastures with me without all the gates being opened first. For instance, if I'd asked Louise, she'd want to know about Chad's death, and I'd have to field a whole bunch of questions. Sarah considered a moment. "I invited Meredith for a Pampered Chef and a lingerie party. She never came, never called. That's about it."

I searched the sky for any sign of sun. "She's lived out here for five or six years, but I don't see her around very often."

Sarah jumped the fence from my pasture to her own. "Gordon Haskett told me he's looking to sell his town house. Thought you might be interested."

What was I just thinking about Sarah always staying with me? "Isn't that in Danbury?"

"Yeah. The one a couple of blocks off Main. His kids graduated, and he doesn't need it anymore."

She couldn't see me roll my eyes at her not-so-subtle hint for me to move. "Danbury is too far from the courthouse."

Apparently, Sarah wasn't done. "It's not as far as Frog Creek, and Ted managed that fine. It's got a fenced backyard so you could get a dog. Michael and Lauren have a couple of pups they haven't given away."

My brother's wife, Lauren, took life in gulps. With two young daughters, she managed to always have several projects going at once, most of them dealing with livestock on their ranch. Currently, she kept a huge flock of chickens and sold eggs, not to mention goats she intended to use for cheese. She'd wanted to keep all the puppies to add to her menagerie. But ever-practical Michael quashed that plan. "I don't need a dog."

"I met the new vet in Hodgekiss. Heath Scranton. He's hot."

A house? A date? Come on. *Et tu*, Sarah? "If you're going to play Louise, you need to be about forty more pounds and a lot more bossy."

She took off the gloves. "You're living at your parents' house. You keep finding things wrong with every place you look at. You won't date, despite the opportunity."

I could count on one hand the times Sarah and I had fought. When the sibs came down on me, she always had my back. "Why are you riding me?"

She let out a sigh. "Because you're on cruise control. It was okay for a while. You needed to take a breath after the whole Ted and Roxy mess. But it's been long enough."

I passed Dwayne and Kasey Weber's place on the right. The barn stood outlined against the pale winter sky. A horse with a thick coat milled in the corral. The few leaves clinging to the oak shivered in the afternoon stillness.

I knew about squabbling. It fluttered around me my whole life with one sibling or another at odds with something, someone, or each other. But not with Sarah. A terrible seismic shift shook me, and I got plain owly with her. "Since when do you get to decide how I ought to live my life?"

Her voice carried a knife's edge. "Be miserable, then. That'll show Ted and Roxy."

"Sheriff's phone is ringing," I lied. "I gotta go."

Sarah's tone didn't match her words. "Happy belated birthday."

"Glad you're feeling better." That's it. My mood swung low as I stopped off to change into a freshly washed uniform. I forced myself to strap on my gun.

The freezing air chilled me before I climbed back into the still-warm Charger, again reminding myself to get that pine deodorizer.

I pulled up at the courthouse and hustled up the back stairs. Steel guitar wound its way from Betty's radio into the quiet hallway as I went in search of Bill Hardy.

Clete was sitting in the commissioner's room when I passed on the way to my office. I stopped in the doorway. "I'm on a hunt for Bill Hardy."

He jerked as if I'd jumped him in a dark alley. "Said to tell you he'd be back. Had to go to the bank."

I backed up to go to my office and ran smack into Ethel Bender, sending her tottering backward into the wide corridor. She clutched her coffee mug to her sagging breasts and frowned at me with her lipless mouth. "Honestly."

Why couldn't I have bumped into a grizzly bear instead? "Excuse me." I stopped short of saying ma'am.

Ethel glanced over my shoulder into the commissioner's room where the coffee pot scorched thick coffee. "Nice of you to show up to do some county business."

Betty bustled out of her office, probably because she heard me and Ethel talking and she didn't want to miss out.

The feud between Betty and Ethel stretched back so many years no one remembered what started it. They might not even know. With not much county business, days could stretch on with no one in the courthouse but these two and the sheriff. Ted said they spoke to each other only when absolutely necessary.

Betty, with her spikey hair, patted my shoulder. "I thought I heard you out here. Glad you made it back to inspect Bill's pickup so quickly."

And the battle lines were clearly drawn. I got the treasurer on my side. The county clerk / assessor would bear watching. The two women stood still while awkward silence billowed around us.

Ethel sent me a stink eye. "I understand the state patrol is taking over the Chad Mills investigation." She plainly wanted to point out that not only was I not in the courthouse to take care of the good citizens with instant auto inspections; I was shirking everything else.

I opened my mouth but didn't get a chance to speak.

Still not looking at Ethel, Betty said, "Kate is busy getting used to being sheriff. This investigation is beyond her scope."

Was that supposed to be in my defense? She evidently thought keeping Newt and Earl from killing each other and inspecting vehicles for auto registrations topped out my list of skills for sheriff. At least I'd been certified to carry a gun. "Actually, the state patrol is assisting me."

Ethel stared at the coffee station behind me. "No one's asked me, but the idea of Chad dying in an accident is plain stupid."

Betty raised her eyes to the ceiling and murmured under her breath. "Here we go."

Ethel ignored Betty but shifted her burning eyes to me. "People like to ignore anything that makes them uncomfortable."

Betty put an arm around my shoulders and drew me away from Ethel. "Do you have a minute? I'd like to explain how the county budget works."

I'd rather stay and ask Ethel what she meant, but she'd already knocked into me to get to the coffee, like a cow on the way to the trough.

I tried to tune out the screech of some woman country singer on the radio and act interested as Betty showed me the ins and outs of fund accounting.

After assuring Betty I'd grasped the concept of budgets—as if I hadn't been running a ranch for years on two bits and a smile—I played my friend card, inviting gossip, something I'd spent most of my life avoiding but might have to embrace as an investigator. "Ethel seems gnarled up over Chad Mills's death."

Betty pshawed. "She likes to stir the pot."

I leaned forward like a conspirator. "What do you mean?"

Betty lowered her head away from me and straightened papers on her desk. "I'm sure I don't know what foolishness she's got herself worked into."

But I think Betty knew full well, and it obviously upset her. I thanked Betty for the information on county finances. I sauntered out of her office, and keeping my footsteps silent, crossed the hall into Ethel's office.

A counter created a narrow space just inside the door with a small reception area beyond it. The bulk of the assessor's office was a vault with a thick door like a bank safe. All the county records lived in ledgers and files in the vault. Ethel worked at a desk inside the inner sanctum, which might account for her troll-like personality. Ethel's clerk, Brittany Ostrander, a sometime girlfriend of my brother Jeremy, typed at a computer at the receptionist desk.

She brightened and started to stand when she saw me. I didn't want Betty to know I was in Ethel's office because I suspected she'd feel two-timed. After all, I was her friend, where Ethel was obviously loyal to Ted. I waved at Brittany as I slipped behind the counter.

I figured I could bluff Brittany that as sheriff, I had special privileges to go behind the barriers. "I just need to talk to Ethel." I kept my voice low to imply private county business.

Brittany nodded understanding and pointed toward the vault. "Sure. She's at her desk."

The rust-colored industrial carpet masked my boots as I passed through the eight-inch vault walls into the silent, cave-like room. It smelled of old banana peels and baloney, what Ethel probably had for lunch.

Ethel didn't look up from her desk piled two feet thick with files and papers. Her fingers flew on an old-school adding machine.

I stopped in front of her desk and tried for a gentle tone so she wouldn't immediately curl up and rattle her tail. "I wonder if I can ask a couple of questions."

She slammed her hand on her adding machine and it whirred a few times. Maybe she didn't have rattles or fangs, but she wasn't shy on the venom. "What are you doing in here? Isn't Brittany at her desk?"

I held my hand up to ward off some of her fight. Might as well jump straight into it, in case I needed to run for my life. "I wanted to talk to you privately. Who do you think had cause to hurt Chad?"

She threw herself back in her chair, and I wondered that it didn't break. Her thin mouth formed a smirk. "I knew Betty wouldn't tell you. Always protecting her own."

I'd have to wade through Ethel's stream to get to the good stuff. "She didn't seem to know anything about Chad."

Ethel's chuckle had the sound of rustling dead leaves. "I don't suppose."

For the love of cheese, this woman made me work for this. "Can you tell me what you know?"

Ethel inhaled until I thought she might explode and looked away as if I tromped on her nerves. "You know Olin Riek is Betty's cousin?"

I traced the family tree in my mind and nodded, wondering where this was heading.

Ethel glared at me as if I were a dunce. She prompted me. "Olin Riek? Sells State Farm and a few other companies?"

"Sure." And what? Man, this sheriffing gig called for buckets of patience.

She waited for me to make a connection, and when I didn't she shook her head in disappointment at my stupidity. "When Chad Mills got to be president of the union at the railroad, he started steering his guys to get their insurance from his buddy in Broken Butte. When he got the union account switched over, well that was Olin's bread and butter. Didn't make him too happy."

The used lunch smell in the closed space clogged my throat. "How do you know?"

She had a self-satisfied smirk. "Garth plays cribbage with Olin on Sundays. Garth says Olin was spittin' nails about Chad. Said he could go hang himself."

That hardly makes him a murderer, but I didn't say that. Olin wasn't someone I'd been around much. Just an older guy in the background of my life. He wasn't a big man, probably around sixty-five years old, not prone to calling attention to himself. "Okay, Ethel. Thanks for the heads up."

She reached for her scorched coffee and sipped noisily. "Ted relied on me to help him out quite a bit. I've been in this office a long time. I know about the people around here."

And if she didn't, she'd be sure to make it up.

I gave her more gushing thanks, waved at Brittany, and slipped out of the office and across the hall to the commissioner's room to see whether Bill Hardy had made it back.

Clete hadn't moved so I ventured in. I didn't take my coat off and perched on a chair. "Have you talked to Trey Ridnoir?" Clete had about as much starch to him as a wet rope.

"Nope. Had my phone off."

Sometimes you've got to let another person unload their sad on your shoulders. "It's been a rough day, I'll bet."

Clete lifted a Styrofoam cup half full of coffee. He set it back down. "Hell of a way to go."

I had to agree with that. "I didn't know Chad well. What was he like?"

Clete raised his eyes to mine. "I thought a lot of Chad. So young."

Something tickled my brain. "Don't you have a son about the same age?"

Clete stared at the table. "My wife's boy."

"Were they friends in high school?"

Clete slid his cup a few inches one way, then back. "They probably played against each other in sports. Ron was only here his junior and senior years."

"Where's Ron now?" I asked out of politeness, not because I cared that much.

Clete was like a grizzle-faced Eeyore. "He allowed as how he didn't want any more snow and took off for California after a couple of years at the university in Lincoln."

"Oh." What should I add to that?

Clete shook his head. "College isn't for everyone, I guess." I'd like to escape to my office, but sitting with Clete seemed like the thing to do.

He sat back and veered off the topic. "Have you heard anything from Carly?"

Speaking of college. She should be halfway through her freshman year. Everyone in town knew she'd run away last spring just weeks before graduation. I shook my head. "Not much."

"Kids can be a real disappointment some times. I always believed in Scripture, 'Train up a child in the way he should go; even when he is old he will not depart from it.' But I wonder how old a kid has to be to not depart."

I doubted he referred to Carly, but I didn't need to go prying into his private life.

Guess he didn't mind a guest. "You try to help them out. Give 'em advice and do everything you can, and then," he sighed, "it all goes to hell."

Never the life of the party, Clete's normal gloom darkened a few shades. "You know, when Chad started at the railroad, I took him under my wing. I helped get him the union rep position. We'd talked about him going for my job when I retired."

"I'm sorry." Union rep. A person couldn't take on that responsibility and not make someone unhappy from time to time. Like Olin Riek.

He stared at his coffee cup. "How could it all go so wrong?"

The shrill of my phone sliced through the silence. I jerked to my feet. "Sorry." I nodded to Clete as I rushed from the room, leaving him to his sadness. I answered in the hallway. "Hi, Michael. What's up?" Michael, my younger brother by five years and twin of Douglas and married to Lauren.

"Meet me at the Long Branch."

Michael, the brother who charged through life at breakneck speed, never had time for a casual get-together. I didn't need Spidey senses to know something was up. I steeled myself in case he plopped a cute and cuddly puppy into my arms. "What are you doing in town?"

"I had to pick up parts in Broken Butte, and I'm heading home."

"And you want to meet me at the Long Branch?" To say it was out of character would be like calling January in the Sandhills cold.

"I just pulled up, but can't stay long. Kaylen has a basketball game at six."

Now it made sense. Michael had an hour before he needed to be at the school to watch his eight-year-old daughter run up and down the court. I can't go as far as to call what they did an actual game of basketball. But even LeBron had to start somewhere.

Going to the Long Branch opened me up to all kinds of questions about the Chad situation from happy-hour drinkers, and I didn't crave that kind of attention. "Meet me at the house instead."

The ding of his pickup said he was climbing out. "I'm already here. Come on, I'll buy you a beer."

Bill Hardy's voice rang out from the commissioner's meeting room. He'd apparently returned from the bank and was jawing with Clete.

If Michael had been in town getting parts, he probably didn't have a puppy in tow. "I've got to inspect a pickup and then I'll be there." If for no other reason than curiosity about what he was up to.

I walked into the commissioner's room and greeted Bill.

He rose and took a few tentative steps as if warming up his legs. He'd been a pro rodeo bull rider, and the spills, breaks, and damage had settled in his bones. Even when his muscles agreed to work, he limped toward the door. "Sorry to drag you into the courthouse. I heard about the train wreck last night. They say Chad Mills was killed. I 'spect you've been dealing with all that mess. That BNSF will be trying to find their way out to making it Chad's fault so as not to have to pay the widow."

I didn't answer.

Bill glanced back at Clete. "No offense there, ranger. But you gotta admit, the damned railroad ain't no Santa Claus."

Clete waved Bill away. "None taken. I just work for them."

"I'll get my inspection form." I hoofed it out of the meeting room and down the short corridor to the door marked "Sheriff."

That's me. Not weird at all. I jangled the stupid key ring with the cheesy sheriff badge. It stabbed me with a memory of my honeymoon with Ted at the lodge on the North Rim of the Grand Canyon. We'd seen matching silver rings designed by a famous Navajo artist in the gift shop. We couldn't afford anything that fine, so we'd given ourselves five dollars each to pick out something for the other in the gift shop. I'd found the key ring with a sheriff's star for him. He'd picked out a tiny wooden pop-gun for me. I'm sure it wasn't oversight that he hadn't changed it. I inserted the key and pushed the door open.

As the sheriff's wife, I'd been in this office countless times. There were the occasional lunches or dinners we'd shared early on when I had to make an unexpected trip to town for penicillin for a sick critter or for a load of salt to throw in the pasture or a couple of times just because. I tried to forget those thrilling moments because that always led to me remembering that he and Roxy conducted some of their business here, too.

The office was cramped and dark, with no window to the outside. I wondered if it had been a supply closet and later converted to the sheriff's office. It didn't matter. The sheriff didn't spend a lot of time there. Well, Ted hadn't anyway. I could see that I might hang out here more than he did, just to escape my parents' house.

Toward the back of the office, behind a thick steel door, Grand County possessed one holding cell. I pulled open the door to see it. I'd expected a cot and sink behind the barred jail door. What I found was a storage area and the door not locked. It looked like a hundred years of spare parts and county records. I took that as a good sign there wasn't much cause to lock up prisoners in this quiet, law-abiding enclave.

If Ted had straightened or cleaned there was no evidence. Papers heaped the metal desk with files tossed haphazardly across the surface. Two ceramic mugs half full of coffee, doctored with Ted's concoction of sugar and powdered Coffee-Mate, grew fluffy white mold. A couple of drawers in the four-drawer metal filing cabinet were open with files lying on top. It's possible Ted skedaddled from the office in a rush, like the survivors of Kilauea, but the more likely explanation was sheer passive aggressiveness. He'd purposely left everything in disarray. I wouldn't be surprised if he and Roxy had spent last Saturday night here, downing a bottle of Jack Daniel's and rearranging the files.

I'm not bitter, though. Maybe he's not either.

I peeked under the papers strewn on the desk. No inspection forms. The slim drawer in the center of the desk held only pencils, pens, free-range paperclips, a few loose coins, and lots of dirt. The top right-hand drawer had a Grand County phone book from 2004, a directory of Nebraska county officials from the same era, and other useless and outdated reference booklets and folders.

The left-hand top drawer was more of the same worthless junk.

I plopped in the desk chair, the low burn of frustration heating my cheeks. The chair, one of those cheap secretary things with three legs on rollers, wobbled, then tilted. I grabbed for the edge of the desk, but the leg of the chair snapped, and I tumbled backward, my legs sailing up. I landed on my back, the chair on top of me. I pushed myself to my knees and grabbed the chair to study the break. I'd never be able to prove it, but I'd have wagered Ted sabotaged me.

"Are you okay?" Bill Hardy's scuffed cowboy boots appeared in the office doorway.

I scrambled to my feet. "Sure. I haven't found the form yet." I flipped through a desktop file folder.

Bill stepped into the small office and snicked the door closed. His voice lowered conspiratorially. "I only brought the rig in today because I wanted a word with you."

His tone caught my attention, and I quit rifling papers on the messy desk.

He lowered himself into the only intact chair in the office, something pilfered from the commissioner's room. "You know Marv and Trish Duncan? They've been out at our Double T place since before Pop's heart attack."

I knew the place. So far back in the hills a person could settle in at Christmas and not be seen until Easter. There were many places like that in the Sandhills. In fact, Indians and outlaws used to retreat out here to hide.

I nodded. "Marv and Dad used to fish on Duck Lake out there." It took about an hour to get to the Double T from Hodgekiss, but the scenery was worth the bother of a four-wheel-drive road meandering between rugged sandhills and shallow lakes. Dad and Marv Duncan had gone all the way through school together. When Dad went into the Army, Marv had married and moved to the Double T.

"I'd forgot about that." He eased his weight to his hip, as if sitting in one position for more than a few seconds pained him. "So you know what a nice place it is. I keep about four hundred head out there year round and some more heifers in the summer."

There's only one reason he'd be telling me this. I folded my arms and leaned back against the file cabinet and waited for it.

He shifted again. "Marv is fixing to retire. Trish wants to move to Omaha to be close to the grandkids, you know how that is."

Here it comes.

"I know you just got sworn in, but I'd sure like to have you take over for Marv." He spoke faster than I'd ever heard him. I supposed he wanted to sell me on the idea. "It's a long ways out for a single person, I know. But Marv and Trish raised two daughters out there and got along fine."

A ranch job. Exactly what I wanted. The life I was used to and loved.

Bill stood. "You don't have to answer me right now."

This was that safety net I'd been hankering for. A house of my own, a solid ranching job, solitude, peace. "When do you want an answer?"

Bill rubbed his left giddy-up. "A week or so. Marv's ready to go and I 'spect you got to give a couple weeks' notice so's they can appoint Ted."

Funny there seemed to be no doubt about Ted stepping back. He'd be thrilled.

Bill reached over my shoulder to the top of the filing cabinet and pulled off a stack of papers. The inspection forms.

10

It didn't take long to inspect Bill's truck and send him back to Betty to jump through the hoops of presenting the spike-haired sharp-shooter with every number, signature, proof of cradle-to-grave protection, and woe-to-who-might-have-forgotten-the-exact-slip-of-paper. January was about to throw the switch on the afternoon and bring on early dusk.

I stood in my office doorway. If I took Bill's offer, why bother to put order to this chaos? I tossed the broken leg on the seat of the wrecked chair and wheeled it down the hall. It clattered down the stairway to the basement and back door.

The cold shocked me, though I should have expected it. I dragged the busted chair down three concrete steps and past the Charger. Up with the Dumpster lid and goodbye to Ted's chair. There had to be enough money in the budget for a new one.

Clete was gone by the time I gathered my coat and keys. Betty's radio clicked off, and she and Ethel both stepped out of their offices, like dueling piano players, inserting their keys into their office doors, one after the other. They turned in sync and, keeping a few feet of distance between them, not making eye contact, walked toward the front hall.

"Calling it a day?" It was a stupid thing to say, but these tough old birds, flip sides to a bitter coin, scared me. As they did almost everyone else in the county.

Spiked-haired Betty perked up. "Looks like another cold one out there."

My voice was too cheerful by half. "They say there's a warm front heading in." We were in a deep conversation now.

Ethel had changed from her one-inch vinyl Sunday school teacher pumps to vinyl black ankle snow boots with rubber soles. I wondered how she zipped them around her thick ankles. She didn't offer me any more than a sullen nod. At five o'clock, the red lipstick she favored had crawled up the fine wrinkles around her lips and smeared, giving her a clown mouth.

The courthouse perched halfway up the hill that Hodgekiss called home. It was around the corner from Main Street, just down half a block from the ornamental windmill that stood sentinel over the business district. The highway ran perpendicular to Main. The Long Branch and First State Bank stared at each other on opposite sides at the bottom of Main. Marching uphill from those anchors were Burnett's Tack Shop, the post office, and Hodgekiss Farm and Ranch Supply on the Long Branch side. Dutch's Grocery Store, the Methodists' Jumble Shop, and a rickety fourplex known as the Apartments on the bank side.

Three blocks on either side of Main made up the north side of town. Crossing the tracks where two highways intersected, one long street bordered the tracks the length of town. This street is where I grew up and where I'd retreated to nine months ago. When

Hodgekiss got 911 service a few years ago, the officials gave all the streets name. No one in town used them. When referring to my street, people said south-along-the-tracks.

Bill Hardy's offer ground in my mind as I glanced at the cruiser and decided to leave her parked and walk. *It*. Leave *it* parked. Sure, it'd be a real chickenshit thing to abandon the office after being duly elected. But a ranch job. Those didn't come along every day, at least not one this sweet.

I hoofed it to the Long Branch, still sporting my lovely brown uniform and Smith and Wesson. With little sleep last night, I was more than ready for a warm shower and an early night.

The smell of work-soiled bodies, beer, onions, and grease so old it could have a high school diploma filled me as I found Michael perched on his usual barstool amid a noisy early crowd. Where his twin, Douglas, loaded extra pounds and had round cheeks like the Pillsbury Doughboy, Michael's muscles had hardened with daily workouts. Even his hair had darkened from the blond of his youth as if growing more serious as Michael pushed himself harder.

The kids' basketball game brought a few young families in for a sandwich, along with the usual postwork bunch, a couple of the guys who worked at Hodgekiss Farm and Ranch Supply, a cowboy or two. No one had fired up the jukebox, which played only country music. I could at least be thankful for that.

I plopped on what everyone knew was my stool, next to Michael. I waved at our Aunt Twyla, from down the bar. Dad's sister, she and her husband, Bud, owned the Long Branch.

She stood no taller than five foot five, and her dark hair was pulled into a messy ponytail that hung between her shoulders. The ravages of cigarettes and booze showed in her bony face, lined with deep wrinkles.

Michael gulped from a Coors Light can. "Everyone's talking about Chad Mills. What's the deal?"

I shrugged as Aunt Twyla caught up to us. "What can I get you?"

I looked at Michael's can. "Not that horse piss, that's for sure."

"Hey!" It was an old argument, going way back to high school.

I punched his arm. "Bring me that IPA you had last week, if there's any left."

Twyla cocked an eyebrow. "There's plenty left. Cowboys around here don't go for the microbrews. But are you sure you should be drinking?"

I shot her a questioning glance.

"In uniform." She indicated my dapper duds.

Oh. I didn't hide my disappointment. "Coffee, then." I was so tired the caffeine wouldn't keep me awake more than ten minutes.

Michael laughed. "The price of power."

"What's up?"

He tipped his beer. "What? I can't buy my older sister a birthday drink?"

Twyla set the coffee in front of me, and I wrapped my hand around the heavy mug. "You haven't bought me anything since that Batman comic book when you were in second grade."

He pointed at me. "I didn't buy that for you. You stole my allowance."

"See?"

"And now look at you all Sheriff and everything. The world is full of irony."

I surveyed the bar while I waited for him to get to whatever point drove him to meet me here. I was surprised to see Josh Stevens sitting at a two-top shoved under a window. He hunched over a half-eaten burger, a bottle of that IPA I'd had a taste for beading in front of him. He stared out the window with that sad Abe Lincoln face.

Michael set his can on the bar. "Okay. Here's the deal. Diane and Louise and Douglas, they all—"

I held up my hand. "You drew the short straw?" If I wasn't so chapped, I'd laugh. Michael, the Fox with the lowest compassion quotient, the guy usually swimming so deep in his schemes and plans he barely took a breath, got tagged to straighten me out.

He let out a long breath and tapped the side of his can. "I had to be in town anyway, and those biddies cornered Lauren."

"Does the term 'biddies' include Douglas?"

"Douglas especially. He's like a supercharged mother hen with sideburns."

I laughed, sipped my coffee, and wished it was that hoppy IPA.

"They gave Lauren a sob story about how you need to 'engage' in life." He did air quotes and scrunched up his face to show what he thought of that psychobabble. "They all got together and decided it would be better coming from me, God only knows why."

"It's the element of surprise. I'd never expect you to give me a heartfelt talk." I hadn't expected it of Sarah, either. My brothers and sisters had known better than to wrangle her into their scheme. Wouldn't it tickle them to know she'd hitched to their wagon anyway?

He held up a finger to Twyla to order another beer. "Right. I told them, 'Kate can manage her own life, and if she wants to be a sad old maid living with Mom and Dad, then that's her business.' "

"Yeah, thanks for that."

"I told them I don't have time to chase after you and make sure your life is all hunky-dory, but Lauren threatened to cut me off if I don't talk to you. So here it is."

Twyla set a cold can of Coors Light in front of Michael, and he tipped it back as if he'd just run a marathon.

Josh hadn't taken a bite of his hamburger or touched his beer since last I looked his way. I don't think he'd even twitched a muscle.

I considered my coffee cup with dissatisfaction. "Duty done, Michael. And might I say, accomplished with your signature warmth and caring."

He gulped his beer. “Right. As if you’d want someone all soft and mushy.”

He had me there.

Michael slammed the rest of his beer down and stood. He grabbed my head in the crook of his arm and rubbed his knuckles across my scalp. “I may be a lousy messenger, but listen to what they’re saying. Get a life.”

I swatted at him, but he jumped back and strode toward the exit. He yanked open the glass door and backed up a pace or two, his head jerking in my direction, a look of alarm in his eyes.

Dahlia, my ex-mother-in-law, sashayed into the Long Branch. She held the door open, something I’d never seen, and Roxy appeared on the arm of my ex-father-in-law, Sid. He escorted Roxy to a four-top in the middle of the bar. Ted limped in, leaning on his cane, and Dahlia let the door close behind them. She acted like ringmaster for Barnum & Bailey.

Circuses always creeped me out.

Roxy was all boobs and fur, shiny lips, and absolutely everything I wasn’t and never would be. Her wide mouth stretched into a greeting and she paused as if stepping onto the red carpet.

I did not roll my eyes.

Well, of course I did, but no one saw me.

Michael glanced at his watch, then back at me, clearly fighting his need to show up to see Kaylen play basketball against giving me moral support. In truth, he was probably trying to weigh which move would score him more points with Lauren.

I waved him off, wishing I’d had the prescience to leave five minutes ago. If I left now, it would look like I was running away. We were much too civilized for that. I managed a smile of hello before I turned back to my lukewarm coffee, now really coveting Josh Stevens’s untouched IPA.

Twyla shoved a draft beer toward a cowboy halfway down the

bar from me. She huffed, pulled an order pad from her back pocket, and started around the bar toward the Conners' table. Twyla hated waitressing and was constantly on the lookout to hire someone, anyone. But three-quarters of the time, she suffered the hardship herself.

I faced forward, annoyed there happened to be a mirror above the bar and my attention couldn't help but wander to it. Twyla didn't say a word of greeting. She stopped next to Dahlia and raised her pad and pencil. Customer service wasn't Twyla's strong suit, but then, folks didn't come to the Long Branch for its friendly staff, good food, or fancy ambience. They came because everyone else came here and had for four generations. Aside from the gas station pizza, it was the only eatery in town. But even I had a hard time calling it a restaurant.

Dahlia raised her head toward Twyla, as if surprised to see her there. She sat back and with a voice inappropriately loud, she said, "We need a bottle of your finest champagne."

A garbage barge sank in my gut.

All I could see of Ted was the back of his head, and it looked as though he pointed his gaze to the table. Dahlia's public drama could embarrass him from time to time. Roxy sat next to Dahlia, as sparkly as the ordered champagne.

Dahlia's perfectly made-up face glowed with excitement. "Bring four glasses but also bring us a bottle of sparkling water. One of us won't be drinking alcohol." Dahlia clapped her hands, then leaned over and placed them on either side of Roxy's head and planted a loud kiss on Roxy's forehead.

Oh dear dread. This could not be happening. Not here. Not now.

Twyla stomped around the bar, slammed the order pad down in front of me, and started her grumbling tirade. "Finest champagne. Like I have that shit sitting around all the time."

Steady breath. I couldn't stop the heat creeping onto my face or the clench in my belly, but I could keep from making a spectacle of myself. One hand gripped the beige, thick warmth of the old-time café mug. The other clung to the edge of the bar.

Twyla rummaged in a beer cooler under the bar and, after a clanking of bottles and muttered curses, emerged with a bottle of Asti Spumante. "Left over from New Year's. S'pose that will do for Her Highness?"

From the mirror over the bar, I watched as Dahlia patted Roxy's hand, then pushed her chair back and stood up. "Everyone, everyone!" Her royal voice commanded the bar to silence. The smattering of families finishing up their suppers before heading to the game, the cowboys at the bar, the odds and ends having a drink before heading home, all gave Dahlia their half-hearted attention.

She didn't seem to care and acted as though she stood at a White House press conference announcing world peace.

My hands cramped where they clutched the mug and bar to keep me from plugging my ears. I clamped my teeth and for all that's holy, forced the edges of my mouth into the best imitation of a smile I could muster.

Twyla clattered ice into a beer mug and slammed it on the bar. "Bottle of sparkling water? For Christ's sake, she can get seltzer from the soda machine." She squirted the fizzy water into the mug and plopped it on a cork-covered bar tray along with three standard wine glasses. Dahlia would balk at the lack of flutes, but I didn't take much delight in that.

Dahlia lifted her chin and gazed around the motley collection of Long Branch patrons and said those words I didn't want to hear. "I'm overjoyed to announce that at long last," she glanced my way at that, "I'm going to be a grandmother!" She clapped her hands again, a reaction more appropriate to a seven-year-old than a middle-aged harpy.

Okay, "harpy" might be unfair. I didn't care. The whole situation reeked of unfair. It basked in cruel irony.

A murmur of congratulations rounded the bar. If the lukewarm reception bothered Dahlia, she didn't show it. Nor did she seem to mind the bar-sturdy wine glasses or lack of bottled sparkling water. She . . . glowed. Authentic happiness.

My hand crept to my belly, and I was surprised there was no gaping hole where my guts leaked onto the floor. I had to escape their happy party. The pop of the Asti cork felt like a shotgun blast to my heart. Ted's laughter sledgehammered into my brain.

I couldn't take one second more and fought to keep from bolting for the door. A warm hand closed on my cold fingers still gripping the coffee mug and pried them loose. Soothing glass cooled my palm, and I opened eyes I hadn't realized I'd squeezed closed.

An IPA bottle, less than half filled with tepid beer, nestled in my grip, and Josh Stevens leaned close.

"Take a drink, then breathe." He nudged my hand.

Listening to his direction, I did what he said. The beer burned as I gulped once, twice, three times. I set the bottle down and opened my mouth as if surfacing from a wild ocean.

He raised two fingers to Twyla, and she dove into the beer cooler. She had the caps popped off and the beers in front of us before I'd sucked in two more breaths.

Josh tapped the top of his bottle to mine and raised his. "Now, enjoy a cold one at your own pace."

I worried beer would spout out the bullet holes Dahlia's announcement shot through me, but a smile slipped onto my face. I nodded back to Josh and took a long pull on the fresh IPA. I swallowed it down. "Thanks."

Josh hunched over his bottle and caught my gaze in the mirror above the bar. "You just needed a minute. That's all."

Already the shock receded, a few inches at a time. “And a good beer.” I tried to make my tone light.

Josh turned halfway toward me, maybe testing to see whether I’d welcome his interference. “It can be awkward when someone you thought you loved starts on a new life without you.”

Awkward. I might come up with a stronger word. “I didn’t get much sleep last night. I think maybe I need to eat or something.”

He acted like what I said made perfect sense. He sipped his beer and didn’t quite smile. “Yep. Cold weather like this can take a toll, too. I was helping preg check Shorty Cally’s heifers today.”

I strained to make conversation with Josh and pull my thoughts entirely away from Ted’s doings. “Dad used to hire on for day labor between trips. He gave that up a long time ago when the BNSF lineups got so unreliable.”

Josh didn’t seem to have any more ease making small talk than I did. “It’s sure a crapshoot when they’ll call you for work.”

Dad spent much of his time at home checking the lineups on the BNSF employee Web site. By law, after finishing a trip, or “tying up” as they said, the engineer and the conductor had at least ten and sometimes twelve hours of rest before they could be called back to work. After that, they were added to the lineup, a nearly fictitious list of trains and crews that supposedly gave some indication when they’d be summoned to work. In reality, the lineups gave only a vague sense of when the crews were called; sometimes it was off by twelve hours or more. It was a crazy way to live.

“So you take your chances with working that far away?” The trains were called in Broken Butte, an hour’s drive away from Hodgekiss, and they only got a two-hour call. So being in the country might make that timeline dicey.

Josh looked uncomfortable. “Yeah.”

While we’d been talking and I was sweeping myself back in one pile, more people had filled up the bar. In the mirror I saw friends of Roxy's, including Kasey and Dwayne, pull up chairs and join the Conners.

"Hi, Kate."

The voice on my right elbow cut through my fog. Trey Ridnoir, face wind-raw and hair plastered to his scalp from his cap, plopped on the stool next to me. He eyed my beer and ordered a Coors Light when Twyla stopped in front of him.

I leaned back. "Trey Ridnoir, this is Josh Stevens. Josh was with Meredith Mills last night when I gave her the news. Josh, this is Trooper Trey Ridnoir. He's investigating the accident."

I couldn't say Josh was warm and easy before, but he looked downright frozen now. It took a might too long for him to raise his hand for Trey's offered handshake. He released quickly and stood. "I need to be getting home."

"Thanks," I stammered. "For the beer." He had to know I meant more.

Josh wove through the gathering crowd. Dahlia's sisters and their husbands had joined the table, and more friends of Sid and Dahlia's milled around. No doubt, Ted's mother had sent out a media blast, and people showed up for a command appearance.

Trey leaned toward me. "Do you know Josh Stevens very well?"

I shook my head and drained my beer. Maybe I could slip out unnoticed now. "He was older than me in school and went to Danbury."

"He and Meredith Mills were alone at her house last night?" Trey asked, still looking after Josh.

"He said she'd called him when she saw the emergency lights."

Trey let his beer sit. "You don't think that's weird?"

I weighed the kindness I'd seen in Josh's eyes and the way Dad obviously liked him against Meredith's strange behavior. "I think they're friends from way back."

Trey considered that. "Josh work for BNSF?"

I nodded, trying to appear casual as I scanned Ted's table and the crowd congratulating them. "How's the investigation progressing?" I didn't figure he'd offer up details since we sat in a public place.

He adjusted himself on the barstool. "NTSB and BNSF declared it not a safety issue, and they've hightailed it back to heated offices." While he answered me, he watched Josh slip out the door. "I drove all the way to Broken Butte, but the trainmaster wasn't there, and none of the employees would talk to me. When I went to Meredith Mills's, her prick of a father chased me away and said I couldn't talk to Meredith without her lawyer there."

I took a sip and nodded at him. Okay, yes, I did feel a little smug. "Clete was here. I tried to tell you the crew wouldn't talk to you, not in uniform anyway."

He squeezed his can. "You never said anything."

Not that he heard. "And I'd say if you're planning to talk to Meredith, which I think you should, you ought to do it soon, before she bolts."

Trey pulled a palm-sized spiral notebook from his chest pocket and flipped it open. He clicked a pen and jotted in the book. He looked up at me. "What do you mean?"

I sipped my beer. "Looked like she was packing when I talked to her this afternoon."

His jaw dropped. "You talked to her? How did . . . ? I told you not to."

I nodded. "I know."

Before he spit out the question or lecture or whatever he wanted to say, I caught a fearful sight in the mirror. Oh no. I hadn't made a getaway when I had the chance. My heart thudded like it wanted to break a couple of ribs. I squirmed on my barstool, thinking to retreat to the bathroom. Too damned late.

Ted slapped Trey on the back of his heavy jacket. “Good to see you, man.”

Trey jumped to his feet, a giant grin on his face. “Conner! How the hell are you?”

Ted’s eyes slid to me, to the gun at my hip, and quickly away. He clasped Trey’s hand. “Not missing having to patrol in the freezing cold, I can tell you that. What do you know about the Chad Mills deal?”

Trey lost his grin and eyed me uncomfortably. “I, um.” There was a moment of silence.

I raised an annoyed eyebrow.

Trey cleared his throat. “I called him. Thought maybe he could give me some pointers about talking to the railroaders.”

With effort I kept from boxing Trey’s ears, as I might my younger brother Jeremy. “I thought I made the point this morning that I’m Grand County sheriff.”

Trey’s face flared. “Yeah. You’re right.”

I nearly crushed my back teeth to powder.

Finally, Trey swept his arm toward the table, now crowded with extra chairs and people hovering around it. “Looks like you’re celebrating.”

A smile battled onto Ted’s face, and he glanced at me again, then back to Trey. “Roxy’s been tossing her cookies for a few days, and this morning she really got after it and couldn’t stop. It scared the bejesus out of me. I rushed her into the emergency room, and turns out, she’s got morning sickness.”

Trey slapped Ted on the back. “Good for you, man.”

“Not like regular morning sickness. It’s on steroids or something.”

Ted maneuvered around Trey until he stood between us. He leaned closer to me, maybe hoping the increasing din of the bar would make his words private. It didn’t. “I didn’t know you’d be here.”

Trey looked straight ahead. No way he couldn't have heard Ted or the pity in his voice.

I waved my hand and surprised myself with the casual tone I manufactured. "No problem. Congratulations to you both. I know you always wanted kids." I wanted them, too. We'd plotted and planned and put it off for years. Three months before I found out about Ted and Roxy's affair, we'd decided I'd stop taking birth control. I'd even thought I might be pregnant once, though it turned out to be a false alarm.

He started to put a hand on my arm and stopped himself. "It's got to be hard, watching me and Roxy get married and you aren't even dating. And now this."

What the hell? Was he trying to be an ass, or was he a dimwit? Trey fidgeted, and I clenched my hands, my jaw, my gut. Back came the easy smile, at least I hoped it looked that way. "It's fine, Ted. I wish you happiness. I'm moving along myself. Really enjoying this sheriff gig."

He frowned, and when he came up with words, they sounded a little less than sincere. "Yeah. It's a good job. Lots to keep you busy. 'Course you ought to let the state patrol handle the murder investigation."

"Murder?" I glared at Trey.

He looked as guilty as a puppy caught chewing a favorite shoe.

I snarled like a caged badger. "Even a rookie knows not to compromise an investigation by giving sensitive information to citizens." I hopped off the barstool and grabbed my coat. "I'll be handling the investigation from here on out."

Trey sputtered, "That's not . . . You can't."

Someone tugged on the collar of my coat, keeping me from shrugging it on. I spun around to the pale, short woman with stringy gray hair. I went cold all over, and I barely got her name out without choking. "Vicki."

She let go of my coat and whipped out a stenographer's spiral notebook and poised her pen. "I want to know about the railroad accident."

What had she overheard? Next week's headline might read "BNSF Engineer Murdered," or it might be "State Trooper Maimed in Barroom Altercation."

I studied Vicki Snyder. If she'd picked up any mention of murder, she didn't give a sign.

Ted slinked backward as I faced the determined newspaper editor. "You have a week before deadline, right?"

She narrowed her slightly rheumy eyes at me. "Five days. And it takes some time to write, you know. It's not like magic."

As I hurried away, I said, "I'll get back to you."

She took a few steps after me and whined, "Ted always cooperated with the press."

I whirled around and nearly plowed into her. I strode to Trey. "If you want to help out, be here first thing in the morning, and we'll take a road trip to Broken Butte." Before Vicki could stop me or Trey could argue, I pulled Ted's cap out of my coat pocket, stuffed it on my head, and stomped into the night.

11

The forecast called for dry but cold. I layered long underwear under my ever-stylish sheriff brown. But underneath that, I added a slightly padded push-up bra. I even managed to put on a pair of simple gold hoop earrings and a touch of makeup. Not Roxy-full-out-twenty-products-complete-with-perfume display, just some mascara to keep my eyes from disappearing and that good kind of Burt's Bees lip balm with the slight tint so I didn't look dead.

Maybe I wasn't on the prowl for a boyfriend, but it wouldn't hurt me to not look like a ranch hand at the end of calving season. I stared at myself in the old vanity mirror my sisters and I had fought for space in front of while we prepped for dates. The glass was scratched and streaked with black from old age. It didn't help my glum image.

Should I take Bill Hardy's offer? Yes. No. The ethical thing to do was finish this investigation before flitting off to another job. I owed Grand County that much, at least. Dad would say I owed them the four years I'd agreed to when I won the election. I wasn't above a little Scarlett O'Hara, I'll-worry-about-that-tomorrow procrastination.

I forced a smile and tilted my head, pulling my curls up and behind my head with one hand.

"You're not a Victoria's Secret model, but you're no dog either." I smooched myself.

A burst of girlish giggles made me close my eyes. Of course. "Aren't you supposed to be in school?"

Michael's two daughters, Lucy and Kaylen, flew into the bedroom and tumbled onto the bed. Lucy, four years old and cuter than was legal, started to jump. "I don't go to school." Just being around her forced me to grin.

Kaylen, grown up at age eight—the consummate big sister—sat cross legged and stared at me through the mirror. "You do too go to school. And you know you're not supposed to jump on the bed."

Lucy flopped her head back and forth while she jumped, keeping a close eye on herself in the mirror. "I go to pretty school." That was Lucy's understanding of preschool. She gave one giant thrust and blew raspberries on the way to landing on her butt with her legs crossed in perfect imitation of Kaylen.

I let my hair fall and picked up an elastic to corral it into a ponytail.

Kaylen assessed me like a model's agent. "You are a very lovely young woman."

I met her serious gaze. "Thank you. I needed that."

Lucy jumped up and threw her arms around my neck, leaned over my shoulders, and kissed my cheek, all the while watching herself in the mirror. "You are beautiful."

"And late." I stood up with Lucy still attached to my back. We bumped down the stairs, and Kaylen followed. I deposited them in the kitchen with their mother, Lauren, and grabbed my sheriff's coat and debated about appropriate headwear.

Lauren held a steaming cup of coffee. No sign of Dad or Mom. Mom was either asleep and would stay that way for forty-eight hours, or she was downstairs in some kind of scary sleep-deprived artist's trance.

Lauren gave me an apologetic wince. "Sorry about that. I hope they didn't wake you up. The heating system broke down at the school. They got it fixed but delayed start for an hour to let the building warm up."

"Things fall apart in this kind of cold. No problem. I was on my way out." It was never a problem. Family came and went, flowing like a noisy tide. At any moment of any day someone was bound to burst in on me. I loved my family. Loved them. Really, really loved them.

I wouldn't allow myself to add the "but" that begged to follow. Without giving Lauren time to press me about taking a puppy, I hurried out the door.

My patrol car didn't get her heat blowing before I parked her behind the courthouse. It. It. It. Ethel and Betty probably got to the courthouse at the stroke of seven. Days start early in the Sandhills. Band practice, sports workouts, and school activities had students in town by six thirty some days, so it made sense for the courthouse and bank to open early, too. I stopped into Betty's office to tell her I'd be in for a while. She didn't need to know, but I counted it as PR to stay friendly and keep her on my side. I left Ethel alone, afraid if I poked my head in and there were no witnesses, she might take the opportunity to lop it off. Her unrequited love for Ted ran deep.

Seven thirty. Trey might show up anytime, ready to get a good start after striking out yesterday. I probably should set the office to rights, but my mind trotted down another trail. Trey didn't show up to interrupt me as I spent an hour on the phone, mostly with Louise. I had to walk her around a few pastures first to throw her off my real purpose.

I ended up with only a few interesting bits of gossip for all the pain of listening to Louise. Chad Mills, though he had no kids of his own, volunteered with little kids' basketball in Danbury. Because he had a railroad job and couldn't plan to be in town for practices and games, he couldn't be head coach, but whenever he was in town, he showed up. According to Louise, the kids loved him because when they did something good, he rewarded them with nice gifts. Last year, when they'd won the holiday tournament in Broken Butte, he'd given them all iPad minis.

Louise's opinion of that galloped on for long enough I worried I might have rusted in place. I speculated about why Trey was so late. While she chatted about the new house Chad and Meredith built and how you could afford that if you didn't have children, but why would you want a life so lonely, I searched an office store online and ordered a new chair to be delivered in seven to ten business days.

She started in about Meredith and her thin model's appearance. And if you didn't have a family to cook for and your husband gone several days every week, you could probably stick to a diet. I Google Earthed Bill Hardy's Double T and was surprised to see an aerial shot of the ranch. The date stamp was from last year so I got a pretty accurate shot of the house roof, green yard, a long stand of lilacs and a new pole barn. Peace and quiet, cows and solitude.

I interrupted Louise mid-rant about how she'd give up a perfect figure for having a family any day. "What about Josh Stevens?"

She made a choking sound. "J-Josh? I don't really know him. He went to Danbury and was a year ahead of me."

"Oh." I waited, curious about her reaction now and in the kitchen yesterday morning. "Thought you might be friends."

Her laugh sounded like a strangled kitten. "No. He's Black Socks, you know."

That might be why I'd never been around him much. From what I knew of the Black Socks, they held tight to their strict Christianity and didn't mingle much with outsiders. Not Amish or Mennonite, but with that mysterious and set-apart air. Obviously, he'd drifted from his restricted upbringing or he'd never have been drinking a beer in the Long Branch.

The back door of the courthouse clanked open, the sound rattling up from the basement above Kasey Musgrave's ranting on Betty Paxton's country radio. "Good chatting with you. We ought to do this more often." I pulled the phone from my ear to the sound of Louise's voice.

"Wait. I wanted to tell you—"

Wearing his gray-blue uniform and clutching a McDonald's coffee cup he'd had to have bought in Ogallala, Trey walked around the corner. Without preamble, he started in, "I plan on going to Josh Stevens's ranch first thing this morning, then back to the depot in Broken Butte to talk to Clete Rasmussen this afternoon."

I sat back in my folding chair, made a point of focusing on my industrial wall clock, and said, "First thing this morning is long gone. If we don't get trucking to Broken Butte right away, we'll be too late."

"Late for what?"

I stood and grabbed my coat from the back of my chair. "I've got to work with the sheriffs' co-op at the monthly traffic stop this afternoon. And the engineer's union meeting's at noon so we'll catch a few railroaders at the depot for their pre-meeting bitch-fest. And Clete will be out of there before noon."

"How do you know?"

I squeezed around him and started for the back stairs. "I have snitches all over. Let's take your car." Not only did it have seats that weren't worn to the nubbins; it didn't smell like Ted.

He followed me. "I'm sorry for that whole awkward scene in the Long Branch, and I understand why you told Ted you were working the case. But it's okay. I'm not going to tell him otherwise."

I stopped halfway down the stairs and craned my neck up to him. "Thanks. Now let's go."

He grinned at me in a teasing way. "You're not serious."

I hurried down the stairs. "I've already spent half the day waiting for you."

A gust slapped my face when I opened the back door of the courthouse and stepped out. I sucked in a breath before the wind whipped it away from me. I ducked into the passenger side of Trey's car, thankful it still held the warmth from his drive. I kicked a McDonald's bag at the same time I identified the telltale aroma of hash browns and sausage.

Trey slid in behind the wheel but hesitated to put the keys in the ignition when the bag of food trash appeared under his nose. He jerked back, surprised.

"One of the first things they taught us at the academy was to keep the car clean."

He turned as red as the ketchup smeared on the side of the bag. "I don't usually eat this stuff." He grabbed the bag. "But this drive is killing me."

"I'm not judging you. In fact, the only reason I want you to get rid of the evidence is because it smells so good."

Compared to the nauseating smell of Dad's oatmeal, the warm grease of fast food smelled like paradise. It reminded me I hadn't had anything this morning except coffee.

He lurched out of the car and dropped the trash in the county Dumpster, where it could keep Ted's chair company.

We drove down Main Street, past the grocery store and the ever-popular post office. A half-dozen people gathered in the lobby of the post office behind the plate-glass windows. This was the unofficial meeting place for those who didn't have the leisure to hang out for coffee at the Long Branch. Mail was always out by 9 A.M., or

Barbie Drake, the postmistress, would be in for it. For rural small towns, the post office took the place of the well in ancient villages or the water cooler in office buildings. A body could wander into the post office somewhere from 9:07 to 9:28 on any given morning and be guaranteed the latest news.

I had no doubt today's headlines included Chad's death. I just hoped they hadn't started wondering about murder. In fact, more than a few pairs of eyes homed in on us as we idled down the hill toward the highway.

I sat up and punched the button on my seat belt. "Pull in here for just a second."

Trey whipped into a parallel spot across the highway from the Long Branch. I jumped out and ran across the highway in front of the car and pushed through the glass door into the small vestibule. I hip-checked that door. Bacon, coffee, and the crush of an overheated room threatened to drown me.

Twyla stood behind the cash register, deep bags under her bloodshot eyes. Wranglers draped from her hips, as lean as a turkey carcass on Thanksgiving night. I could almost see the headache from her usual hangover. Her raspy, cigarette-abused voice greeted me. "Hey, Sweet Pea."

"Can I get a couple of your cinnamon rolls and two large coffees to go?"

Twyla nodded and winced. I followed her to the window between the kitchen and the dining room and leaned on the counter while she went through the swinging doors. She appeared on the other side and reached for the Styrofoam boxes. "They say the funeral is tomorrow."

I pulled two cups from the stack next to the coffee machine. "Already?"

She grabbed a spatula with the surface area of a small airport runway. “They say Meredith’s dad railroaded the whole affair. Seems he doesn’t want to stick around here any longer than he has to.”

I filled both cups with steaming brew not much darker than a yellow lab. “Is this tea?”

Twyla looked up and I showed her my cup. “Oh for Chrissake. That bimbo Bud hired is about as good as a four-sided penny. I’ll make another pot.”

Twyla’s mood tended to improve as the day went on and the hangover faded. I waved her off. “That’s okay. We’ve got to go.”

Twyla thrust the spatula into the pan of cinnamon rolls like it was a sword into the bimbo Bud hired. She lifted a brick of baked goodness, slathered with cream cheese icing and thick with gooey cinnamon heaven. “Can you believe they wanted to have a private service at the Episcopal church?” She plopped the first roll in a box and stabbed the spatula with deadly purpose back into the pan. “But the priest, what’s her name, you know, the one they send from Broken Butte. . . .”

I didn’t know the name of the priest and poured another cup of weak coffee.

“Anyway, she talked sense into them. They’re having the funeral at the high school.”

This wasn’t unusual for a young person, well known and liked.

“But they’re having a private reception at Chad’s house.” Twyla landed the second roll in the box and smacked both the lids down. “That’s snooty if you ask me. Like we’re not good enough for the likes of them.”

“I’m sure that’s not it. It’s probably the way they do things in Omaha.” I paid Twyla, grabbed my rolls and a stack of paper napkins, and bolted for Trey’s cruiser.

Trey might deny being a junk food aficionado, but he didn’t turn down the roll. Smells of warm cinnamon tickled my nose, and the sweet icing melted on my tongue.

I sipped with dissatisfaction. "Sorry about the coffee. Uncle Bud and Aunt Twyla don't offer a big menu, and the food is mostly fried or heavily calorie-fortified, but they generally make a good cup of joe."

He smacked his lips. "Best rolls ever, though. You said uncle and aunt?"

I swallowed and said, "Uncle Bud and Aunt Twyla own the Long Branch. My father's sister and brother-in-law."

"Are you related to everyone around here?" Only one bite remained of his roll.

I took another sip of coffee. "There are dribs and drabs of the county where I couldn't even tell you a person's name."

He shoved the last bite in. "But not much."

I pushed the second half of my roll at him. "I'm done."

He picked it up. "You sure?"

I nodded and didn't say anything while he finished the roll and licked his fingers. He kept giving me a sideways stare, and I finally couldn't stand it. "What?"

He colored like Lucy when I caught her snitching cookies. "Nothing."

I gave him the evil eye my nieces and nephews knew well.

He laughed. "Okay. It's just that you're . . . well, you're not what I expected."

Damn. This conversation took a fork I hadn't intended. "You expected something?"

He squirmed. "Not really. I don't know. It's just . . . Well, a woman, only six weeks of training at the academy. I didn't think you'd be so . . ." He trailed off.

"So what?"

He kept looking down the road, his face blazing. “Never mind.”

I was happy to never mind. I could never mind it forever.

He waited a beat, maybe as disconcerted at the personal bend as I was. “So.” He cleared his throat. “You interviewed Clete yesterday?”

12

I settled back in strained silence and watched the dried prairie zoom past. Last winter, I would have been in my tractor with the farm and ranch report blaring, twisted to watch the arm of the hydro fork as I grabbed hay and deposited it in the pasture for the hungry cows. Now I was sheriff. I'd better act like it.

Trey had brought along a too-thin folder containing all our investigation notes and photos. I pulled out the photos of the crime scene and flipped through them again. "Someone had to climb up to secure all that hardware without being seen. Even if they did it at night they'd have to dodge highway traffic, not to mention trains and anyone on the county road."

Trey said, "It had to be more than one person."

"Not necessarily."

He squinted an eye. "Have you ever tried to lift a railroad tie by yourself? Those puppies are heavy. No one could secure one up there alone."

I rifled through the photos and pulled one out, trying not to focus on the red and gray mush that looked like hamburger stuck to the end of the tie. It was one thing to talk about Chad's death, another to see his brains splattered on the railroad tie. I swallowed a sick feeling and focused on the tie. "Pulleys. He didn't have help."

Trey nodded. "Or she."

I gave him a questioning look.

He opened his hands. "What did you find out from Meredith?"

I mulled it over. "Weird family. But Meredith looks so frail I'd doubt she could manhandle a stick of firewood, let alone install hardware under a bridge in the middle of the night."

Trey considered. "What about that guy, Josh Stevens, who was with her that night?"

We hit the flat that took us into Broken Butte. "I don't think he's involved."

"Why?"

I wanted to have a good reason but had to settle for the truth. "He seems like a good guy."

Trey laughed. "Good vibes? That's some solid investigative work."

So much for Trey's impression I had it all together as a professional. Didn't they always say to trust intuition? But then, I had a strict policy against *they sayisms*. Still, Dad respected Josh enough to have him in our home, and even if I couldn't trust my judgment, Dad's was infallible.

"What we've got is that someone hooked up a railroad tie and dangled it in front of the engine on a dark night, when the crew couldn't see it. It might have been a random killing. I mean, not necessarily meant for Chad," I said.

Trey pointed a thick finger at the photo of the underside of the bridge. "That's a pretty complicated mechanism. It'd take a freaking engineer to figure that out."

"You think someone wanted Chad dead?"

Trey shook his head. "It would have to be someone who knew trains and who knew when Chad's train would travel under that bridge."

I gave a humorless chuckle. "That's a big pool. All railroaders, which would include anyone who uses their computers, have access to lineups. Basically, they all can see the dispatcher's screen so they know where every train is on the line. Might narrow it down if the killer knew Chad would be looking for a yard light."

Trey brightened. "Who would know Chad lived there?"

I directed Trey through Broken Butte to the east side of town and south to the rail yard. "About anyone on this line, or anyone who knows anyone on this line, or any person at all who had enough interest in killing someone and the smarts to find out where he lived."

A twelve-foot-tall chain-link fence surrounded a parking lot Walmart would have called overkill. Trey pulled through the open fence. "This is bigger than I thought."

I collected the trash from the back seat. "Lots of coal trains running from Wyoming and then the usual freight."

I set a brisk pace to the brick depot. If I walked fast enough, I could survive without smashing a cap over my head. Not that I cared what I looked like.

Okay, maybe I cared a little.

Cigarette smoke cut through the cold air at the entrance of the depot. They weren't allowed to smoke inside but wouldn't want to get too far away from the door.

A large empty room greeted us. Old linoleum and several vending machines gave the place a less than homey feel. Off to the left, an arched entryway led down a corridor. Another room, lit with fluorescent ceiling fixtures, contained a long table. The lights were on, and a few men milled around. The whole place smelled like burned coffee, oil, and fuel, and nothing clean.

I headed toward the corridor and Trey followed. "You've been here before?"

I shook my head. "Dad's been with BNSF longer than I've been alive, and I've never seen where he goes to work."

"Then how do you know where to go?"

The corridor ended in a brick wall, giving us a left or right choice. I took the right and Trey stayed with me. "I don't. But you have to start somewhere."

Clete's baritone rumbled from down the hall. I gave Trey a *see?* look and hurried to the doorway.

Clete looked up, frowned at me, and said into his phone, "I'll call you back." He put the phone down. "What's wrong?"

Trey followed me in. "We need to ask you a few questions about Chad Mills."

Clete's expression went from sucking a lemon to kidney stone passage. "Did we have an appointment?"

Trey pulled a chair from where it was pushed against a wall. "Do we need one?"

Apparently, whatever attacked Clete wouldn't kill him, and his expression improved to mild stomach cramp. "No. Seeing Kate made me nervous, that's all."

I found another chair and pushed it in front of Clete's desk.

Trey settled himself in his chair. "Why's that?"

"I'm just waiting for the heat in that damned courthouse to go belly up, and I figured she was here to tell me that very thing." Doom hung so close over Clete's head I was surprised he didn't duck.

"Far as I know, it's toasty on the home front," Trey said.

Clete didn't look at me. "So, she's helping you out with the investigation?"

Trey pulled out the small notebook he kept in his breast pocket. "Is that a problem?"

Clete let out a painful breath. "I can't say as I like it. I mean, murder is pretty ugly. Don't you think?"

Too ugly for a girl, he meant.

Trey earned points for not agreeing. "Did you know Chad well?"

Clete concentrated on Trey. "About like the rest of the boys. I see 'em occasionally when they get on or off a train."

This was a different tune than he was humming yesterday.

Trey jotted something, then looked up at Clete again. "Why don't you tell me what you know about him."

Clete splayed his hands on his desk, elbows bent, and disapproval sank into the folds of his face. "I pulled up his employment sheet here. He was hired on in 2000. Got fired for running through a dark signal in 2008, not much else since. Got elected union rep two years ago."

Trey leaned forward. "You say he was fired?"

Clete made a face like a gas bubble lodged in his gut.

I could take this one. "Getting fired at the railroad isn't like it sounds. It usually means a temporary punishment. Getting fired means getting put on unpaid leave because you've broken some rule or something. But going through a dark signal is serious, isn't it?" I asked Clete.

"Can be," Clete agreed. He eyed Trey and sighed as if put upon. "You got signals like on the road—red, green, yellow. In various combinations they mean to go, stop, slow down. In the case of a dark signal, you better stop the damned train because no one's telling you jack and it can mean all kinds of trouble. In this case, some fool kid shot out the light, and it didn't mean anything." He rubbed his chin. "Chad's got a pretty clean record."

Trey scribbled in his notebook. "Can you think of anyone who would want to hurt Chad?"

Clete leaned back, dragging his hands but leaving them on the desk. "I been giving this some thought, and I come up with nobody.

So I think maybe it's some kids or somebody. Not really after Chad, just out to do some damage or a prank gone wrong."

Trey rested his hands in his lap. "That's an awful lot of effort for a prank."

"What's so hard about hanging a tie to a bridge?" Clete asked.

"It wasn't that basic. There were precise measurements and timing. Like a professional engineer set it up."

Clete sucked in a breath as if sucker punched.

"What?" Trey's eyes brightened. "Did you remember something?"

Clete picked up his phone. "Nope. Nothing. But now I've got to get back to work."

Trey acted as if he hadn't heard the dismissal. "I'd like to talk to Bobby Jenkins."

Clete rubbed a weathered hand along his grizzled chin. "Nope. Can't allow you to do that without a BNSF representative."

"You can attend," Trey said.

Clete burped. "Can't. Got to head to Ravena. Broken rail."

He was putting off Trey. The trainmaster didn't need to be on site for a broken rail.

Trey held up his hand to halt Clete. He looked down at his little spiral notebook. "I'll contact BNSF. What was on the train that night?"

Clete set his phone down, crags deepening on his face. "Well, I'm not for sure. Usually, that time of night it'd be a coal train."

Trey took that in. "Where would that train originate?"

"In the coal mines up by Gillette, more than likely." Clete's hands flattened again on his desk, and the knuckles tensed.

I thought about walking the train that night. Pictured the frozen ground, the blue light of the moon. "It wasn't a coal train."

Both men jerked their heads toward me, as if they'd forgotten I sat with them.

Clete's brow furrowed more. "Pretty sure it was coal."

I nodded at a hulking desktop computer on a table behind him. "You've got Chad's last call record on the computer, right? Why not pull it up."

His hands clenched. "We've been having some trouble getting online today. This cold mucks up everything. Like that broken rail by Ravena. Maybe you could come back."

His cell phone rang. My cell phone rang. Trey's brought in the trifecta. Even Clete made a facsimile of a smile. Trey shrugged and all three of us answered.

"Sheriff's . . ." My mind was still on the train. I stood and walked to the corner of the room.

The voice, scorched from a millennium of cigarette abuse, rasped out, "This is May Keller, and I've got a house for you to buy."

Really? In the middle of a murder investigation, I have to deal with this? I eyed Clete. His typical kettle drum of a voice was hushed. Trey had pushed back and walked out to the hallway. "Thanks, May, but I'm not looking for a house right now."

I waited out her gurgle cough, impatient to get back to my job. "That's what Diane said you'd say."

Oh for the love of Pete. "My sister Diane?"

The unmistakable intake of smoke from her cigarette. "The same. She heard about the house. And don't ask me how because I'd only told Aileen Carson."

One possible scenario is that after hearing about May's house, Aileen walked into the bank, told someone there, and by some twisted trail, word landed in Diane's orbit at her bank in Denver. But it could just as bizarrely have found another route.

May blew out the inhale—much too long to hold the poison in her lungs, but then, it wasn't going to make much difference in her life now. "It's not good for you to be bunking with your parents. You're the sheriff now, and it sends a bad message. You know, like you're not man enough to have your own place."

I wanted her off the phone and my attention back on the case. "I don't think—."

"Don't interrupt me," she coughed. "You and I both know I don't have time to argue."

She had plenty of time to natter about her opinion.

"It's hard enough for folks to respect a woman."

She ought to know. May Keller had been ranching on her own since her cheating husband disappeared about the time the cool cats were jitterbugging to Glenn Miller and his home boys. She'd out-toughed and outsmarted, not to mention outlived, the old boys she'd ranched alongside. That took buckets of guts. But she wasn't gaining me any respect from the state patrol by interrupting me now.

"To tell the truth, I hadn't thought about you until Diane called. I always liked that missy. She's got balls. You take a page from that book, I tell you. Grow a pair. Move out of your mommy and daddy's place."

Clete spun his chair around to put his back to us and bent forward, his voice practically a whisper. Trey stood in the doorway, his phone back in his pocket.

I lowered my voice. "Can I call you back?"

A coughing fit delayed her response. "It's that little ol' house on the north side of Stryker Lake. I gotta be in town tomorrow afternoon for the Episcopal women's meeting, so I'll meet you out there at three." Guess she ran out of time for me, because the phone went dead.

Clete continued to mumble into his cell. I caught a couple of ominous-sounding words, like "lawyer," "plead," "sentence." Clete looked over his shoulder at me and Trey watching him. "I gotta go." He nodded with impatience. "Fine. I'll see about it." He punched his phone and set it on the desk, looking like he'd rather fling it across the room. His face twitched.

He knew we'd heard, and I thought I ought to break the tension. I tried for sympathy. "That your son?"

He rubbed a hand over his face, pulling the canyons into flat plains and letting them drop back. "My wife's boy."

Since he didn't dig any deeper, I let it go.

Trey stepped forward and dropped his card on Clete's desk. "Thanks for your time. E-mail me Chad's call record when your computers are up again."

We stepped into the hall. Clete followed us to the door and shut it behind us.

Trey set a strong pace. "That was Bobby Jenkins. I'd tried to get hold of him earlier. He said he's here for a union meeting, so we can interview him."

I should have thought of calling Bobby to meet us here, but it didn't matter whether Trey contacted him or I did. At least the investigation moved ahead. "Great."

"Who was that on the phone?" Naturally he'd assume I was also working on solving the murder.

I kept my eyes straight ahead. "Personal call."

He didn't respond, but I was sure that knocked my professional cred back to zero.

13

My ropers clicked on the linoleum. Trey's lightweight hiking boots whispered. A door opened to my right with a table and chairs, and a whiteboard stuck to the wall. It looked like an empty meeting room. I tapped Trey's arm and pointed to indicate he should bring Bobby in there.

In a few minutes Trey's whispering boots mingled with the soft drag of tennis shoes, and Bobby shuffled into the room. Trey closed the door, and Bobby sank into one of the padded black chairs.

He looked considerably better than last time I'd seen him, but he seemed made of glass. He walked with a halting step, as if each hesitant movement might shatter him. His skin was transparent and pasty, and a watery sheen filled his eyes.

I pulled my chair close and spoke in a soothing voice. "How are you, Bobby?"

He humped his shoulders up and let them fall, and his mouth twisted.

I spoke in the same crooning voice I used to get Lucy to sleep. "Can you tell us what happened that night?"

A burst of laughter from the crew room next door made Bobby duck his head. He squeezed his eyes shut.

I put a hand on his arm. "Bobby? Are you okay?"

He opened his eyes and let his gaze travel over my head to Trey standing behind me. It took him a moment to lower his focus to me. He nodded, and his Adam's apple bobbed down his smooth throat. "I haven't slept much since . . . since then. I keep hearing that explosion and feeling the st-st-stuff on my face."

I sat back. "Of course you do. Have you seen a doctor or a counselor?"

He nodded, again swallowing. "I have some pills. They kind of take the edge off, but I'm not supposed to drive when I take them, and I had to get out of the house. My mom . . ." He ran a hand along his head, brushing back his hair. A gleam of sweat covered his face. "She's in my face all day asking if I'm okay."

Trey leaned against the wall and folded his arms. "Can you tell me what happened that night?"

Bobby eyed me, then Trey and settled on his chair. "So, we got on the train late. The paperwork had to be updated."

Trey unfolded his arms. "Is that usual?"

Bobby seemed to relax at the question; maybe it shifted his thoughts from the details of Chad's death. "It happens a lot. We needed to switch some cars around. Not a big deal."

Trey led Bobby down the road. "Who gives the orders for that?"

A little life came back to Bobby's eyes. "Trainmaster."

Now that we'd pulled Bobby back to the living, we started him toward the horror. I shifted closer. "So the trip from here to the bridge at County Road 67. Did anything unusual happen?"

Bobby shook his head. "No."

From all the years of Dad being an engineer, I knew these trips were mostly boring rides, cruising down the rails, not much to keep the crew from falling asleep. "Did you and Chad talk a lot?"

Bobby's voice shook. "Chad, you usually can't get him to shut up. We all make fun of him."

Trey walked closer and leaned his backside on a table. "Why's that?"

Bobby almost smiled. "Because he's so happy all the time. He's a real Boy Scout."

"Did that irritate people?" I asked.

Bobby considered that. "Not really. I mean, we gave him a hard time because that's what we do, but really, people liked Chad. He was helpful."

"How do you mean?" Trey asked.

Bobby shrugged with forty times more energy than when he sat down. "Like that night, we had to set out a car. He helped me."

Trey leaned forward. "What's that mean? Set out a car?"

Bobby responded with kind patience, as if talking to an ignorant child. "Things can go wrong with a car. Like that night, the tires were hot, which means a brake might not be working right or something. Anyway, you got to pull into a siding and uncouple the car and leave it. You know, set it out." A siding is an extra set of tracks where trains could pull over to wait for another to pass or where troubled cars could be left.

"So how did Chad help you?" Trey asked.

Bobby's face showed appreciation for someone giving him a hand. "He got out and checked it all to make sure I hit the clearance marks."

"You said that you were both looking for the yard light at Chad's house," I prompted him.

The scant bit of color faded from his face again. He nodded, and his lips moved before sound escaped. "Yeah. No light. Then that's it. The whole world exploded." Tears dripped from his eyes. He swiped at them and sniffed, his mouth contorted and watery. "His head was gone. Gone."

We sat in silence with only the sounds of men joking in the next room and Bobby's heavy breathing as he struggled to get himself under control.

His eyes pleaded with me. "Honest. That's all I remember. Can I . . . ?" He drew his arm across his face to dry off the moisture. "Can I go?"

I stood and put my hand on his shoulder. "Sure. Thanks, Bobby."

Trey walked him to the door, giving him a firm handshake. "Say, can you remember what kind of train you were running that night?"

Bobby sniffed. "Yeah. It was a stack train."

"Thanks." Trey handed Bobby a card. "If you think of anything else, give me a call."

Bobby dropped his head, pocketed the card and shuffled down the hall.

Trey turned to me. "Stack train?"

At least he acknowledged I might know something about the railroad. "Freight. Container cars of freight that are loaded off ocean liners and shipped across land. They can be like semitrailers stacked two high."

"Not coal."

Laughter erupted from the crew room. I held out my arm to send Trey in that direction. "Let's see what the guys have to say."

Trey fell into step beside me. "They wouldn't talk to me yesterday. What makes you think they'll talk to us today?"

The crew room sported the same faded tile floor and cigarette-smoke yellow walls. Windows lined the north wall toward the ceiling, casting a beam on three vending machines as if spotlighting poor eating habits. The soda, candy, and salty snack machines hummed their siren song to men—mostly men, though a few women engineers and conductors were among them. The Bunn coffee maker, producing fifty-gallon barrels of coffee per brew, spewed its toxic sludge, adding the acrid aroma more like dead highway skunk than fresh-brewed coffee. Four men lounged at the ten-foot blond pressed-wood table in their puke-colored plastic chairs, tall paper coffee cups in front of them.

I slid a chair next to a man who appeared to be two hundred years old. "Terminator. When are they going to let you out of the zoo?"

With a bony face that kept from being a skeleton only because it was covered with skin colored with a zillion tiny red lines, and with thinning gray hair longer than mine, the man tossed an arm around my neck, caught me in the crook of his elbow, and hugged me to his bony ribcage. "K-K-Katie! What's got you skulking in the underbelly of the world?"

Trey hid his shock well, but I detected a smidgeon of alarm in his eyes. He stood at the head of the table.

I pushed back from Terminator's grasp and turned to Trey. "Dave, this is Trooper Trey Ridnoir. Trey, my father's oldest friend, Dave Turmin."

"Who you calling old?" Terminator grinned, and his cheekbones nearly sliced his face open.

I knew one of the other men at the table. Lawn Dart. That probably wouldn't work for a police report so I struggled for his real name and fell short.

Lawn Dart sniffed and spit into a Mountain Dew can. He sipped his coffee. "I heard they made you sheriff down in Grand County. I never cared for that bonehead, Ted Conner."

A younger man, in canvas Dickies and a ratty hoody, jumped up and leaned across the table with his hand extended. He had the look of a prison camp survivor, nearly bald head and scratched face. "You're Kate Conner. I'm Tim Strong."

"Fox," I corrected him when I shook his hand, wondering at his exceptional friendliness.

Terminator tipped his gray bird's nest of a head at Tim. "That's ol' Two Names."

The light bulb came on. "Oh. Two Names. I didn't recognize you."

He ducked his head. "Yeah. I got drunk one night and my buddies shaved my head. Didn't even leave my beard."

I filled Trey in. "Two Names dated my sister Susan when they were in high school."

Two Names's smile looked extra big on his hairless head. He pointed at my uniform. "This is not a surprising look for you." He glanced at the other three railroaders. "This big sister here wouldn't buy us beer on prom night."

"Maybe she kept you from gettin' your hair shorn sooner," Terminator said.

The other railroader's phone bipped. He read the message and pushed his chair back. "No loss there." He rubbed the top of Two Names's head. "Come on, our train's here."

They trudged out, steel-toe boots giving them the look of astronauts.

Trey must not have been able to contain his curiosity. "Why Two Names?"

Terminator and Lawn Dart acted as if Trey was invisible.

Interesting. I gave my voice a little chill, hoping Trey would get the message. "Tim's mom divorced his dad and remarried, and Tim took his stepfather's name. When he graduated, he hired on with BNSF, and they always use last names on the lineup. About a year later, Tim took his father's name and changed it on the lineup. So it confused people, and he got the nickname."

Trey eyed me, then let his attention shift to Terminator and on to Lawn Dart. Neither of them added anything, just drank their coffee and looked at each other. Trey backed up a step. "I'm going to see if Clete has that paperwork."

With my back to the railroaders, I winked at Trey. "Good idea." Later, I'd fill him in on Lawn Dart's nickname. Several years ago, he'd gone skydiving on a dare. His chute only partially opened, and he'd made a connection with the ground that broke an arm and a couple of ribs.

When Trey was gone, Lawn Dart sniffed and spat again. He didn't have more fat than two strips of lean bacon. I wouldn't be surprised if, like a lot of railroaders, Lawn Dart spent most of his off-duty hours with a beer attached to his right hand. "What's a nice girl like you doing hanging out with that bad element?"

The laugh escaped before I knew it was on the run. "He's not so bad."

Terminator rubbed his hand down his beard. "I s'pose this is about the General."

"General?"

Lawn Dart supplied the information. "Mills. When we elected him union rep, it swelled up his head. So we started calling him General Mills."

Trey would love that. "Clete said everyone around here liked Chad."

Terminator laughed. "The way a gopher likes a rattle snake."

I pushed. "Bobby Jenkins said Chad was a good guy."

Lawn Dart leaned back with a sour look. "Baby Bobby thinks Clete Rasmussen farts pixie dust."

I wasn't sure what that meant and must have looked confused.

Terminator helped me out. "He means Baby Bobby isn't the sharpest tool in the shed. He's a sweet kid, you understand. But he's no brain trust."

Lawn Dart rattled his chair and took a few steps before he limbered up enough to walk to the coffee pot for a refill. "He's a damned idiot. They had no business hiring him. Blew through a slow order his first trip. Nearly got me fired."

Terminator winked at me. "That wasn't Baby Bobby's fault."

"Screw you." Lawn Dart filled his cup and clomped back to the table.

Terminator tipped his chair back. "As soon as the General got his new title, he started pulling shit like calling safety meetings and bull like that."

Lawn Dart blew on his coffee. "I'll tell you who don't like the General one iota."

Terminator winked at me.

"That Olin Riek." He nodded with finality. "And with good reason. When the General took away all his business."

Terminator agreed. "That was a dirty trick to play on Olin, for sure. And after Mills took over the union, he didn't work many trips."

Lawn Dart peered over the top of his cup. "But that still didn't satisfy that hoity-toity wife of his."

Terminator scolded Lawn Dart. "Now you don't know that's true."

Lawn Dart sneered. "It's true enough." He set his cup down and swiveled to face me. "She was here having it out with Clete and some of the guys heard it."

This sounded unlikely. "Meredith Mills was here? Why would she do that?"

Lawn Dart seemed satisfied he'd engaged me. He settled in his chair. "Well, she was going on about how Chad was working too much."

"You heard this?"

Terminator chuckled and folded his arms, waiting for Lawn Dart to answer.

Lawn Dart stuck out his bottom lip and wagged his head, chin thrust in a defensive mode. “I didn’t directly hear it. No, I did not. But that doesn’t mean I don’t believe she did it.”

Terminator nodded at me. “There you go. I, personally, don’t buy that Meredith Mills would drive all the way down here because her loving man wasn’t home more. She’s classier than that.”

Knowing how gossip spread through the railroad crews like butter on warm toast, I leaned toward Dave’s opinion.

I nodded at Lawn Dart to indicate I’d take his story under consideration, then addressed Terminator. “Is there anyone else you can think of who has a grudge against Chad?”

He opened up his mouth and poured the remains of his coffee straight back his throat. He ran his hand down his beard again. “Aside from his all the sudden getting above his raising with the union rep thing, he made plenty of the guys unhappy when he pushed the addled idea of making this a run-through.”

Trey appeared in the doorway and glided into the room, hardly making a sound. He pulled out the chair vacated by Two Names and sat. “What’s a run-through?”

I knew something about this battle from hearing Dad’s one-sided phone conversations. “Right now, crews run west from Lincoln to Broken Butte. A new crew gets on and takes the train to Denver. It’s the same going east. But there is a proposal to eliminate the crews in the middle and have the trains run between Denver and Lincoln. So everyone in this western Nebraska pool would have to relocate.”

Lawn Dart sniffed, spat, gripped his Mountain Dew can and his coffee cup, and jerked to his feet, sliding the plastic chair back with his knees. Without a word, he stomped out of the room.

Terminator shrugged at Trey. “Don’t worry about Lawn Dart. He hates everyone.”

Losing Lawn Dart wasn’t a tragedy. “Who was mad about Chad taking BNSF’s side in the run-through fight?”

Terminator chuckled. “Who wasn’t? You got wives and kids to

uproot. Not to mention the cost of living in either of those places. You can have a decent three-bedroom house with a yard here for the price of a one-bedroom apartment in Denver."

"One guy was particularly pissed about it." The curdled voice belonged to Lawn Dart, who must have decided to put up with the odious state patrol to get in on the good gossip.

"Who's that?" I asked. Trey wisely kept quiet.

Lawn Dart pulled his chair up to the table. He set his Mountain Dew can and empty coffee cup in front of him. "Josh Stevens."

I didn't like that. "How so?"

Lawn Dart rested his elbows on the table and grabbed his forearms, leaning in. "We had this meeting." He stopped and wrinkled his skinny brow. "Must have been three, four weeks ago. Union meeting."

Terminator sat back and smoothed his beard.

Lawn Dart pointed at him. "Don't you say nothing. You weren't there. It was for engineers. Bunch of us were not happy about the proposed change, as you can imagine. And there was a ruckus."

"A fight?"

"Naw, not fisticuffs or anything like that. But folks were yelling."

I glanced at Trey. His face was the color of a hot burner, and it didn't take Columbo to know he was holding back questions. I asked for him. "Was anyone particularly angry?"

Lawn Dart scowled at me. "If you'll hold your horses I'm getting to that." He sent a growly aside to Terminator. "They get like this from always having smartphones and iPads and having everything instant all the time. They have no patience."

I'd like him to patience this, but I did my best conciliatory wince and hoped it would appease him enough he'd continue.

"So, everyone is carrying on like that, and there's a lull in the uproar, like it happens sometimes, you know?" Lawn Dart stopped talking. Apparently the question was not rhetorical.

"Yes, I know. What happened?" Dang it, I sounded as annoyed as I felt.

Lawn Dart tilted his chin to his chest and looked out the top of his eyes at Terminator. "See what I mean? Gotta have everything right now."

Terminator sighed and shook his head. "Just tell her."

Lawn Dart deflated, as if Terminator had taken all the fun out of it. He flicked his shoulders and snapped his head like a girl in a snit. "Somebody—maybe it was Flubber McGee—says, 'Someone ought to take a two-by-four and knock some sense into you.' All of a sudden it's quiet, like people are taking a breath together, and Josh Stevens says—sort of under his breath like he didn't intend for anyone to hear—he says, 'A two-by-four wouldn't do it. The only way you could knock sense into him is to hit him upside the head with a railroad tie.'"

Lawn Dart thrust out his chest and raised his chin. He crossed his arms and sat back in his chair, a satisfied grin on his face.

Terminator stared at Lawn Dart, then at me. "Huh."

I narrowed my eyes at Lawn Dart. "You heard this with your own two ears?"

"Indeed I did, missy." He nodded with satisfaction. "But it wasn't only me. Word got back to Clete, and he fired Joshy-boy for threatening Chad."

14

We hit the drive-through at Hardee's and headed back to Hodgekiss. Twyla's cinnamon rolls had worn off, but the thought of a greasy burger didn't thrill me. I opted for a side salad. Trey ordered the third-pound Velveeta Patty Meltdown with a monstrosity serving of fries and a chocolate shake. The name of the burger alone curdled my stomach.

I watched him mow down his food like a half-starved coyote.

Trey squashed his wrappers into the Hardee's bag and held it out to me. "I'm thinking Josh Stevens is our guy."

I pitched in my salad bowl and took the bag from him. "Not sure." I didn't have the conviction he did.

He ran his tongue around his teeth. "It makes sense. He was out at Meredith Mills's house when Chad was murdered. Why would he be there unless he and Meredith were having an affair? Add that to his obvious animosity toward Chad."

"Weren't you the one warning me about jumping to conclusions?"

"When did I say that? And there's plenty to support my theory. What about what Lawn Dart said? Heck, Josh was fired for threatening Chad."

"Suspended from service temporarily." I thought a moment. "But why hadn't Clete mentioned that?"

Trey shrugged. "Just trying to protect his employees, don't you think?"

Clete never struck me as a Daddy Warbucks type. But hey, did Trey really ask for my opinion?

There was a warm pulse pumping at the base of Trey's neck, right where he'd loosened the top button of his shirt. I turned the heat down in the car. "The first time I met you and told you Chad had been murdered, you accused me of being hasty. Now, you're ready to pin the tail on the first bull in the corral."

His hands tightened around the wheel. "He said, 'It would take a railroad tie to the head to knock sense into him.' And that's exactly what he did."

"I've been known to say something in a temper I didn't mean. Haven't you?"

"Sure I have. But a tie to the head is pretty specific."

Maybe too specific. "Could be someone set Josh up."

Trey guffawed. "And maybe my granny did it. Come on, you're reaching, and that's not very professional."

That smacked into my belly like a fist. "Before you convict Josh, don't you think we ought to check out Olin Riek?"

"You really think an insurance salesman would kill someone over a lost account?" He made it sound ridiculous.

With confidence I didn't feel, I said, "I think we ought to check it out."

The wheels bumped on highway cracks. I adjusted the heat back up.

Trey broke the silence as if he'd been stewing for a while. "What gives you such faith in Mr. Stevens?"

I tried not to sound defensive. "Not faith so much. But it's too soon to tie the noose for him."

He smirked. "I suppose your gut instincts honed from years of law enforcement experience are telling you Josh is innocent."

He didn't know how close his condescension brought him to a smack on the back of his head. Or how worried I was that he might have a point. "Okay, tell me why you think Josh didn't kill Chad." He sounded almost apologetic.

My gut? Because Dad believed in him? Even to me it sounded lame. "Bits and pieces of this and that."

Trey cocked his head. "What's that?"

I waved it away. "That's what Gramma Ardith would say. It means there are small reasons that add up to the logical conclusion."

He shook his head.

I tapped the dash. "Who else had a reason?"

Trey didn't like my answer, I could tell. "There's always his wife."

I considered this. "Why would she go to all that trouble to kill Chad?"

Trey held his fist up and flipped a finger. "She's a city girl and tired of living in the middle of nowhere."

"She could get a divorce."

He flipped up another finger. "Maybe Chad's been having an affair and she's mad."

"Again. Divorce."

Another finger went up. "He's abusive."

"Chad?"

Trey shrugged. "Sometimes it's the guy you least expect."

"Even so, why not divorce? Why go to such an elaborate setup to get rid of a husband?"

Trey thought about it. "That's what makes her more suspect. Whoever did it must have hated Chad. Planning and constructing it with pulleys and winches and getting it installed without anyone seeing was not something done in the heat of passion. This is a hatred that steeped for a long while."

"And you think Meredith would be capable of that?"

Trey shook his head. "Not really. It's more the work of a man, I think. That's why I'm putting my money on Josh Stevens."

I had Trey drop me at the courthouse for my car. He made tracks back to Ogallala, and I stopped at my folks' place. If I was going to conduct traffic stops, I'd need a few more layers.

I walked into the kitchen to Dad's legs splayed on the floor, leading to his head under the sink. I nudged his foot. "The sink leaking?"

He grunted, tightening a pipe. "David dropped Esther's ring down the sink. I'm saving the day."

David and Esther were two of Louise's kids. At fifteen, sandwiched between two girls, and with the twins, Zeke and Mose, way younger, David's hobby seemed to be picking on his sisters. "Nice."

Dad wormed from under the sink and sat up. He held up a cheap silver ring with a gaudy green stone. "Don't think Davie meant to drop it. But he's clumsy. Through the tears, I gathered the ring belongs to Marcee Bolton and Esther's life would be over if she didn't return it."

I held a hand out to yank Dad to his feet. "What do you know about Josh Stevens?"

He washed his hands. "Comes from a good family. They mostly keep to themselves; you know Black Socks."

I handed him a dish towel. "There's something between him and Louise. What is it?"

Dad didn't meet my eye. "You'd have to ask them."

Louise wasn't talking. Dad was a clam. I didn't know Josh well enough to ask him. I'd have to stay curious. "Would Josh have any reason to kill Chad Mills?"

This time Dad gave me one of his come-to-Jesus looks. "No."

That's about what I'd figured Dad would say. "Why are you so convinced he's innocent?"

Dad threaded the towel through the handle of the oven door. "He's a good man, and you can tell that as well as I can."

In the face of this frustration, Bill Hardy's offer looked mighty good. "That's not going to help with the state patrol or the courts. I can't stake my reputation on 'Because Dad says so.'"

Dad gave me the same look he'd leveled when I was in fourth grade and hadn't turned in my report on France. It made me feel lower than a pygmy snake. "Then you're gonna have to find out who really killed Chad yourself."

15

With my thermal underwear and two layers of socks inside my Sorels, Ted's brown sheriff cap pulled low and my warmest winter gloves, I reluctantly left the cruiser and hurried over to Milo. Two other county sheriffs gathered close.

Lee Barnett from Spinner County threw a salute my way. Pete Grainger from Chester County tipped his chin in greeting.

Grainger sniffed, a ball of energy in his compact frame. "I'm giving it two hours. It's too cold for you to be standing outside."

Barnett, eyes red-rimmed and baggy, like a hound, agreed. "Anyone committing a crime in this weather can go ahead as far as I'm concerned."

My tingling nose couldn't agree more. But as a woman and the newbie of the group, I needed to prove my Sandhills grit. "Where would you like me, Milo?"

Grainger and Barnett didn't say anything. They turned to their four-wheel-drive county sheriff vehicles.

Milo spat a stream of tobacco in the old snow on the side of the road. “Don’t know why they’re grousing. They’ll be tucked into their rigs. We’re the ones with the short straw.”

I nodded and watched with envy as they fired up their vehicles and drove off, Grainger to the east and Barnett to the west.

While I wore the brown ski cap, Milo opted for his beige felt cowboy hat. His cheeks and nose were lit up like a jolly garden gnome with broken veins highlighted in blue. “We’ll set ourselves up here in my Bronco and wait ’til they give us the signal.”

We sat in Milo’s idling county Bronco for Grainger or Barnett to alert us when someone crossed their radar.

“How’d they treat you at the academy?” Milo asked after we warmed a bit.

I’d spent six weeks of training and terror as the instructors had pushed and prodded and taught us how to deal with all the bad guys. “I learned a lot but probably not enough.”

He nodded. “No substitute for experience. How’d you do on the shoot / don’t shoot training.”

I hated to admit I’d barely squeaked by. My reluctance to pull the trigger concerned the instructors. “I was raised by pacifists, so I feel about guns like I do my crazy cousin Bart. It’s always good to know where he is, and it’s best to keep the safety on.”

Milo guffawed. “I know Bart. That’s about right.” He didn’t let me off the hook. “Hauling it around on your hip feels uncomfortable at first. Like a snarling Rottweiler, but you’ll get used to it.”

I wasn’t sure I wanted that kind of familiarity. I changed the subject. “I rocked the PIT training.” Pursuit intervention techniques. They trained us to use a couple of tricks to stop a fleeing suspect’s car.

Milo laughed. “Everyone does good at that. That’s playing around in cars.”

Barnett keyed his mic. “Not much going on out here; maybe we ought to talk about a deputy.”

Grainger piped up, “We got to get someone hired soon. The wife and I are taking the kids to Cancun the end of the month. I got two weeks stored up, and the kids deserve a nice vacation.”

Milo grunted as he reached for the mic. “It’s not like we ain’t been trying.”

Since a deputy needed all the certification of a sheriff, they weren’t easy to come by. The four sheriffs planned to hire one deputy to rotate weekends in each county and give us all a free weekend each month.

Barnett said, “What about Conner?”

My face didn’t twitch, but my gut squeezed. The last thing I wanted in Grand County was Ted working for me.

“I’m all for that,” Grainger said.

Milo keyed the mic. “That won’t help you with your Mexico trip. Ted’s not getting around too good.”

At least there was that.

Barnett grumbled, “Gunshot wounds don’t take that long to heal.”

Grainger piped in. “He’s already walking.”

To my way of thinking, a sheriff who shows up to a crime because he’d been in his mistress’s bed and gets shot for the favor shouldn’t be hired for a deputy spot within a year. The good ol’ boys in this co-op might not see it the same way. I needed to get a deputy hired right away.

The radio went quiet, and Milo and I talked about his grandkids for the next half hour.

Several cars whizzed by us before Grainger radioed. “Gray Ford Taurus. Clocked at eighty-three miles per hour.”

Milo grabbed his cowboy hat and slapped it on his head. “Lez go.”

He flipped on his lights. The pickup pulled over, and Milo flicked his chin at me. “You go ahead.”

I knew the driver and walked with confidence until Milo growled at me. "Is that what they taught you at the academy?"

"But this is a buddy of my brothers'."

Milo's face hardened. "I don't give a green goddamn if it's the queen of England. Follow protocol. Learn to trust your training."

Chastised, I stepped closer to the side of the car. I placed a hand on the trunk to make sure my fingerprints were captured in case I ended up dead on the side of the road and they needed to ID the car. I kept my eye on Tuff to make sure either of his shoulders didn't dip to indicate he shoved something under the seat or perhaps grabbed a weapon. Getting closer, I inspected the back seat for any passengers or contraband. Finally, I stayed close enough to the driver's door so he couldn't swing it out and knock me down, but with my right hip far enough away he couldn't reach for my gun.

I spoke into the driver's window. "Howdy, Tuff. I'll need your proof of insurance and license."

He grinned at me. "Wow. I didn't know you'd already taken over. You're looking good in the uniform."

Being a friend of my twin brothers wasn't enough to get him off the hook. "License."

The sunshine clouded from his face. "How about a warning?"

I tilted my head away from a gust that blasted ice crystals into my cheek. "How about your license."

He propped himself up and wrenched out his wallet, snapped out the license and handed it to me. "Registration and insurance," I prompted.

His manners didn't improve after I'd made him wait ten minutes while I ran his docs through the system. He was right to be irritated since this would use up the remainder of his points. He snatched his license, registration, and citation from my numb fingers and rolled up his window without even a "nice day."

I threw myself back in Milo's Bronco and huddled in front of the heater.

He nodded. "See? Not much to it. But now it begins in earnest."

"What begins?"

He spat into a Mountain Dew can. "You're stepping back from regular Kate Fox to Sheriff."

I shook my head. "That's not going to happen. Everyone knows me."

He gave me that *we'll see* head tilt, and I dropped it.

We made a few more speeding stops. Milo seemed satisfied I had the routine down and stayed in the warmth of the Bronco. Two of the stops were folks from Grand County that I knew. They took it a little better than Tuff, but both eyed me with disappointment.

I barely banged the door closed when Barnett came over the radio. "Suspicious vehicle. Late model Chevy Malibu, rusted white."

Milo replied, "Speeding?"

Barnett: "No. Indian. Looking weird."

Milo gave me a sheepish look and didn't say anything. We flagged the car down, and Milo got out of the Bronco and approached the car when it idled at the side of the highway.

The man inside the old beater looked to be not quite thirty. He had his paperwork ready to hand out his opened window. I took it, but didn't know what I was looking for. His plates showed he was from Spinner County, Grand's northwest neighbor that ran to the border with South Dakota.

He gave me a nervous smile with white, even teeth. "What's the stop for?"

Milo stepped up. "Routine traffic stop."

The man's face took on a skeptical smirk. "Not racial profiling?"

Milo waved that away. "We're pulling over everyone. Checking license and registration, the like." Milo took the documents from my hand. "I'll run these and be right back."

I stood beside the car, thankful for my Sorels and Ted's cap to protect my cheeks. "What part of Spinner County are you from?"

He stared out the windshield. "North. On the border. The Rez."

I couldn't blame him for his attitude. "Badlands? What brings you down this way?" I regretted it as I spoke. It must sound like I was interrogating him when I was only trying to make small talk. Maybe my brain was freezing into stupid slush.

He didn't answer for a moment. Then he peered up at me. "Honestly? I was going for a job interview in Antelope County."

"Oh?" I tried for casual. "What kind of work do you do?" I still sounded like a cop questioning a suspect.

He wasn't enjoying it. With barely contained hostility, he said, "I was up for appointment for sheriff."

The current sheriff of Antelope County had been indicted for embezzling from the treasury. It'd been a statewide scandal. I stuck out my hand. "Glad to meet you. I'm Kate Fox. Newly sworn in Grand County sheriff. It'll be good to have another novice around."

He turned to the windshield again. "It won't be me. I didn't get the job."

I shoved my hand back in my pocket before it shattered in the icy wind. "Sorry to hear that." I turned to check on Milo. He had the mic up to his mouth, sitting in the warm Bronco.

"You've been through the academy?"

He nodded.

"Certified?"

Our conversation took a more interesting turn before Milo returned. He handed Kyle Red Owl his papers. "Have a nice day."

That was all? Kyle nodded and took the docs. I thrust my hand into his dumpy car again and he shook it. "Very nice to meet you."

A slight grin crept onto his face. "Likewise." He rolled up his window, turned on his blinker and pulled onto the highway.

"Welp," Milo said and led the way back to the Bronco.

By this time, my lips were numb, and I couldn't tell if I smiled or if my face looked like a death mask. Cold had climbed through my boots and socks, and my fingers wouldn't be able to write a ticket if I had to.

Static scratched the air, and Barnett's irritation slashed through the radio. "This is bull. We're heading back."

Milo grinned at me. "I knew they'd call it off soon. We couldn't do it, you know. Me being the old man and you being not a man." Milo picked up the mic. "You're a couple of softies. We'll do one last stop and call it good."

Barnett keyed the mic. "Do your one more all day if you want. We're done."

Milo winked at me and held the mic to his face. "10-4."

We didn't have to wait long. A gold Monte Carlo popped over the hill to the east, followed by a turquoise one. Milo blipped his lights and they pulled over.

I followed procedure. Hand on trunk, approach from the rear, check the back seat.

I stepped up to the window as Earl rolled it down. When the smell hit, I drew backward. He'd either been skinning muskrats or hadn't showered for a year. Even the crisp breeze couldn't wipe out the lingering odor of dead rat.

Earl started talking before he got the window down. "I know I ain't over the speed limit. This ol' car don't even run faster than fifty-five."

I raised an eyebrow. "I know that's not true. But we're doing a standard stop. Checking everyone."

Newt ambled from his car. A black bruise ringed his left eye.

I held up my hand. "You'll need to get back in your car, Newt."

He stopped but didn't return to his car. "Are you checking for drugs? 'Cause I know this is a drug alley. People are forever transporting marijuana across here."

Earl shot Newt a warning hiss. "Shut up, you igit. You open your mouth, and the heat will think we're mules."

Newt's mouth hung open. "We ain't never."

Earl smiled at me, his teeth the color of margarine. "You gotta excuse my brother. He don't know what the hell he's talking about half the time."

I took inventory of the back seat. Several bulky black garbage bags, a child's car seat with one side of the plastic busted, a pile of rusted iron pipe that had split, what appeared to be a broken sucker rod for a windmill, heaps of wadded paper, a VCR player, and a boxy computer monitor circa 1995. "Where you been today, boys?"

Earl took on a professional demeanor. "We've been conducting business."

I nodded. "Junk dealing business?"

Earl looked offended. "Recycling."

Newt leaned forward. "The new term is repurposing."

I couldn't resist. "What do you do with this stuff, anyway?"

Newt eyed the back seat to consider the junk. "Right there, that is good steel and iron. We can take that down to Ogallala and sell it for cash. Most of that stuff won't amount to much, but you never know. And the deal we make is that we'll take it all off your hands."

Earl frowned at Newt. "People don't know the treasures they got."

They performed a valuable service, really. It might only be relocating junk from others' homes to their ranch, but at least it was concentrated in one place. "I'm glad to see you don't have anything strapped to the roof this time."

Earl nodded. "We learned our lesson, that's for sure."

Newt joined in. "It would have been a real shame to lose that ladder. It didn't come easy and it's gonna come in handy for us."

Earl hissed at Newt again, "Shut up."

I rested my arm on the edge of the open window and pulled back at the smell. "What do you mean it was hard to come by?"

Earl chuckled. "He didn't mean nothing. Junk is all, you know. We clean up people's sheds and that's hard work."

Newt reached in and shoved Earl. "That didn't come from no shed and you know it."

Earl growled, "Shut your pie hole."

Newt shoved Earl again. "We had to dig that out of the bottom of a dump."

Although the government had recently tightened down on it, for generations, every Sandhills ranch had its own dump. It sounds terrible that any old yahoo could go out on their ranch and create a garbage heap, but it didn't work that way. Ranchers typically picked a blowout. This was a raw bit of exposed sand. As the incessant wind blew, a small scar could turn into a dune, eroding at an increasing rate until huge swathes of land became exposed sand desert. A rancher could stop this before it started by throwing tires, old appliances, even a car or farm implement into the small area. That stabilized the sand and kept the erosion from spreading. Instead of a giant sandbox, the rancher now had a small dump, a private landfill, and the surrounding hills kept their grass cover.

"You were digging around someone's dump?" I asked Newt.

Earl gave Newt the evil eye. "No sir. We were not."

Newt shrugged. "We were out there anyways, doesn't seem like a big deal."

Earl rested his head on the steering wheel. "Pea brain."

I was nearly as irritated with Newt as Earl seemed to be. I wanted to clear the brothers, send them on their way, and get myself back to my cruiser. "You cleaned out someone's shed and stopped at their dump on the way home?"

Newt took my question for acceptance. "They don't want their stuff or they wouldn't leave it in the dump."

"And you found the ladder?" I prompted.

Earl didn't look up, just rubbed his head on the steering wheel.

Newt nodded. "It's a damn good ladder."

The only thing I cared about at that point was getting out of the wind before my nose froze off my face and landed at my feet.

"Okay, boys. You're bumping up to your third strike with me, so straighten up your act. No hunting on other people's land, no rummaging around dumps. To be on the safe side, don't tie junk to the roof of your car. Don't speed—"

Earl threw himself back in his seat. "I ain't never."

"That's good. Keep it up."

I waited for them to drive away. When Newt slipped past me, easing onto the highway without benefit of a blinker, I casually looked in his back seat. I'm sure I didn't see correctly, but it looked like a stack of boxes with the Dell logo. And it looked like they'd never been opened.

16

Louise and Mom sat at the picnic table in the kitchen when I rushed into the house. I shed my coat and locked my Smith and Wesson in the gun safe on the top shelf of the pantry. I wanted to stand under a really hot shower for about a month and maybe then my blood would start moving again.

Mom's heavy teapot, the one she made in a state of deep mourning, sat between them, along with heavy mugs she'd painted with an owl motif. She brought this set out at least once a year.

I ignored it, already feeling sad.

Louise turned red-rimmed eyes my way. "Sit down and have a cup of tea with us."

For once, there were no sugary treats to go with the hot brew. I hesitated, feeling a pull of guilt. Mom might gain some comfort from having another daughter sit with her. Louise always advocated family for what ails a body. But this kind of gathering wouldn't do anything except tug me down into the gray loss I'd successfully ignored all day.

I hugged my arms. "I'm going to take a shower."

Mom nodded, her gray mass of curls sliding up and down her thin back. I put a hand on her shoulder and squeezed. What words could possibly heal the gaping wound that oozed with constant pain?

I slid my hand over Louise's head on my way past her.

She sighed. "It wouldn't kill you to lean on your family sometimes."

Kill me? Probably not, but sitting around in gloomy memories wouldn't help. I trudged from the kitchen to the living room.

Two blonde and scantily clad twentysomethings bickered on TV while Ruth, David, and Esther sat in the darkness, lit by the blue tones from the screen.

Ruth sat up from where she'd been stretched out on the couch. "Hey, Kate."

A thump on the ceiling followed by giggles told me the twins were causing chaos upstairs. Sounded like they were in the boys' room, so maybe they hadn't rifled through my stuff. Maybe.

I stopped for what I hoped would be a second. "Are you guys ready for Chester County next week?"

Ruth flopped into a boneless slouch. "Coach is killing us with wind sprints."

I inched toward the stairs. "Probably a good idea. Those Bosch twins can run a whole team into the ground."

David didn't take his eyes from the TV. "Doesn't matter how many sprints they run, Hodgekiss girls aren't gonna beat Chester County. Not gonna happen."

Ruth barely offered a retort. "Shut up. The Bosches got fat this summer. They're not as good as they used to be."

I had a foot on the first stair, ready to make an escape. "Good luck. I'll make it to the game if I can."

I was halfway up the stairs before Ruth started up. I poked my head into the boys' room. "Hey, little dudes. What's up?"

Mose and Zeke had the blankets off the beds and were in the process of building an epic tent. They managed a mumbled hello, too busy in their mission to bother with an old auntie. Good enough for me.

Ruth was already stretched out on her stomach on my bed when I entered my room. I thought of the days, not more than nine months ago, when I had my own room in my own house. I had whole evenings when it was only me and my old boxer, Boomer. Even after Carly moved in, I could easily find privacy.

Carly was fourteen when her father, Brian, died. Since Louise and Norm had kids around Carly's age, we all thought the best plan would be for her to move in with them. That hadn't worked out, and I'd gladly taken Carly. I'd never be able to fully hate Ted because he'd welcomed Carly into our home and seemed to enjoy her living with us.

Despite Hurricane Carly, with her passion and often explosive energy, Frog Creek had been my sanctuary. Grand Central Fox didn't have quite the same feel.

I unbuttoned my brown shirt and shrugged out of it. Off went my pants.

"I hate this day." Ruth rolled onto her back, staring at the ceiling.

I cringed at the thought of removing my long underwear and wool socks. I might have to share my room with every niece and nephew, but I didn't have to give away all of me.

Ruth didn't notice my silence. "I mean, yeah, we all miss Glenda. It's, like, a total tragedy she died and everything. But, you know, doing this whole sadness thing every year is, like, really messed up."

Ruth didn't inherit Louise's deep attachment to ritual. I loved all of my nieces and nephews, of course, but I enjoyed some more than others. "One day each year your grandma and mother take the time to remember and mourn the loss of someone we loved. I don't see that as such a bad thing."

Ruth shot me a look of betrayal. She clearly hadn't expected me to side with the grown-ups.

As if competing for the world title in speed undressing, I shed the final layer, wrapped my fluffy robe around me, and started for the bathroom.

Ruth sat up. "You know who I really feel sorry for? Carly."

Yeah. Me, too. Carly had lost her mother, then two years later her father died. She'd just been getting her bearings when her grandfather was murdered. Now she was off God knows where on some foolish mysterious mission.

By the time I'd defrosted and my skin took on a rosy glow, Ruth had gone back to her reality catfight on TV.

Mom and Louise still sat in the kitchen, and Diane had joined them via Dad's laptop. I passed in front of the screen and waved. "Hi, Diane."

She frowned at me. "A hoodie? What, are you in high school?"

I stuck out my tongue at her.

She rolled her eyes. "Nice. When are you moving into May's lake house?"

Mom turned surprised eyes on me. Louise spun on the bench and jumped all over me. "You didn't tell me. That would be a perfect place for you."

Mom watched me without saying anything.

I pulled my canvas barn coat from a hook by the kitchen door. "Gotta go."

"You chickenshit," Diane said.

Louise slapped the table as if she really wanted to slap Diane. "My kids are in the next room. Language, please."

Diane snickered. "Lighten up, tight-ass."

Louise reared back as if punched. “That was uncalled for.”

I zipped my coat and wound my damp hair into a makeshift bun. A bright purple and red wool cap tipped over the shelf above the coat hooks, and I reached for it.

I tugged the cap over my head and tucked in stray hair to keep it from freezing as Diane continued to bait Louise. Mom held her mug close to her chest. A hint of a smile played on her lips as she watched my sisters.

I reached for the doorknob, and Diane’s voice smacked the back of my head. “Oh no you don’t. You can’t leave until you tell me you’re taking May’s house.”

Mom lost her smile and gazed at me with no expression.

Louise lumbered from the picnic bench and grabbed my arm, jerking me back to stand in front of the computer screen. “Tell her it’s time to get over Ted.”

Diane laughed. “For the love of God, Louise, let her go.”

Louise didn’t. She clutched a handful of my coat.

Diane sighed. “Man up, Kate. You’ve got a psych degree for fuck’s sake.”

Louise gasped, and I swear Mom sipped her tea to keep from laughing.

Diane had her CEO mojo juiced up, and I let it run. “You know you need to take charge. Get your own place. Get laid. Maybe even get a dog.”

Louise let go of me. She put her hands on her hips. “That’s it. I’m hanging up on you now. You can’t talk like that in front of my kids.”

Mom placed her hand over the keyboard to keep Louise from cutting Diane loose into the ether. I scurried to the door and caught Mom’s wink as I slipped outside.

Since I was off duty, I left my gun locked up and opted for Elvis, my 1973 Ranchero. I didn’t lose much body heat on my drive to the courthouse. I commissioned an unwieldy wooden chair from the meeting room and dragged it to my office and shut the door, turned up the heat, and set the ceramic space heater on turbo mode. The place still had the feel of a ransacked crime scene, but I didn't have the energy to deal with filing and straightening.

I sank into the hard wood of the commissioner's chair. On this dreadful anniversary, Mom and my sisters always had a strange sort of wake to mark Glenda's death. If I was more like Louise, I might cry or pray or even sit in Mom's kitchen. I kind of envied her ability to turn herself inside out, instead of letting all the feelings burn and molder like a compost pile.

If I could, I'd apologize to Glenda. She'd left me her beloved daughter. And I'd failed. Carly was out there somewhere. Alone, maybe in some kind of danger.

I ached to pull Carly close. On this day, we usually curled up together on the couch and watched a movie. Sometimes a sappy romance but usually a stupid teenage boy flick like *Dumb and Dumber.* I hated them. But I loved being close to Carly.

I clenched my fists as if in solidarity with my heart. I let go and turned on my computer. Anything to distract me from the loss of two people I missed so much.

I Googled "railroad accidents" and found more scenes of cars smashed on crossings than I'd ever care to see. Typing in "railroad crime" brought up several murders but mostly by transients or those who prey on them in rail yards.

An article caught my attention, and I clicked on it, interested to read about thefts on trains. I reached for the case file on the edge of my desk and rifled through it. I came up with the business card from the BNSF investigator and punched the railroad security officer's number. I glanced at the clock. It wasn't too late.

"Burke." He answered, all business.

I took his cue. "Kate Fox, Grand County sheriff. In Nebraska."

He paused. “Nebraska? Is that the decapitation?” It sounded like he was in a car with a radio broadcasting news.

I confirmed, asked whether it was a good time to talk, and when he said yes, I started. “What can you tell me about train robberies?”

He laughed. “The history going back to the Wild Bunch?”

“I was thinking a little more contemporary. I’m trying to find some motive for this murder.”

The radio clicked off. “There is more loss than people suspect.”

Clete hadn’t mentioned theft as a possible motive. “What kind of loss?”

He hmmed. “Mostly merchandise from container cars.”

“How would someone go about stealing from the container cars?”

“A lot of theft takes place in busy rail yards. You see it in places like New Jersey and Pennsylvania. Basically, a person climbs onto the car, slips inside, and tosses stuff out. If they’ve got a gang, they have an accomplice on the ground to haul it off. If they’re solo, they don’t get away with as much, of course.”

“What kinds of things do they steal?”

He sipped something and slurped into the phone. “That could be anything. Unless they’ve got an insider at the railroad telling them what’s in the cars, they’re hit and miss. They can get a container of fifty-pound rice bags or hit the jackpot with microwaves or smartphones.”

I flipped a pen through my fingers, remembering Louise saying Chad gave great gifts to his basketball boys. “They haul a bunch of coal through here, but what else comes down these tracks?”

“Just about anything you can think of. The railroad is a big land bridge. Used to be, ships would go through the Panama Canal if they needed to haul from Europe to Asia or whatever. But the ships are bigger or the traffic is too hectic, and for the time being it’s cheaper and faster to off-load on one coast, strap the containers onto the tracks, shoot them across the country, and load them back on a boat on the other side."

I doodled on the back of an envelope from Ted's old mail before realizing it was an order form for Victoria's Secret. I jerked my hand away from it as if it were a spider. I wadded it up and tossed it. "How often are the cars inspected to make sure they haven't been tampered with?"

He chuckled. "They aren't."

"Then how can you pinpoint where a theft took place?"

"Unless you catch them in the act, you really can't."

"That doesn't seem like a very smart system."

His booming laugh made me pull the phone away from my ear. "Sometimes you get lucky. Like what happened in the desert outside Needles."

I waited, and when he didn't go on I asked, "What happened?"

"Oh, sorry. I just pulled into my driveway, and my two-year-old is waving like a terrier on crack."

He had a family, a life to go home to. I should let him get on with his evening.

"Basically, there was a whole gang. One guy worked on the railroad so he got his hands on the manifests, what they call wheel reports. So he knew what train was carrying what. They threw a bunch of debris on the track at a highway intersection and the train went into emergency and stopped. Then three guys jumped up and started throwing stuff down to others who loaded the back end of the pickup, and in five minutes, they made off with a ton of big screens."

"They got caught?"

Thumping, like little hands on a car window, and the shouts of a happy baby voice wiggled through the phone. "Yeah. Hey, you can look it up. *Saunders versus BNSF.* They went to trial last week."

I wrote it down. "Anything else?"

His voice was lighter, as if he smiled. "Well, I heard of a case where the railroader tampered with a car and down the way they had to set it out at a siding. Then, the thieves had more time to steal the goods since the car had to sit there until it got repaired or some other train came along to pick it up."

I pictured a young dad with a toothy grin for his kid. "Thanks, Burke."

"You bet. Call tomorrow if you need more."

I thought about thefts on the BNSF, but in no time my mind turned away from the railroad, and I stared at my computer screen, the silence closing in on me. I pushed away images of Glenda bouncing a squealing Carly on her back, galloping around Mom's backyard. The two of them adored each other, and I missed them both so much my bones hurt.

I searched *Saunders v. BNSF* and was rewarded with court transcripts, which I dug into, anxious to distract myself and learn something concrete.

Burke hit the high points for me. This gang had made off with forty-five 52-inch Sony HDTVs at a value of about $3,000 each. Except they'd been caught and would spend time in jail. It didn't take a math whiz to figure out that if they'd been successful, as Burke said many were, there was big money involved.

By the time I finished reading the report, I felt tired enough I could probably drop off to sleep and end this awful day for another year.

I stood, the scrape of the wood chair legs on tile sending a chill up my spine. I reached for my phone. It jangled as my fingers closed on it. My scalp tingled even before I saw the 714 area code. I didn't doubt myself and answered, "Carly?"

She squeaked in surprise. "How did you know?"

"How are you? Where are you? Come home. Now. Please." I don't know how I managed to say so many words when my heart was booming like an August thunderstorm.

She drew in a sharp breath. "Oh, Kate. I miss you!"

I gripped the side of my desk. "Are you okay?"

I couldn't see her nod. "Yeah. I'm good. I've still got a bunch of Granddad's money left, and I'm figuring some things out."

"Figure them out at home."

She sniffed, maybe trying not to cry. "Usually I get along fine. But today was hard."

"Why did you run away?" I stopped short of telling her how broken I felt. She didn't want to be away, I knew that.

"Dad's death wasn't an accident." She spoke it without emotion, as if she dammed up all her feelings.

Carly's father, Brian, died when he crashed his plane into a hillside. Of course it was an accident, but Carly couldn't accept that. "Come home. I'll help you."

"I can't explain now. I don't have the proof. Just trust me, okay?"

She wanted me to trust her instincts? I winced, hearing myself say the same to Trey.

An engine sounded in the background. A city? It sounded more isolated, not like traffic. Maybe a small town or even a rural setting. On the West Coast, I guessed, because of the time of day and the area code. But maybe it was the East Coast, and it was late at night. Carly couldn't sleep because of the grief weighing on her heart.

"I miss Mom," she said. "I miss Dad and you. Grandma and Grandpa. And Granddad Eldon."

Carly had lost so much. "Come home, then. We can't give you back your parents or Eldon, but the rest of us will love you until you can't stand us anymore."

Carly laughed through her tears. "I know. But I can't."

"Why? Whatever it is, we can figure it out together."

"I can't come home yet. This is bigger than I thought, and the more I find out, the more I need to learn."

I clenched my fist with the effort to pull her to me. "I'll help you. Please."

Carly sounded as if she pulled her face away from the phone. "You can't help me. That would only put you in danger."

What? "That means you're in trouble, too. Let me protect you. I'm sheriff now."

"Ha! I'll bet Roxy lost her shit at that." A smile lit Carly's voice.

I pictured her face in the sunshine, the green grass of a spring meadow dotted with the first buttercups and bluebells, a scene I'd seen her in so many times. Her blond hair highlighted with summer, cheeks pinked, and her wide smile of delight in the freedom of the ranch. "Come home. I love you."

Another engine sounded but didn't move past. Carly's voice hardened. "I've got to go."

"No. Wait."

She spoke quickly, "Listen, I'm okay, so don't worry. But you need to understand. You can't trust anyone."

I was losing her all over again. It felt like my hands clutched a mountain ledge but they were slipping. "Why do you think your father was murdered? Let me help."

"Don't tell anyone I called. No one." Her mouth moved away from the phone again, and a man's voice asked a question. I couldn't understand what he said. Was it because the sound was muffled or did he speak in another language? Spanish? Something else?

"Carly. Wait. I—"

The phone went dead. I hit redial. Nothing. Redial again.

Damn it! I jumped to my feet, took two steps, whirled around, pounded my fist on my desk. Flopped back in the hard chair and lowered my forehead to my arms. All the useless frustration moving through my body couldn't bring her back.

She hadn't acted surprised when I told her I was sheriff, and in fact, had gone right after Roxy. I hadn't talked to her since she ran away and yet, she hadn't asked about Ted, someone she loved. When she'd disappeared, he was still in a coma, with doubt he'd ever walk again. It's as if she knew Roxy and Ted had married. She didn't ask who'd killed her granddad. Somehow, Carly had kept up on Grand County. How?

I picked up my phone and hit speed dial. Baxter answered on the first ring. He sounded worried and pleased at the same time. "What's up?"

I leaned back in my chair and let out pent-up air. Don't trust anyone, Carly had said. Her father murdered. I hesitated.

"Kate? Are you okay?"

"Um." What did I know about Baxter? He owned the largest twenty-four-hour cable news network. He had more money than God, was an outspoken advocate for the environment. He'd gone to military school with Brian, Carly's father, from the time they'd been in fifth grade until they graduated.

Baxter sounded almost frantic. "Kate, talk to me. Is something wrong?"

"I'm fine," I managed to say, but nothing more. My pulse quickened while I tossed my knowledge of Glenn Baxter onto the scales. He'd come to the Sandhills last spring to help Carly's granddad, Eldon, figure out how Brian came into a pile of money. He'd stayed after Eldon's murder to find Carly and protect her. He'd promised me he'd find Carly, and since then, I'd talked to him at least once every week.

"You don't sound fine." His voice had a strength I hadn't heard for a while.

"The treatments must be working." I needed more time to consider Baxter. Should I tell him about Carly? She said trust no one.

"There's marked improvement in my lungs, yes. But what's going on with you? Are you upset?"

That didn't get me much. "It's cold here." My gut told me Baxter was good to the core. But then, I'd been married for eight years to Ted, who'd lied to me almost from the beginning.

"Talk to me, Kate. What's going on?" Worry ringed Baxter's words.

But I'd always had a smidge of unease about Ted. Even though I'd dug deep into denial, I'd had to shove aside doubts about Ted all along. I didn't have that unease with Baxter.

Carly needed help. I couldn't give it to her if I couldn't find her. "Baxter?" It sounded like a kitten's mew and I flinched.

"I can be there in four hours. The jet will be ready by the time I get to the airport." His words jumbled as if he jogged.

"No." I got that out with some force. "I'm okay." He had no idea why I sounded like curdled milk, but the cause didn't seem to matter. He knew something was wrong, and he was on his way. "Carly called."

Silence for a beat. "Carly?"

I nodded and sank to my chair. "We didn't talk long. Area code on the phone was 714."

Concern deepened his tone. "Did she sound okay? Did she say why she left? Is she coming home? I can fly to wherever she is. Meet me at the Broken Butte airport, and we'll go together."

I waved my hand to stop him. "She's not coming home. She said Brian had been murdered and she's finding out things."

The air let out of Baxter's balloon. "She's been to see some of our classmates. What is she after?"

"I wish I knew. But I know her. She's not going to give up."

"Why did she call?"

I told him about the anniversary of Glenda's death and the sounds in the background, the man's voice.

He didn't speak for a long time. "Okay. I'll turn this over to the investigator. Text me the number she called from, though I'll bet it was a disposable phone."

I huddled in my hard chair. "Thanks."

We were both silent for a second or two until Baxter's words eased through the phone. "I'm here with you. We'll find her."

Somehow he knew how alone I felt. I leaned into his assurance. "What if she's right? If Brian was murdered and she's poking around, the killer might go after her."

Baxter sighed. "If my investigator can't locate that little escape artist, I'd say she's pretty good at hiding. Try not to worry."

I laughed. "Or breathe or have a heartbeat."

His chuckle made me feel a raccoon's hair better. "Okay. Tell me what else is going on, maybe I can distract you."

I sat back in my chair and propped my feet on the desk. I told him about May's house on the lake, my nieces and nephews, and Mom's latest meltdown. He told me about a glittery fund-raiser at the St. Regis in New York City and how he'd asked some Hollywood dilettante because she advocated for the protection of wildlife and he believed she'd bring a shiny glow to the event. But how she'd been more concerned that the paparazzi photographed her new designer gown in the right light and then she drank too much champagne and ended up falling off her four-inch heels on the way out, which, of course, is the picture that graced *People* the next week.

We hit a lull, and I realized with a start that it was after nine o'clock. That made it after eleven where Baxter was, and yet he hadn't made any move to end our call.

"Thanks," I said.

I felt his smile. "Anytime."

Talking to Baxter had eased the ropes around my innards and knotted in my head. But the moment I hung up, my fists clenched on my desk and my heart started thumping. Carly, Chad, the ranch job offer from Bill Hardy, what to do with my life? I'd never be able to sleep, and I sorely needed to.

Diane wanted me to move out, Sarah wanted me to date. May had a house, Bill Hardy a job. And I teetered on the crumbling ledge, bits of rock tumbling into the bottomless canyon. I couldn't stay like this forever. That much I knew.

With no hope for sleep, the only thing to do was take Elvis for a moonlight spin.

17

Another storm warned of its arrival with a roar of frigid wind battering Elvis. This afternoon's chill had been only the ice breaker for tonight.

Ever since I'd bought the Ranchero when I was fourteen, a couple of years before I could legally drive him, Elvis was my happy place. Even more so than Frog Creek, because I'd bought him with money earned over several summers in the hayfield, and no one could take him away from me. I pointed him east and cruised out of town, letting the heat warm me and the rumble of his engine sing me a lullaby.

I hummed along to an old Beatles cassette of Glenda's and tried to let my mind drift into the dark winter sky.

The sheriff's phone rang and I reached for it. The caller ID startled me with my own name. Then I realized who had programmed the phone. "Hi, Ted."

He laughed. "Already being a great detective."

I didn't want to talk to my ex-husband. But I fell into familiar territory. “It doesn’t make me a member of Mensa to figure out ‘Kate’ would be Frog Creek. What do you need?”

“I heard you were doing the traffic stops today. Earl and Newt, they’re always entertaining.”

“Are you listening on the police scanner?”

“Not really listening. It’s on and sometimes I catch something.”

After so many years of being his wife, I really didn’t know how to talk to him now. “Well, stop it. I’m sure Roxy’s not thrilled with you keeping tabs on the new sheriff. How’s she doing, anyway?”

Ted hesitated. “She’s tired all the time. In fact, she’s in bed already, so I’m out in the shop.”

I jerked the phone from my ear and punched it off. I banged the heel of my hand on the wheel. “Damn it.” A film of guilt dusted onto me. When Ted was having his affair, he’d go to the shop at night and talk on the phone to Roxy. I’d had a certain pleasure talking to him just now. But I hadn’t known I was a secret call from the shop.

I cranked up the tunes to keep from thinking. The headlight of a westbound train flashed into my eyes and continued down the tracks. I watched its hulk black against the dark night until it blinked a red light and faded from view. My gaze brushed across another train car parked at a siding. It sat isolated, no engine, no other cars attached. I’d probably seen a zillion of them in my lifetime, just like that. Sitting on the side of the tracks. I’d never given it a thought.

Bobby said he and Chad had set out a car at a siding sometime before the overpass at Highway 67. This had to be the one. I thought of what Burke said about thefts. Could this have something to do with Chad’s murder?

I took the first turn off the highway, a county-maintained gravel strip, and gripped the steering wheel as I pointed Elvis off the road and down to the railroad access toward the siding. A steep ridge rose on the north side of the tracks. After a half mile, the container car came into view on the tracks of the siding.

This was a double-decker car. The trailer parts of the big eighteen-wheelers that roam the interstates were stacked two deep inside a sort of steel egg-crate base. The back doors of the bottom trailer wouldn't open more than a foot or so before hitting the ledge of the railroad car. But if someone climbed the lower trailer, the doors of the trailer stacked on top would be fully accessible. I might be able to see whether the doors had been tampered with.

I braked and cut the engine. Too bad I wasn't driving the cruiser. I'd have Big Dick and probably my Smith and Wesson. I can't say as I missed the gun all that much.

Climbing out into subzero temps didn't thrill me. I zipped up, mashed my cap down, and pulled on my gloves. I really ought to get a ski mask like Trey wore. Or maybe resurrect my old Elmer Fudd cap. I braced for the wind.

Why couldn't we put a moratorium on crimes committed outdoors for the months of January and February? I opened the door and climbed out, not wasting time as I hurried to the containers.

I'd parked with my lights shining on one end of the car. I assumed it was the front because the two containers didn't have doors on this side. The railroad car had hitches on both ends so the car could be attached to a train heading in either direction.

Moonlight outlined the dirty white containers that rose fifty feet into the night sky. Colorful graffiti nearly covered the Maersk logo printed on the sides. I had no idea what the bubble letters spelled, but I didn't mind the bright reds, yellows, and blues, even though it's a crime to mark the cars.

The flatbed of the railroad trailer reached about chest high on me, with three-foot metal walls running around it to create a sturdy well to place the loaded trailers. A person could clamber onto the flat car at the front or back using a step next to the hitch.

Growing up in a house facing the tracks, I'd been warned about getting too close to trains. At crossings, flashing arms lowered, keeping drivers a safe distance with clanging and wild, blasting lights. Just being this close, even if the car wasn't attached to an engine, brought up fear hammered home since infancy.

By now my nose hairs were stuck together, and the night air nearly burned my cheeks with biting cold. The rocky right-of-way crunched and a 'yote howled in the distance. I walked along the tracks, making my way slowly alongside the car, studying the sides, scanning up and down, leaning over to look underneath. Nothing like giant freight carriers on top of a railroad car, steel on steel, every bolt or rivet the size of your fist, to make you feel like a fragile china figurine.

Toward the back end of the car something on the ground caught my attention. I hurried over to find a bolt on the ground next to yellow bolt cutters with a black handle. I spun to look up the back of the stacked trailers.

From my Web surfing earlier, I'd been shocked to discover the seals the transporters used were flimsy locks. Some styles looked like the zip ties I used to secure pole beans to the scaffold in the garden. Some were like the worthless locks on suitcases.

This trailer used the more substantial bolt seal. In this case, it wasn't any more effective than a zip tie at keeping someone out. One end of the lock dangled from a chain looped loosely though one of the double doors at the back of the top trailer.

Whoever had a mind to steal the contents had made short work of the bolt by simply cutting it off and dropping the cutters. And that person could still be inside the trailer now.

I held my breath and listened.

Did I imagine it, or did I hear a faint thud from inside the top trailer? If there really was sound, it could have been an icicle dropping from the lip. Or it might have been my adrenaline manufacturing noises. I stayed still until I risked freezing in place, and still, the night held only eerie silence.

I snuck to the back, where metal grab irons were welded into the car next to the hitch. I scrambled to the base of the railroad flatbed and stood on the metal platform. Both of the container cars had double doors that opened toward the base of the trailer. If the container was on the back of a semitruck, a man standing on the ground would be able to loosen the latch and open the door. I stood next to the container and tilted my head up to the one stacked on top.

The moon didn't give me nearly enough light. The cold metal sent a scatter of goose bumps over my skin like baby spiders released from their nest. A few metal rungs were welded on to the side of the trailer so a truck driver could climb to the top. If I'd actually heard a sound, it would have come from the top car.

Careful to keep the leather soles of my ropers from slipping on the rungs, I climbed. My breath billowed with each exhale. My gloves made holding the rungs difficult, but without them, my fingers would be numb in seconds. Six times my slick soles slipped on the metal bars. I pulled myself up until I perched on the top rung, within arm's distance of the door latch on the second stacked trailer. My breath sounded like a steam engine to my ears as I balanced on the rung and clung to the side of the top container.

I gripped the side of the top container through bulky gloves and wondered what to do. If I'd brought the Smith and Wesson, I'd pull it out and yell, "Freeze! Sheriff."

My best option right now appeared to be climbing down and sneaking back to my car for my phone. I could call Trey, then wait for the thief to emerge. With no gun, no handcuffs, and only my authority as sheriff, I didn't know what I'd do when he came out.

I pulled back and dipped my head to see the rungs, but before I took one step down, a terrible crash sounded from inside the trailer by my head. The left side of the double doors on the back of the top trailer, the one I clung to, swung open.

I tipped back; the slippery leather of my boots on the icy metal rungs caused me to tilt. My left arm jerked from the socket, and I succeeded in pulling my fingers out of my glove. I lunged toward the trailer, my left hand frantic to find some purchase. But the door flung wider, as if someone inside pushed it. It knocked me in the forehead with a white-hot pain like my noggin splitting wide. I clutched at the swinging steel door, desperate to keep from plunging backward. My numb fingers scrabbled on the edge of the door and grabbed it only long enough to wing it back.

The man inside had been halfway out of the container, and the door smashed his fingers. He cried out in pain. Or maybe surprise that I was hanging on the side of the trailer. The door flew at me again. I'd quit trying to do any damage to the thief and concentrated on saving myself. One glove on, one glove off, I was able to hang onto the door only long enough for it to put the finishing touch on my slipping feet and throw me out like a kid on a rope swing over a pond.

It might take only a blink to sail off a narrow rung. But living through it felt more like a month. My heart nearly burst through my skin, reaching, balancing, knowing I was losing the fight, tipping backward beyond the point of rescue. My hands opened and closed on air, trying to thrust my body forward when it already gained momentum backward.

A moment of total panic when I was free-falling, and then I was squeezing my eyes shut, waiting for impact with the frozen ground.

The slow motion stopped about the time my back whammed into what felt like concrete. Air escaped in a whoosh from my lungs, and my mouth opened while my chest hitched. I struggled in paralysis, willing my legs and arms to move, my lungs to take in air.

But the hulk of flesh I called my body was less reactive than a bag of cattle feed.

The door at the back end of the container car swung closed, hit the frame, and flew open with force. A dark figure emerged from the shadows. In his heavy coat and hood, gloves and boots, and this far away at this wonky perspective, there was no way I could identify him. One hand cradled the other. With clumsy movement, he grabbed the handholds and swung himself on the metal ladder. His boots slipped from the rung and he dangled for a second before pushing off and landing on the ground with a muffled *oooof!*

Still unable to breathe, I struggled like a turtle on my back. My legs and arms barely moved. I sucked unsuccessfully to draw in air, helpless as the man pushed himself to his feet and took off with a lumbering run. He stumbled over the tracks and up the hill.

"Stop!" I yelled with as much force as a week-old puppy. "Sheriff. Stop!"

By the time he topped the ridge, I'd managed to push myself to my knees. Blood gushed from my forehead, the only warmth in the whole state of Nebraska. Wiping my eyes, I hauled myself up on shaking legs. I hadn't scrambled more than halfway to the top of the hill before the rumble of a diesel engine sent a wave of frustration through me.

It took another couple of minutes before I struggled far enough up the hill to look over the other side with the eye not constantly washed out by blood. By then, whoever had been there was a frozen memory.

18

I found a towel behind Elvis's passenger seat and pressed it to my aching forehead and waited for the heat to thaw my right hand. Every time I pulled the towel away to assess the damage, the blood coursed before I could get a look. I'd need stitches. My options were limited.

A drive to Broken Butte to the emergency room, an hour away, with me pressing and wiping and the blood dripping, didn't make sense. I didn't want to alert the rescue unit and pull several people away from their beds.

It might be a good time to introduce myself to the new vet Sarah told me about. Heath Scranton. I drove back to Hodgekiss, past my parents' house to the end of town. The street spilled out to the open front lot of the vet clinic. A few years ago, Doc Bunner, long-time vet, built a Morton Building with a barn and clinic on one side, an office between, and a two-bedroom house on the other. Then he up and died. For several months, the ranchers in Grand County had been hard pressed to find veterinary care. Now we were back in business with this new guy.

Lights shone from the clinic side, and I let myself into the office, towel pressed to my forehead. Like a hospital, veterinary patient care wasn't a nine-to-five kind of job. The clinic smelled of antiseptic and horse, with a smidgeon of rusty birth fluid. An old black lab lifted his head from a dog bed in the corner and thumped a tail at me.

"Doc Scranton?" I walked behind the counter, through the exam room with its stainless steel table and floor-to-ceiling cupboards and counters, and thudded through the open door toward the lights of the barn.

Rapid footsteps on the concrete of the barn headed toward me, and a blond man, midthirties, muscular build, rounded a corner. "Here."

Wow. Sarah had been right. Heath Scranton was hot. Sizzling. About six four, he had broad shoulders and a face like a Disney prince. But my forehead throbbed and stung, and my arm was tired from holding the towel up. I'd have to charm him with my feminine wiles some other time. "Sheriff Fox. Kate. Can you sew me up?"

His friendly grin dribbled from his face. "Stitches? For you?" He focused on my forehead, no doubt seeing the blood-drenched towel and my reddened fingers and wondering what was going on.

I made it seem as normal as possible. "It'll probably only take a couple."

He stood in front of me, in his insulated coveralls, all handsome and confused.

"I ran into a door. Not a big deal."

He kept his eyes on my injury. "But I'm a vet. I'm not licensed to work on, you know, people."

I pulled my hand away, glad the bleeding had let up enough it didn't waterfall into my eye again. "Sure. And I won't tell anyone. But I've got some things I need to attend to, and I can't run all the way to Broken Butte. I grew up down the street. With a lot of brothers and sisters. Believe me, we kept Doc Bunner in cigars with all the stitches he supplied over the years."

Still, Scranton didn't twitch. "But it's your face."

I shrugged and wiped at the dribble of blood sliding down my forehead. "Gives me character. Can you help me out?"

It took more coaxing than it took to convince Mose and Zeke to go to bed, but he eventually agreed. He settled me in the clinic exam room and swabbed the gash while I practiced not wincing.

"You say you ran into a door?" He sounded skeptical.

"Chasing a bad guy. Which is why I need to get back to work." I clenched my teeth as he dabbed on topical anesthetic.

"This is against all principles. I shouldn't be practicing medicine on a person." Worry lines danced between his eyebrows. But I focused on his blue eyes. Whether he'd think it was lucky or a bother, every single woman in Grand County, and some who weren't single, would be all over him like gravy on mashed potatoes.

"You're aiding in the apprehension of a criminal. It's perfectly legal."

He grinned despite himself. "Really?"

By the time he'd put three stitches into my noggin, I was ready to down a fifth of Jack Daniel's and sleep until it healed. Unfortunately, I wasn't done with my night. Heath wouldn't take any money, and I respected that ethic. I'd figure out some way to compensate him. But that would mean I'd need to get to know him a little better.

Darn.

I might be able to slip that plan into a conversation to appease a sister or two later, but the idea of getting to know someone held little appeal for me now. God, my head hurt.

My next stop involved a short drive to the other side of town. It was after eleven, so I didn't expect any lights on. They weren't. I knocked and waited. Knocked and waited. Knocked and the door finally opened.

Clete Rasmussen filled the doorway like an angry grizzly wearing a purple terry robe, his white hair sticking out six ways to sundown. "What?" His mouth opened at the sight of my bloodstained forehead and what must be swollen flesh.

Behind him, his wife's voice floated out. "Who is it?"

Clete twisted his head over his shoulder. "County business. Go back to bed." He opened the door wider to let me in.

I stood in the entryway, illuminated only by a hallway light. "Actually, it's railroad business."

He frowned at me and ushered me around a corner to the kitchen. In a big city, they might call Clete's house a midcentury brick bungalow. In Hodgekiss, it was an old brick house they hadn't done much to update. The kitchen was closed off from the living room on the other side of the front door. With a booth under a window, there wasn't a lot of room left for counters.

"What's this about?" Clete whispered, a volume I didn't know he possessed.

I relayed my adventure at the tracks. "You need to call the BNSF security and get them up to investigate. I'll go out to meet them."

Clete put a hand on my arm, the most caring gesture I'd ever seen from him. "No. You need to get some rest. I'll make the call and go out there. I'll wait for the investigator to show up."

I didn't want to, but I agreed to let Clete handle it. As trainmaster, it was his job.

I should do it myself. Probably ought to call Trey and get him up here. I wanted to think everything through and figure out who was out there, who killed Chad. But my head throbbed, and before I could be useful, I needed to get some sleep.

19

Cold morning light left the kitchen as gloomy as I felt. My boots clunked on the kitchen floor, making a racket in the quiet house. I felt as though someone had pounded me with a sledgehammer. My back felt especially tender. Next time I took a swan dive from the top of a double-stack railroad car, I'd make sure someone provided a net.

"You look nice." Even though they were spoken softly, the words startled me. Mom slumped at the table, resting her head on one hand, the elbow propped on the surface. Dark circles sagged under her eyes. I doubt she registered any more detail about my appearance than the splash of color. She looked like three-day-old road kill. "Thanks. Funeral."

She wore a vague expression that matched her disjointed voice. "Oh. That railroad accident."

In her working phases, Mom didn't pay much attention to the real world. "How's the new piece?" I asked.

She waved the hand not responsible for keeping her head from slamming into the table. "It's junk. I think I've lost the creative juice. I don't know. Maybe I'm done sculpting."

This pasture was well trampled. But her normal low cycle coinciding with the anniversary of Glenda's death was a double whammy. "I'll bet it's a great piece."

She straightened the scaffolding arm, and her head sank to use it for a pillow. "We'll never know. It's in a million bits, scattered on the studio floor."

This, too, seemed to be part of her process. "You'll do another."

She closed her eyes. "I don't think so."

I lowered myself to a chair next to her, stifling a moan. She reached out and ran a finger along the embroidery of my jacket. "This is an extraordinary work."

She'd bought me this wool blazer from a boutique in Santa Fe several years ago. She was showing at a gallery and made a rare appearance at a First Friday Art Walk. She said the jacket called to her from across the plaza. It had been searching for the woman it was made for and begged her to bring it to me. In Mom's world, things like that happened. I'm sure she'd spent a good portion of the show's commission on the jacket. I loved it. If I ever had a daughter, she'd probably love it, too. It had that kind of timelessness.

I ran my hand along the soft wool. "Ted always wore his uniform to funerals." I had considered it. It didn't seem right.

Mom's hand dropped, and her critical inspection took in the midcalf flared skirt and dress cowboy boots. "It's a sign of respect to dress for a funeral."

I got up to make coffee. "Would you like some tea?"

She didn't answer so I made her a cup while my coffee brewed. I set our cups on the table.

We sat together in silence for a while. Misery drifted off Mom. She hadn't showered for a few days, probably hadn't eaten much, and maybe hadn't even gone to bed after Louise left last night. The piece that had consumed her and then led to her despair might have been great. But after a few days in her condition, she'd be no judge. Several times I'd tried to convince her not to destroy something when she was in this strung-out state. When she'd come out the other side and was planted more or less in sanity's garden, she agreed her perspective could get skewed and delusional while on the tail end of her manic surges. But she could never seem to avoid that slide.

In the stew of mental illness, the Foxes had learned to swallow the bitterness of Mom's gravy.

"I had no idea the house could be so quiet," I said.

She closed her eyes. "It roars, doesn't it?"

"After all those years of kids fighting and playing, you must love this peace. I'll bet you work better without us around."

Mom opened her eyes and, with what appeared gargantuan effort, pushed up and let gravity flop her back in her chair. "I like the noise. I tried to fill the house with children so the silence wouldn't swallow me."

"But you hide from the chaos in your studio."

Mom had a diamond of a smile. Seeing it slide onto her face made me feel like a prospector spotting the glint of fortune in his pan. This morning, her smile struggled through exhaustion. "I wasn't hiding. If I could, I would sculpt in the middle of the kitchen with all the coming and going."

"But we weren't even allowed into your studio."

"That's more for your protection than for mine. Your father insisted and I acquiesced."

"Why?"

She indicated the silk kimono wrapped loosely around her. "Although I believe in the beauty of the human form, you father is a little more inhibited. Even more than that, this town has a repressive streak. So, since I can't be encumbered with clothes when I work, he thought I ought to have my own space."

"You worked down there so we wouldn't see you naked?" I'd never understood how she didn't freeze to death. Her basement studio hunkered below the house with a side patio scraped outside to create a walk out with a bank of windows, giving her light and making her feel open. When she worked, it was as if a fire burned inside. As the work high faded, she'd gradually add thicker layers until, like the rest of us, she'd venture out in heavy sweaters to survive the winter.

"I hated it when you all traipsed off to school. For those hours, the walls creaked and the ghosts whispered. But then, your footsteps would pound on the ceiling, and you chased it all away."

I had no idea.

"These days I've had to make peace with the ghosts. They've been cooperative for the most part. Then you come back for a day or a few hours. The grandkids run and you kids argue and my soul settles."

"I always thought we distracted you, and when you're working, you wished we weren't around."

Mom's haggard eyes moved to my face, as if she were too tired to turn her neck. "You kids were the only reason I could work. You made it possible for the flames to leap around me. Now, with most of you gone, the fire that filled my work has to heat the rest of the house."

I'd thought of her as flawed and maybe a little crazy—okay, more than a little. I'd accepted her stretches of neglect and indulged her affection when she rejoined the family. All along, I thought I was the more stable and adult in our relationship, understanding she loved on her own schedule.

I often wondered why she'd had so many children. Now I knew.

She needed us to hold her to the earth. With all our noise and drama, we crowded her soul back into her body.

The kitty clock ticked. I shoved my chair back. "I'm sorry. I've got to go. Get some sleep, Mom. You're teetering onto the crazy side."

She narrowed her eyes at me. "What happened to your face?"

Without thinking my fingertips brushed the stitches on my forehead. "I fell off a railroad car."

She shrugged in an *it happens* sort of way. "It'll leave a scar but the stitches are even."

"Maybe I'll wear bangs from now on."

She chuckled. "So adventurous, like your namesake."

I bent over her and kissed her forehead. I don't know how much I acted like Kate Hepburn, but I wished I had her height and dignity—and a few of her dollars wouldn't hurt, either.

20

Funerals for young people draw crowds. No church, and not even the Legion hall, could contain the two or three hundred people expected for Chad's service. The district cancelled school for the morning and used the high school theater, with spillover herded to the wooden bleachers in the gym to watch on a remote feed.

I stood in the gym doorway and searched the bleachers. Sarah and Robert sat with Michael and Lauren. Jeremy, the second-to-youngest Fox, named for Jeremy Irons, dropped down next to them. Louise and Norm huddled up a row with their two oldest kids, Ruth and David.

An arm draped around my shoulders, and I tilted my head to Douglas. Mom lucked out the year the twins were born when Michael Douglas won for Best Actor. Douglas, never Doug or, God forbid, Dougy, pulled me close. Five years younger than me, and often under my supervision, Douglas never said much. He was like a gentle bear. Even as a little kid, he knew when I needed support, and he'd magically show up by my side. "Fall on your face when you passed out at the Long Branch?"

I scanned the bleachers. "Bull-riding accident."

Though she rarely spoke of it, we gathered Mom grew up in a status-obsessed family in Chicago and hit the hippie trail early. She'd met Dad in San Francisco after he'd finished his Vietnam tour. I couldn't imagine the conversations that led them to move back to Dad's hometown, among the provincial and clannish Foxes and all their extended, eccentric relatives, but Mom made few concessions to Sandhills conventions. She didn't feel obligated to attend funerals or weddings or high school sporting events.

Dad, on the contrary, knew what was expected of a Fox. He made sure we all knew, too. Aside from Diane, who'd made her escape to Denver, the sense of obligation Dad dribbled into our midnight bottles soaked into our veins.

Douglas and I joined the rest of the family to watch the sad service on the TV that Principal Barkley wheeled in on a utility cart. I gave various explanations for my face, from running into May Keller in a dark alley to skydiving at midnight. None of my family members seemed too concerned about a few bruises. Standard operating procedure for me.

I settled next to Sarah. Movement at the doorway caught my attention. In his crisp state trooper uniform, Trey Ridnoir filled the gap. He studied the crowded bleachers. Maybe he scanned for suspects. I watched him watching us. He was far enough away I couldn't actually see his eyes, but I knew they'd be keen and assessing.

Ted used to stand in the doorway of events, just like that. In his uniform, he provided safety and authority. I dropped my eyes to my skirt and embroidered jacket. When I looked up, Ted and

Roxy filled the gym doorway. Supported by his cane, Ted leaned close to Trey, and they spoke with serious faces.

Even though she seemed pale and subdued by her normal standards in a long skirt and leather duster, Roxy still flashed like a neon bar sign. She kissed and hugged everyone trying to enter the gym.

I needed distraction and turned to Sarah. She looked too pale and maybe even a little green around the gills. She wore her chestnut hair in a ponytail. That wasn't unusual for everyday, but she believed ponytails were lazy. For dress-up occasions she generally wore it smoothed with the blow dyer, a process that took ages with her thick hair. Her eyes and smile had a limp quality that worried me. "Are you feeling okay? Still got that bug?"

She gripped the seat of the bleachers and clamped her lips as if waiting for a wave of nausea to pass. "I need to tell you something."

Just then, Roxy's high-pitched laughter hit us from halfway across the gym. We both whipped our heads to look. I said, "She's going to act like she's the only woman who's ever had a baby."

Sarah swiveled toward me. "Roxy's pregnant?"

I nodded, knowing my mouth curled in contempt despite trying to appear unconcerned.

"Oh," Sarah said. I waited for the string of expletives or a witty insult, but Sarah gave Roxy a contemplative stare.

Principal Barkley tinkered with the controls. Static blizzarded across the screen and roared over the speakers. His face fired crimson. A few more tweaks, a hasty confab with Marty Jean Stavick, the current high school IT geek, and the mournful strains of organ music pressed against us. The live feed showed two sprays of purple iris and glads bookending Chad's casket, which was covered in white roses. The screenshot was stationary with no images of the family or those in the theater.

Ted and Roxy found a place in the first row next to the door. Everyone quieted.

I hadn't known Chad well, but that didn't stop me from absorbing the grief of everyone around me. He'd never celebrate his fortieth birthday. So much potential squashed.

I hunkered down, hating to sit through the service of another young person, and when it ended, I jumped up and joined the rest of my family filling the aisles. I headed for Trey, who stood just inside the gym watching as the mourners exited.

Lauren, my sister-in-law, whispered into our family bunch, "They didn't mention the burial and funeral dinner. Aren't they having one?"

Robert looked confused. "They're from Omaha. Maybe they don't do things like that."

Douglas shrugged. "Doesn't seem respectful to just send everyone away."

Louise tsked. "She's having an invitation-only reception at her house."

Sarah asked, "How do you know that?"

Louise's love of gossip oozed. "Twyla got invited. I guess Meredith knows her from the Long Branch." She reminded us that Mose and Zeke played their final basketball game of the season tomorrow evening. She suggested we gather at Mom and Dad's afterward for cake, which she'd bake, of course.

We gave her the usual noncommitment. A few days ago, that suggestion would drop a gallon of dread into my tank at the thought of the invading hordes to disrupt a quiet evening of reading. Now that I knew how important it was to Mom to have her house filled with life, I had a little more tolerance.

I made my way to where Trey waited. The closer I got, the more his face clouded. "What the hell happened to you?"

I ignored him. "Anything new in the investigation?"

We'd marked the end of a life with a solemn ceremony, and now we were going back to our lives. We made plans for family get-togethers, plunged into work, refocused on our own problems. It didn't seem fair or right. And yet, what else could we do? I fought the guilt that blossomed every time I walked out of a funeral. And I remembered Glenda.

Trey's focus stayed on my face. "Tell me."

I took a few steps back from the doorway with people still meandering through. "I checked out the car Bobby said they set out on the siding. I don't think Chad was the target. They wanted to stop the train."

"What are you talking about?"

I'd rather lay it out for him in my office, but he looked ready to hog-tie me for the details. With a low voice I told him about the car and the man who escaped. I added the details Burke explained about train thefts.

He crushed his back teeth together. "Why didn't you call me?"

I stepped back. "I talked to Clete. He was going to contact the BNSF investigator. If they need any help from us they'll call."

I braced for his indignation for me relinquishing the investigation. His face tightened like a twisted rubber band. "You shouldn't have gone out there alone. You got hurt and it could have been worse."

"This is my job."

He clenched his fists. "But you're not experienced. What if he'd attacked you instead of escaping?"

Now I was running hot. "You think you need to protect me?"

We stared at each other while the gym emptied. Gradually he calmed down, and his color returned to normal. "Okay. It's over. But I'm not convinced Chad wasn't the target. Let's look into it a little more. I heard there is a gathering at Meredith Mills's house. You should go."

I held my hand up. "I can't do that. I wasn't invited. I barely knew Chad, and I don't know Meredith at all."

Trey considered that. "I understand. But there's no way Meredith's father will let me past the door." He tipped his chin toward my skirt. "You look like a friend."

"What is it you think I'll find?"

Trey tilted his head. "Anything, maybe nothing."

"Bobby Jenkins said everyone knew how devoted Meredith and Chad were to each other."

He nodded. "But the yard light signal of their devotion didn't flash that night."

I paused. He had me there. The light had been on when I drove there later.

Trey shrugged. "No, I don't think Meredith killed her husband. But it would be good to rule her out. Maybe you can find out something useful about Chad from his family."

I looked out the gym door. Sarah and Robert made their way down the hallway with the rest of the crowd. She threaded her arm through Robert's and leaned into him. He bent his head and kissed her hair. Concern zinged through me. Tenderness wasn't their public face.

Trey waited for my response. "I'll go out there and see if I can find out anything. But there's something I want you to do."

He raised an eyebrow, probably in response to me giving him an order. "What's that?"

"Yesterday I thought I saw some new Dell boxes in the back of a citizen's car. Since that's something Burke mentioned is often taken from railroad cars, I think you should investigate."

He got all huffy. "You were going to tell me about this when?"

"Now." I gave him directions out to Newt and Earl's. "We can meet at the courthouse and compare notes later."

He didn't look happy about his assignment, but I'd have gladly changed places with him.

21

By the time I reached Meredith's house, expensive foreign sedans and shiny tasteful sports cars with Omaha plates lined the gravel road in front of the white fence. A smattering of mud- and dust-encrusted pickups and SUVs with Grand County plates mingled with the classier herd. I slammed Elvis's door and raced for the house, hoping to get inside before my body heat vanished.

Emily opened the door and pulled me inside. She wore a simple black sheath dress—I only know that's what it's called because my sister Diane tried to give me one of her hand-me-downs, and that's what she'd called it. Diane's dress didn't love me nearly as much as Emily's adored her by embracing her thin curves. The same delicate silver chain with a glinting diamond circled her neck. She held out a pale hand. "Kate, isn't that right?"

I envied her name recall, especially since she'd probably been presented with a gaggle of Sandhillers over the last couple of days. "Good to see you, Emily."

People milled around the living room and toward the dining

room. The folks from the Sandhills wore crisp jeans and boots, with one or two women in dresses.

The people in black wool dresses and suits, with pumps or wingtips, those wearing ties or pantyhose were, I assumed, Meredith's family. Heels clicked and thumped on the gleaming hardwood floors. The faltering sunlight and dead white of the sky seeped through the bank of southern windows that ran from above the couch to the breakfast nook.

The lingering scent of burning pine from the fireplace mingled with brewing coffee and the unusual smell of perfume. Delicate perfume that smelled like money. The Sandhillers I recognized looked as out of place as I felt. Our traditional post-funeral protocol involved a meal served at one of five churches in town. Roast beef cooked overnight in roaster pans, buckets of mashed potatoes, and brown gravy.

For our usual funerals, the churches not hosting the dinner divvied up desserts and salads, and the ladies of the various congregations were then assigned their contribution, which they delivered whether attending the funeral or not. In some instances, the roast beef could be switched with ham, in which case, the roaster pans were filled with "funeral potatoes," a magical mixture of sliced potatoes, cream cheese, sour cream, and cream of mushroom soup, all covered with crushed corn flakes and melted Velveeta.

The food would be strewn on long tables covered with plastic cloths. People would fill paper plates, their voices rising in the church basement. Everyone had been to these dinners in these same basements all their lives and knew what to expect. When they cleaned their plates, they'd deposit them in the big Rubbermaid trash can by the front door.

Here, a lace table cloth covered the dining table. Delicate white china cups and saucers were lined like soldiers at attention next to a coffee urn. An honest to goodness sparkling urn. Not a decrepit five-gallon percolator with tepid, weak coffee. A full bar was laid out on the counter between the kitchen and dining room with crystal of various shapes and sizes waiting for anyone knowledgeable enough to mix a cocktail. Instead of stained roaster pans of greasy or fat-infused comfort, Meredith served uniform platters of cheese and fruit, some kind of spring rolls with raw salmon, and fancy finger food that would send Twyla into apoplexy.

While not a woman of the world, I had occasion to eat sushi and other Asian and fusion food. I loved me some spicy Thai green curry. It's true I usually skipped the chopsticks and embarrassed companions by asking for a fork, but I wouldn't run from the food lining the table.

I placed a few tidbits on a china plate and wandered over to Clete, who held up a wall between two windows. He gripped a china saucer in one hand and wound a gnarled finger through the delicate handle of a tea cup.

He glanced at me then dragged his attention to the crowd of city folks cheerful as if at a cocktail party. "Can't believe he's really gone."

"What did the railroad investigator find out?"

Clete slurped and looked irritated enough to crush the cup and saucer. "They confirmed a theft, but no telling where."

"But the bolt cutters and cut seal were right there on the ground. What did they steal?"

Clete bent over and set the saucer on an end table and clinked the cup on top of it. "They counted thirteen missing computers."

"Dell?"

Clete's face pinched and he shifted. "How'd you know?"

I changed topics, hoping Clete would understand my reluctance to discuss an investigation. "Are Chad's folks here?"

Clete's hands clenched. "Too busy being missionaries in the Amazon or some godforsaken place to get to their boy's funeral."

It wouldn't make much difference to Chad now. "No other family?"

Clete shook his head.

Twyla stomped over to us. She'd wound her hair into a bun and applied eyeliner and blue eyeshadow. She even wore a black skirt and Western shirt with pearl buttons. She curled her lip at my plate and patted Clete's arm. "Sorry day for you. I know how close Ron and Chad were. How's he taking it?"

Clete's frown deepened. "I don't s'pose Ron and Chad were that good of friends. Ron, well, he's pretty busy with work. I'm not sure he knows about this."

Twyla blinked in shock. "You haven't even called him?"

Clete's head sunk into his shoulders. "Mostly it's his mother that talks to him. She probably let him know."

I tried to smooth it over. "People move away. They lose touch."

Twyla eyed Clete, and he cleared his throat and studied the leaf-wrapped dolmades on my plate. "What is that?"

Twyla sniffed. "Fancy-ass hord-de-vores."

I offered the white china to him. "It's some really good stuff wrapped in a grape leaf. Give it a try."

He searched my eyes as my old college roommate would after I told her to "smell this sock" or I would at one of my sisters telling me to "taste this and see if it's off." I guess he must have seen something trustworthy in me. With great trepidation, he inched his gnarled hand to my plate, and using two fingers, as if it might be poison, he lifted the dolmades to his mouth and took a bite. In a second he shoved the whole thing in and chewed. With his mouth still full, he said, "Holy cow. That's good eats."

I nodded, chewing on a bite of well-aged cheese. Clete backed away from me and headed to the table.

Twyla watched him. "He's a real asshole."

Before I could comment, she wandered away to talk to other offended church ladies who hadn't been asked to bring food.

I spoke to a few people I knew. Several congratulated me on my new position. Most had a lame joke about my stitches. No one asked about the investigation, but they all gave off the whiff of curiosity. Thank goodness they didn't know Chad had been murdered.

Like a junior high dance with boys on one side of the gym and girls on the other, the Sandhills contingent loitered in the open dining area or leaned on the breakfast bar wall away from the tonier set. They whispered. No one laughed. More than one of them checked a watch as if wondering the minimum time they had to stay for politeness's sake.

Emily and Mrs. Sterling rose to some secret signal and slinked into the kitchen like lionesses. I followed them. With a murmur and nod, the older woman directed Emily to collect a few of the Tupperware and casserole dishes full of food brought by Meredith's Sandhills neighbors. Mrs. Sterling filled the sink with sudsy water and searched in the cupboard under the sink. She emerged with yellow plastic gloves. While Emily pulled containers from the rows of knotty hickory cabinets and transferred food from original dishes to Meredith's plastic, Mrs. Sterling started to wash the original containers.

Mrs. Sterling was the mature model of the sisters. A few shades darker blonde, she wore her hair in a tasteful French twist. Her body, no doubt sculpted under the direction of a personal trainer, traced the same sleek lines as the younger versions. Black wool draped over a gazelle frame, accented with two long strings of pearls, with matching pearl clusters on her earlobes.

She braced herself against the bottom of the sink with one arm and sawed a scrubby on the remains of "Potato and Cheese Perfection." That was Twyla's specialty. It appeared at funerals and pot lucks. Despite the foreign nature of Chad's funeral, some of the Sandhillers wouldn't dream of showing up without food.

Mrs. Sterling hesitated and studied the dish. She brought it out of the suds and lifted it, turned it over, and squinted at the bottom.

Mom did that sometimes, when she wondered whether the artist signed the piece. I imagined Mrs. Sterling was more interested in the authenticity of the old dish.

When I approached, Mrs. Sterling splashed the dish back into the water as if embarrassed to be caught sizing up the bakeware. Emily rushed over and pulled the plate from me. "Here, let me take that."

The older woman twisted her head over her shoulder and offered a perfunctory smile. "You can set it there, Emily. Grandmother would roll over in her grave if we put it in the dishwasher. The gold plate will wear off."

Emily set the plate on the counter and winked at me as if we understood the eccentricities of picky mothers.

Twyla pounded into the kitchen. "Oh, honey." She threw a hip at Mrs. Sterling, nearly knocking her into Choker County. "You don't need to worry about doing these up now. Just throw some tin foil over them and pop them in the deep freeze. They're for Meredith, and no one expects to get their dishes back for a long time."

Mrs. Sterling held her left hand under her right, catching the drips from one but letting the other hand splash onto the wood floor. "It seems far simpler to send the clean dishes home today."

Twyla plunged her hands into the dishwater, and with muscle Mrs. Sterling could only hint at, scrubbed the burned potato from the casserole. "Oh no. The point ain't the food exactly. It's that it gives Meredith the excuse to get out of the house and see folks. Or sometimes, it's the duty to return the dishes that forces people out of theirselves. You know what I mean?"

Mrs. Sterling raised a gloved hand toward the sink as mothers automatically throw an arm across a child in the front seat when they put on the brakes. "Careful. That's an antique."

"What it is, is my granny's old dish I've had since dirt was young." She lifted it from the water and grinned at it. "I always kind of liked the blue flowers. Makes me glad and reminds me of Granny. Plus, it's the right size for Potato and Cheese Perfection."

Emily stepped back and kept her eyes on her mother, as if gauging the exact moment of the explosion. Mrs. Sterling dripped on the floor.

Twyla tugged the dishwasher door down, fought with it, and accidentally slid it out. "I'll be darned." She popped an excited face to me. "Did you see this, Kate? It's like a giant drawer. Now ain't that clever?"

She picked up my plate and plunked it onto the bottom rack. More plates followed in rapid succession. She yanked out the top rack and deposited several crystal cocktail glasses. Mrs. Sterling stood in horrified paralysis.

Probably out of genuine concern for Twyla and maybe to save the day from another murder, Emily inserted herself between Mrs. Sterling and Twyla. "Please, you're a guest here. We don't expect you to do the dishes."

Twyla waved her off. "Oh honey, we're here to help any way we can. Now you and your mama go back in and sit with Meredith. I'll get this kitchen spick and span and put the food up. Don't you worry."

Emily pulled Twyla away. She reached into the sink and tugged the stopper. "I insist. It would make us uncomfortable for you to do this work. Really. Leave it."

I had to admire Emily for the deft way she handled the situation.

I left the kitchen negotiations to Emily and went in search of a bathroom. Of course, in this house, with this crowd, the correct nomenclature was probably "powder room." I loved the layout of this house, with the kitchen, living room, and dining room on one side of the stairs. The bedrooms were probably on the second story. On the other side of the stairs, a giant polished mahogany desk looked out of northern windows to the pasture. The space under the stairs opened to a laundry room and a wide hallway. I assumed my expedition ended with a bathroom somewhere around here.

Meredith stood in the corner, her head propped against the wall. If she wanted to hide, there were better places. It looked like she'd simply stalled out.

Meredith's mother popped around the other side of the stairway. She drew up and gasped. I hadn't heard many people actually gasp, and then, only if something threatened their life. "You have guests!"

Technically we were guests, but I believe funerals have a different set of hostess responsibilities. In that case, the people stop by to help out those grieving, not to be entertained.

Meredith cringed. "Yes. Of course."

Mrs. Sterling appraised Meredith. She wetted her thumb with her tongue and dabbed underneath Meredith's right eye, then produced a lipstick from midair. "This will be a good color on you."

Maybe she kept it in a hidden pocket. With that trick, I ought to frisk her for concealed weapons. She dabbed it on Meredith's lips and mushed her own together until Meredith imitated her. "The true test of character is not how we behave in good times, but how we bear up under tragedy."

It looked to me like Meredith wanted to slap her mother's hand away. She closed her eyes and her nose flared. When she opened them again, she rubbed her lips together and smiled. "You're right, of course, Mother."

Mrs. Sterling stepped back. "You go out first and I'll follow in a moment so it won't appear as though I came to retrieve you."

With her long legs in the sheer black hose and the three inches of spikes on her heels, Meredith stepped around her mother. I wouldn't be able to move with that smooth precision and grace if I wore a satin gown and went barefoot.

Meredith's shoulder blades settled into a well-worn slot in her back, straightening her spine.

I wandered around the corner as if just arriving on the scene. "Am I anywhere near the powder room?"

Mrs. Sterling didn't seem delighted to see me, but she managed something close to a pleasant expression. "You've come to the right place."

I leaned back a little. "You have such beautiful daughters." Gushy, I know. I'd never say that, but I thought it might hit a soft spot with Mommy Dearest. I stopped short of saying, "They take after their mother." Even for a diva like Mrs. Sterling, that might be over the top.

Mrs. Sterling agreed and warmed to me. "We've been blessed with good genes."

"The girls are obviously close." Maybe close meant something different in Omaha than it did in Hodgekiss. Close for the Fox clan meant dropping in uninvited, sharing clothes, cars, houses, child-care, money, time, and support. It also meant disruptive squabbles but a united front for the rest of the world. "It must be hard for Meredith to be so far away from all of you."

Mrs. Sterling sighed deeply, a sure sign of exaggeration, if not out and out lie. "I have to admit, when she started getting serious with Chad and he mentioned moving out here, her father and I did all we could to persuade her not to."

"You didn't like Chad?"

Mrs. Sterling radiated a moral and social superiority like a noxious odor. "You don't have children, do you?"

I could have told her about my nieces and nephews, but I suspected she didn't care. I shook my head.

All knowing, she said, "You love your children, of course, and want their happiness. But, having lived and experienced the world, you know romantic notions of love, while they're exciting, don't necessarily ensure lasting contentment. I've always believed making a good match involves more than the giddy rush of romance."

Since my parents didn't lecture on life, I was ill prepared to listen to lofty philosophy from a woman more concerned with appearances than with comforting a grieving daughter. "Seems like Meredith and Chad were good partners."

Mrs. Sterling melted. It started with her eyebrows, sank through her cheeks. Her shoulders drooped and she shrank. Unlikely as it sounds, tears filled her eyes. "I was wrong. I thought Meredith would tire of Chad and the rural life. In no time, she'd be begging to come back to Omaha. But she thrived here. I believe she was truly happy with Chad."

I could tell her I was sorry for her loss. Or maybe murmur something about what a tragedy it was, how Chad was too young, how terrible it was for Meredith. I sorted through all the cardboard comments. My natural reaction would be to touch her arm or lay a gentle hand on her shoulder, maybe squeeze her hand. But touching her would be like stroking a scorpion.

As quickly as she'd broken down she resumed her royal demeanor. Through her core and shoulders, up to her chin, and finally her eyebrows rose. She inhaled as if marking completion of the transformation. "I suppose an accident like this is inevitable when you work such a dangerous position."

Accident? Meredith hadn't told her mother Chad was murdered. I couldn't blame her for that. She probably had a better idea how Mrs. Sterling would react to that scandal than I did, but I'd imagine news like that would shoot Mother into orbit.

Mrs. Sterling raised fingers that shook slightly to pat her updo. "At least Meredith is young enough to remake her life. Now that she's had her adventure in country living, she can settle down to a more appropriate match."

Did people really think that way? And to speak to a stranger about such private views seemed truly odd. Maybe talking to me was like having a conversation with a cat or stuffed animal. Mrs. Sterling was too controlled to be honest with her family or friends, but she could unburden herself to the likes of me.

I gave her a noncommittal smile-and-nod combo and slipped into the bathroom. When I emerged, she'd retreated to the living room to attend to the guests. I found Meredith at the kitchen sink with a water glass half raised. She stared out the window.

"How are you doing?" I knew it was a lame opening. I also knew from the days following Glenda's death, it was a question a person can answer on autopilot.

She seemed to have forgotten to drink the water in her glass. Maybe she'd taken strength in a pill to help her through the demanding day. She cleared her throat. "Kate." She seemed to yank herself back to the moment. She turned from her dreamy contemplation beyond the window and swept her gaze beyond me as if checking to see who watched us.

In a quiet voice, she hissed at me, "What are you doing here?"

I hadn't expected hostility. "I stopped by to offer condolences."

She glanced around nervously. "It's not the sheriff's duty to attend private receptions, is it?"

Maybe her meds produced paranoia. Or maybe she was hiding something.

Meredith's eyes shifted out the window as if against her will. Emily clicked in, her thin heels a staccato on the wood floor. "Mr. and Mrs. Carstenson are leaving." Spoken with almost no inflection, yet her tone carried a smidge of contempt.

Meredith gave the faintest smile, serene, as if she hadn't just bared her teeth at me. "I'll be right there." She glanced out the window for a split second then back to me. Her animosity burned into me, though her words were perfectly polite. "Thank you for coming."

It was a phrase that flowed from her throat as spring runoff. I imagine she'd said it thousands of times in the last few days. *Fine. Thank you for coming.* What else was there? Because you couldn't cry anymore. You couldn't throw yourself on the ground and scream and plead with God to return your loved one. That person was gone forever, and you were left with *Fine. Thank you for coming.* And soon, that would fade, too. Then you dealt with the gaping hole as best you could.

God, I missed Glenda. And days like today only made the ache deeper. The days after her death had been the worst in my life. Who knows what confused and unkind things I might have said at the time? I was reading too much into Meredith's reaction. After all, I was the one who brought the terrible news of Chad's death. No wonder she didn't like the looks of me.

I raised my eyes to the window. I'd thought Meredith had been staring at the dead prairie. But she'd had a more concrete subject.

Josh Stevens stood with his back to the house. A full white plastic trash bag dangled from his fingers. He wore a plaid shirt and leather vest but no coat. He also wasn't wearing a hat or gloves against the bitter wind, and yet he remained as still as the naked cottonwoods. The only thing moving besides bits of brown grass and dirt caught up in the restless air was a massive ball of gray fur that I assumed was a barn cat. It darted across the dirt ranch yard toward Josh.

I braced myself for the cold. At least I wore long underwear under my skirt and a few layers hidden by my jacket. I slipped out the back door and across the cement patio, striped with pale sun from the pergola.

"Hi Josh." I thought I ought to warn him of my approach since he hadn't moved.

He twitched and turned his head away from me. He raised his free arm and scrubbed his face on his sleeve. When he turned to me, his eyes were damp and red.

I sucked in a rush of cold air, and my heart slammed against my ribs the moment I saw his wrapped right hand.

"Hey." He seemed to notice the bag he held. "Just taking out the trash."

The cat arrived and rubbed against Josh's jeans, leaving a thin trail of gray fur.

I reached out to rub the cat's back to give myself a second to recover. Its silky fur warmed my shaking fingers. I plastered on a casual expression. "What did you do to your hand?"

He nodded at my own goose-egged forehead. "Looks like you met with a bear. I got a little too close preg checking heifers at Shorty Cally's yesterday. You?"

If he'd been stealing computers from a railroad siding, would he really be this relaxed? Checking with Shorty would be easy. "Slipped on the ice."

Skepticism crossed his face but he let it go. "Cold doesn't seem to want to shake loose."

I stopped petting the cat, and he rubbed against my legs so I started again. "It's tough to lose a friend."

A swell of tears threatened his eyes before he blinked them back. "Yeah."

I waited, wishing we could take the conversation inside but suspected Josh would clam up once indoors. Better to stay in the open.

He stared at a tumbleweed, dull brown against tarnished gold grass. "He was a townie." I knew what that meant. As townies, the Fox house served as Grand Central for prom and homecoming preparation, quick meals for ranch kids between basketball practices and play rehearsals, a stopover after school before parents could make it into town from a day working cattle.

"I used to wait at the school. Mom couldn't always get away to come to town in the afternoon. But after Chad moved in, I'd hang out at his house during the week. It sort of became routine. During the school year, I think I spent more time with them than I did at home."

His flow of words surprised me. "Did he ever go to your place?"

The cat meowed long and high. It wound around Josh's legs, letting out another plaintive yowl. Josh set the trash bag down and ran a hand along the cat's back, making it arch. "Bet no one's fed you."

He picked up the trash. "Come on." I didn't know if he talked to the cat or to me, so I followed anyway.

With fluid movement, Josh crossed the ranch yard to slip behind the barn. The cat sprinted ahead, then zipped around and raced behind us. Typical behavior for crazy cats. I trod after them, considering the wisdom of traveling farther from the house's central heat. A county Dumpster and an elevated fuel tank nestled close to the steel barn, shielded from the house. He raised the Dumpster lid, tossed in the garbage bag, and let it clang closed.

Without pausing to see whether the cat or I followed, he slipped into a door at the front of the barn. The giant sliding doors remained closed, but this human-sized one opened easily. If anything, the interior of the building was even colder than outdoors. The feeble sun must afford a little warmth. The cat bounded between my legs and nearly tripped Josh in his enthusiasm. He meowed and put up such a racket it sounded as if he'd been starved for months. Josh pried the lid off a metal trash bin and bent in. The dry food rattled into a metal pet dish. The cat fell to it, and Josh dropped in the scoop and smashed the lid back on.

I backed out to make room for him to step through the door. He closed it behind him and stopped, staring at the dead pasture. It was as if he'd had a plan, executed it, and had run out of steam.

More to keep me from freezing, but also to jumpstart our

conversation, I prompted him. "So, you spent a lot of time at Chad's house. Did he ever go to yours?"

Josh's eyes lost focus. "Yeah. On weekends. But when he came out, we usually worked. Fencing or cattle. I taught him how to ride a horse, which he never really liked. But we had an old Honda 350 Scrambler. We'd tinker with it and get it fired up and take off. The summer we were fourteen, we'd sneak out after my folks went to sleep. We'd push that old 350 down to the county road, then fire it up. Roggin Lake wasn't too far away cross-country. Chad and I used to park the bike and sneak down to the shore. People would pull their campers down there and leave their coolers out. We'd snitch a beer or two from a few coolers. Not enough so anyone would know they'd been robbed. They'd probably just look in the cooler the next morning and be surprised they drank so many the night before."

I admired the logic of that. It made more sense than stealing a case off the Miller truck when it made a delivery to the Long Branch. That stunt could have landed me, Robert, and Sarah in a lot of trouble if Dad's cousin, who was a lawyer in Broken Butte, hadn't spoken to the judge on our behalf.

Josh sniffed. Maybe the cold was getting to him after all. "But that jig was up when the motorcycle broke down. We walked back to town, and Chad's dad had to take me and the bike home. They never found out about the beer, but my folks were kind of strict. After that, Chad wasn't allowed out to the ranch."

"But you still got to hang out with him in town?"

He warmed, which is more than I could say for me. "There was an empty lot next to his house, and we used to play a game we made up called run-tackle-kill-smear." His faraway face told me he relived the good times. "One time, we were probably in sixth grade, his mother came out and told us it was supper time. It was one of those fall days where it's warm all day, but as soon as the sun starts down, it gets cold. We wanted to get one more play in. I don't know what happened, but Bucky Volks tackled me hard. I broke my arm."

The cold didn't seem to penetrate his thin layers. My fingers were numb.

"His mom had to run me to Broken Butte because my folks were out on the ranch. Chad knew how much I loved McDonald's and how I hardly ever got the chance to eat there." It surprised me when he brought his focus to me to give me an aside. "My folks didn't go to town very often. They worked a lot and they hated fast food, so when we did get to Broken Butte, Mom usually packed a lunch."

From what I knew of Black Socks, they preferred frugal and simple.

"I remember Chad convincing his mother to take us to McDonald's after I got my arm set."

His talk of football sparked a vague memory. "Didn't you and Chad play on the Danbury team that went to State?"

The transformation of a smile, even the small one, made him almost handsome. "What a year. We'd done okay our junior year, came within three points of winning districts. But our senior year, Coach switched us and put Chad as quarterback and me as receiver. We were unstoppable."

I looked down to make sure I still had feet since I couldn't feel them anymore.

The back door banged open. Meredith's father stormed out. He glared at the covered patio furniture as if it was an invading army and he threatened to destroy it. With the gait of an angry bull, he took the patio steps two at a time and advanced on us. "Where the hell is some kind of tank or heavy-duty four-wheel-drive that can get me out of this goddamned black hole so I can make a f—" He halted and started a few decibels lower. "A phone call. I can't get a signal in the house."

I wrapped my arms around myself, unable to stoically tolerate the cold.

Josh indicated the barn. “Take the white Dodge dually. I just fueled it up.”

Mr. Sterling seemed to notice the weather for the first time. “Damn. Chad couldn’t die in April. The bastard always had to do things the hard way.”

Neither Josh nor I had anything to say to that.

Mr. Sterling tilted his head at Josh. “Oh. Hey. You’re Josh Stevens.” He transferred his phone to his left hand and stuck out his right. “Good to see you.”

Josh shook his hand. “Sir.”

Mr. Sterling studied him a moment longer, as if not sure what to say. “Well. Okay.” He galumphed to the steel barn, and we watched him struggle to slide the big door open.

Josh noticed my shivers. “You best get back to the house. They’ve probably got another full trash bag already, I’ve been gathering dust out here so long.”

I watched Josh’s purposeful strides to the side of the barn away from the house. He was sure familiar with the place, knowing where the Dumpster was hidden, entering the barn and feeding the cat, filling up the pickup from the locked fuel tank. And how did Josh know Mr. Sterling?

22

I let myself into the back door wanting to moan at the wave of warmth. Emily had taken Meredith's spot at the window above the sink. She handed me a mug of coffee, and I gratefully wrapped my frozen fingers around it, letting the steam thaw my nose. "Bless you."

Her perfect smile with even white teeth in flawless skin drew me in. "Just don't tell Mother I gave you that mug instead of Mere's china."

I mimed a zipper on my lips.

Emily leaned back and surveyed the house. "I love this little house, don't you? I mean, at first, you think, 'How could anyone live here full time?' It's more like a quaint cabin, really. But having everything just a few steps away is nice."

"How is Meredith holding up?" Stupid question, but I wanted to pry some sisterly gossip from Emily, so I eased into it.

Emily glanced behind me and lowered her voice. "Honestly?"

I nodded. That was easy.

Emily rolled her eyes. "All the tears and drama are over the top. Even for Mere."

I'd seen more drama from Grandma Ardith when she napped than what Meredith showed today. "Losing a loved one is difficult."

Emily kept an eye out for eavesdroppers and continued in conspiratorial mode. "Oh, please. Until today she's been bawling and carrying on. Now it's all sighs and tragic looks, tears hanging in her eyes. Manufactured to get sympathy. Mere loves being the center of attention."

I felt like a schmuck for egging her on, but I wanted to hear more. "It can feel good to be the star. Even if you have to fib a little."

"Right?" Emily's enthusiasm grew. "She's always liked to lie, even when the truth works. It's like her telling you the other day that Daddy gives her money to buy art."

"He doesn't?"

Emily laughed. "The last time Daddy spent money on either of us was our weddings. He gave our husbands the same speech, basically, 'She's yours now.' And he meant it."

The paintings and bronze sculpture captured light from the southern windows. All of this on Chad's salary? "She didn't have an inheritance?"

Emily rolled her eyes. "Not yet. We'll both inherit when Daddy and Mother pass, but we'll probably be too old to enjoy it."

"She has some nice things." I let that hang with a touch of bitterness to fuel Emily.

"Meredith always had expensive tastes. That's why she went into engineering in college."

Engineering? Interesting. "So she could earn a good living?"

Emily tossed her head back and laughed. "You don't know Mere very well at all."

My questioning look prompted her.

"She went into mechanical engineering to find a husband. She's not smart enough to pass those math classes. It's the same reason I went into pre-law."

Emily laughed at what must be a horrified look on my face. "We were raised to be professional wives. In the old days, we'd have gone to finishing school. Now. Well, now we have to be more clever about it."

I might have been more tempted to pass judgment if I hadn't married Ted. I maintained I didn't marry him because I'd get to live and work Frog Creek. It was a real perk for me, though. "But Meredith ended up marrying a railroader. That's not known to be real lucrative."

Emily emphasized her words with big eyes. "I know!"

"Then she must have loved Chad."

"You aren't listening. Mere is all about the drama."

"And the railroad is drama?"

Emily shook her head and leaned in again. "No. It's Daddy."

She'd galloped off to a whole other pasture, and I hadn't even opened the gate. "I'm not following."

She sighed. "In college, Mere was in the engineering school at the University of Nebraska. Daddy was already at his limit with her because she'd flunked out of Creighton, where there are more of the people . . . ," she hesitated as if searching for the polite way to mention wealth, "who are like us. So she's slumming at UNL until next semester when Daddy can pull some strings and get her into a better school. And she meets this other engineering student, Josh Stevens. They start dating and get all serious."

A jolt of electricity shot through me. "Josh Stevens from here?"

Emily nodded. "I saw you talking to him. Almost didn't recognize him. I mean, when Mere dated him, he was, like, alive and happy. Now he looks mad and sad and so skinny. But back then, he was the bomb."

"What happened with Meredith and Josh?"

Emily considered her story. "Everything was good until they got engaged."

Wow. Josh and Meredith, both with an engineering education. Engaged.

Emily continued, "Naturally, Daddy did a background check on him. Found out he came from here and that his parents weren't anything. He forbade Meredith to date Josh."

I couldn't imagine that kind of parental interference. Mom and Dad believed in letting us all tie our own nooses.

"Oh my God. You can't believe the tears and slammed doors and hysterics. No one does drama better than Meredith."

I'll bet Roxy could be a contender.

"Mere was all, 'He'll provide for me.' Because of being an engineer and all of the opportunities. But Daddy didn't listen. In fact, he ignored her. So that's when she suddenly announced her engagement to Chad."

"That doesn't make any sense. If your father wouldn't accept Josh, why would he feel any differently about Chad?"

Emily's gaze drifted toward the living room where Meredith endured Twyla's embrace. "Sometimes she just gets crazy. I don't know what it is. Personally, I think she's got like a real mental disease. But she'll do things to hurt herself just to hurt someone else."

"My grandmother would say she cuts off her nose to spite her face."

Emily nodded sagely. "Exactly."

"So she married Chad to spite your father?"

Emily gave a sorrowful click to her tongue. "Yes. I think that's exactly what she did. I mean, Josh was bad enough. But he'd have a good career. She might have to tone down her life a little, like not the biggest house and stuff, but he'd do okay. But Chad, he was in agronomy or something. I think he wanted to be an FFA teacher like his father. We all thought it was hopeless."

"She seems to be doing okay, though. New house, nice art, expensive car." Not to mention a big refrigerator and all those other sexy appliances.

Emily looked puzzled. "Yeah. She says they made some good investments and the cost of living out here is really low."

"Josh didn't become an engineer, though."

Emily's eyes sparkled at this twist. "Right after Chad and Meredith got married, Josh quit school and came back here. He loved her so much he just couldn't go on there."

For the last eight or nine years Josh had been living only a few miles away from his college sweetheart, selling them land that had been in his family for generations.

I probed, "People say Chad and Meredith were devoted to each other."

Emily twirled a strand of smooth blonde hair. "That's just Mere's way. She wants everyone to think she's got the best of everything. She'd never let anyone know things weren't amazing between her and Chad. But I know the truth because I've seen them together." She leaned in closer to me. "They slept in separate rooms."

"Maybe they hit a rough patch, the seven-year itch. They could have been working it out."

Emily eyed me. "They've been itching for way longer than that."

Nobody knows what really goes on in someone else's marriage. In my case, sometimes you don't even know what's going on in your own. "If Meredith didn't love Chad and wasn't happy about living in the Sandhills, why did she stay?"

Emily acted as if that were the dumbest question ever. "Money."

The house was nice, sure. The art and car, but she'd get spousal support and would have a chance to find an even better financial ride if she got back to a city. "Chad couldn't be making that much."

Emily laughed. "Oh, not Chad's money. Daddy's."

"I don't understand."

Emily gave an annoyed click with her tongue. "We all knew Meredith married Chad out of spite and assumed she'd divorce him after a year or so. After Chad, Josh would look good by Daddy's standards, and he would give her his blessing. But don't ever try to outsmart Daddy."

She gathered up my coffee cup and placed it in the sink. She had a cagey smile, and I figured she wanted me to ask.

"Why is that?"

She raised her eyebrows. "Right after the wedding, when we had a little tea at Mother's to open the gifts, Daddy brought us girls into his office and sat us down. We thought maybe he was going to give us a portion of our inheritance. With Meredith's marriage and me practically engaged, we both could have used a pile of cash."

"And did he?"

She shook her head in irritation. "The opposite. He showed us the investments and the accounts he'd set up for us, still in his name, of course. Then he said that if either of us ever embarrassed him by divorcing, he'd change the plan and leave our portion to charity."

So if Meredith divorced Chad, she'd be cut off from all that gooey, sweet money. Her next-best option was to play house with Chad and enjoy an affair with Josh, her hunky, brooding neighbor.

But maybe the pretense was too much for them. They killed Chad, and after a suitable time, they'd hook up and, with Daddy's blessing, live in marital bliss, holding out for the cushy inheritance.

I fought the evidence, circumstantial though it may be, that planted Josh six feet deep in the suspect field. But even with Dad's endorsement, it was hard to ignore that he had motive and means. Not to mention that damned injured hand.

23

I stopped at the house and changed into my browns and hiking boots. It may not be as swank as the Sterling women's ensembles, but it was a darn sight warmer than the skirt and jacket. I considered rubbing a little Icy Hot on my sore back and arms but didn't want to smell terrible all afternoon. My feet cuddled into thick wool socks. For good measure, I even pulled the brown ski cap on top of my waves.

I would have welcomed a nice long nap, snuggled deep into my quilts. That wasn't going to happen.

At the courthouse, Trey Ridnoir huddled over pages of notes spread on the conference table in the commissioner's room. He leaned back in the heavy wood chair when I walked in.

I unzipped my coat. "What did you find out at Newt and Earl's?"

He shook his head. "Good God. They weren't home, or else they were buried under so much junk we'd never find them without search and rescue dogs."

I should have known. "Did you find any computers?"

He shook his head. "Even if I had a search warrant, I didn't know where to start. We can go out there together tomorrow." He pushed his notes aside. "What did you come up with?"

I wandered over to the table and glanced at the pages. My head and gut wrangled. I knew the right thing to do was tell Trey everything, but I didn't want to. "Meredith's family is upper crust from Omaha with everything you'd expect. And yes, I know that's stereotyping. But they'd be repressed even in Stepford."

Trey laughed. "People keep saying Meredith is stuck up."

I paced, still trying to work blood back to my feet. "You can't rely on what 'they' say. Folks around here are skeptical of anyone who drinks wine with a cork."

"Same as in Ogallala. You went to college, though; how does that sit with everyone?"

I waved that off. "I'm a Fox. We go so far back around here, most folks will overlook any eccentricity." I paused. "Although my mother still rattles them from time to time."

"What's wrong with your mother?"

"She's an artist. Around here, it's a condition to be tolerated or even pitied, sort of like cancer of the common sense."

Trey leaned forward. "Your mother is Marguerite Myers?"

I pivoted toward him. "How do you know Marguerite Myers?"

He colored like a cute little boy. "I was an art major my first year at UNL."

I didn't mean to, but I laughed out loud. "How does an art major wind up a state trooper?"

"It's a boring story. Ending with me realizing I wasn't anywhere near good enough to make a living with art."

I raised my eyebrows. "It's not the most stable profession."

"But my sculpting instructor was a huge Marguerite Myers fan. I think he loved the fact that she lived in a tiny Nebraska town and thought it would inspire us that she'd gained such success."

Mom could inspire a lot of people. She inspired Louise to be the perfect nurturer, she inspired Diane to go into corporate life with a definite career path. She even inspired me to follow my heart, which might have sent me on a murky road.

Trey placed his bulky hands on top of the papers and grinned. "Wow. Marguerite Myers is your mother. Go figure."

He stared at me like I'd stepped from a genie bottle, so I blurted out, "Josh Stevens was out there."

Trey sat up, all fan-boy aura gone. "And?"

"He seemed pretty shaken up by Chad's death."

Trey huffed. "I'll bet. It's upsetting to kill someone."

I lowered myself to a chair, hesitating. Was I misguided about Josh? If I was going to keep believing in him, I'd need to come up with something solid quickly. "He and Meredith were in engineering school."

"For the railroad?"

I pulled my hat off and rubbed my hair, probably making a mess, but it felt good. "Not running trains, mechanical engineering at the university. They were engaged before Meredith and Chad were married."

Trey plopped back in his chair. "Holy crap. And you still don't think Josh killed Chad?"

I balled my hat up in my fist. "I don't trust the source. It came from Meredith's sister, and I get the vibe that Emily has a gripe against Meredith."

He sat forward in agitation. "Vibe? Like this stubborn streak about Josh Stevens being such a great guy. You just don't *believe* he could hurt someone?"

"All right. Yes. I think Josh is a good guy."

Little ridges ran in parallel lines across his forehead. "Here's what we've got: Josh mad enough at Chad he threatens to put a railroad tie upside his head. Josh is a trained mechanical engineer, someone capable of rigging up the tie. Josh is in love with Chad's wife."

I didn't want to say it but I needed to. "Josh's right hand is wrapped."

Trey pounded a fist on the table. "As in the hand you smashed on the train last night?"

I nodded. "He said he had an accident working at Shorty Cally's yesterday. I called Shorty."

Trey zeroed in on me. "And?"

"Not in. I left a message to call me."

Trey jumped to his feet. "Why do you have any doubt Josh killed Chad and is stealing from the railroad?"

I folded my arms. "It's easy to get hurt working cattle, and if Josh is stealing from the railroad, what's he doing with the money? He's living pretty simply."

"He's probably saving for his getaway with Meredith."

Was I fighting so hard for Josh because Trey fought so hard against him? The Fox stubborn streak was a well-known joke among Sandhillers. As the clues piled against Josh, I dug my heels deeper into the sand. Josh's injured hand ought to be the final barb on that wire. I opened my mouth and kicked more sand. "We need to see Olin Riek."

Trey dropped his hand to the table. "Really?"

I shook open the hat I'd been squeezing in my fist and started out. Trey grabbed his coat from the back of his chair. "This is a waste of time."

No sense in arguing with him. The icy air battered me for the ten seconds it took to throw myself into Trey's car, and then it pressed against the bare skin on my neck and cheeks. In May, I'd happily traipse up the hill and around the block to Olin's bungalow. But today, if I could cut a few seconds off my time away from a heater, I'd do whatever it took.

I directed Trey to the green-sided manufactured home. Olin's wife, Jan, collected yard art. Although "art" was a loose term for the plastic whirligigs, plywood statues of silhouetted cowboys leaning on imaginary fences, and brightly painted metal Huskers signs that adorned the frozen yard.

I hurried up the front walk and rang the doorbell before Trey even slammed his car door. Heavy footsteps lumbered toward the door, which was thrown open. Jan, an older woman with fleshy arms and hips like a double-wide trailer, unlatched the screen with a grin. "Katie! Get yourself inside here before you turn into a glacier."

Trey and I crowded into her foyer, and she slammed the door closed. It felt like Honduras after a rain. The hot, humid air blanketed me, and the smell of thousands of meals and cakes pushed into my head.

Jan's voice was that of someone hard of hearing. "What in the world happened to your face?"

It's always nice to feel pretty. "Ran into a door."

Jan seemed to buy that and started on a full gallop. "Oh my, what a cold snap. You know, we're usually down in Ajo this time of year. Sure wish we were there now. Come in, come in. Let me get you some coffee. I baked rolls yesterday but they're all gone now. But I have some cookies. Just you settle yourselves in the living room, and I'll be right back."

I finally jumped in with a voice louder than hers. "That's so nice, Jan. This is Trooper Trey Ridnoir. We really need to talk to Olin. Is he in?"

She dropped her arms and her face fell. "You don't have time to visit? Most folks don't know we are wintering here this year so nobody's been by."

Dad would brain me for not giving Jan a few minutes of my day. Just another brick of guilt. "I'm sorry. We're really busy." I thought about what she said. "Why aren't you in Ajo this winter?"

Her face fell even further. She eyed a hallway leading toward the back of the house and lowered her voice. "Olin didn't make his usual commission this year. We couldn't afford it, you know. It's been hard, because my arthritis is terrible in the cold." She brightened and clapped her hands. "Nothing to be done. At least we have central heat."

I glanced at Trey, lifting an eyebrow to comment on Olin's obvious motive and opportunity. He remained deadpan.

"Is Olin around?" I asked again.

Jan fluttered both her arms, and her flab, hemmed in by a baggy cardigan, waggled back and forth. "Of course." She turned and hollered, "Olin! Olin!"

A *thump, scrape* sounded, followed by more, and from the end of the hallway, a figure emerged. *Thump, scrape. Thump, scrape.* Olin Riek slowly advanced with his walker.

Trey nudged my shoulder, and his eyes clearly told me that, yes, I had indeed wasted his time. No way Olin was climbing around on a railcar last night.

His huge salesman grin greeted us as he struggled into the light of the foyer. "Katie Fox. Been thinking about you. Probably ought to get your policy changed. Beneficiary is Ted Conner, and my guess is you maybe want someone different. And with your new job, might be smart to up the policy."

I didn't need the policy anymore since I was insured through the county now. But if I canceled the policy, it might mean another winter in Nebraska for poor Jan. I didn't have the heart to do that to her. I smiled at Jan, then at Olin, and wondered how to get us out of there. "You heard about Chad Mills?"

Olin lost his grin. "That is a tragedy. Wish he was insured with me. I'd have a check right now for his wife. But he went with the cheapest and now . . . ," he trailed off.

Trey followed up. "You wouldn't know anyone who had a grudge against Chad, would you?"

Jan's mouth gaped, and she turned to Olin. "He was always so polite and sweet. Can't imagine anyone thought ill of him."

Olin looked sad. "I know I should have been madder than a hornet at him for getting the union to switch insurance. But the honest truth is that I know he was trying to do what's best for his guys. Can't fault him for that."

I don't know about the sincerity of Olin's statement, but it didn't matter. He couldn't have killed Chad. And that plopped Josh right back into the fire.

24

The cold had eased, but only because the clouds hovered low. We drove past Meredith's house. Most of the shiny cars and dusty pickups were gone. There are few things sadder than the hours after the funeral. I looked the other way, across brown weeds and a tumbleweed-clogged barbed wire fence. Hard to believe that in a few months knee-high green grass would ripple in soft spring breezes. Life and seasons.

That's too philosophical for a small-town sheriff on a cold winter afternoon.

Trey drove with one hand on the wheel, the other holding a travel cup filled with the evil courthouse brew.

A few miles west from the Millses', a narrow dirt road led to the right. Two whitewashed corner posts held a plywood plank with "Stevens Ranch" painted in black letters. Another few miles in brought us to a second wooden sign indicating "Stevens Ranch" to the left.

Trey settled his cup in the holder. "Ogallala is pretty rural, but this Grand County is a whole other dimension."

I might not know every hill and valley, every shallow lake or the name of all the pastures, but Grand County was home. The remote ranches and distances from one landmark to another were just the way it was.

Stevens Ranch wasn't the most impressive place in the Sandhills. What it lacked in sparkle, new and improved, it made up for in neat and clean. A freshly painted white picket fence surrounded the picturesque, if small, ranch house, also painted white with forest green trim around the windows and doors. A front porch faced south and held a swing and two bent willow rockers. No dust, dirt, leaves, or trash marred the tidy front yard.

Trey parked the car in front of the fence, and we climbed out to pelting ice crystals.

An old wooden barn with corrals in back and a windmill towering behind sat fifty yards from the house. It, too, showed signs of loving attention, the white paint and green trim flawless. Josh's black pickup was parked in front of the closed barn doors.

The pinging of ice pellets on the ground added to the clanking and banging from behind the barn. I threw Trey a curious glance and headed off in that direction. When I got closer, I heard grunts and the banging grew louder. I followed the commotion behind the barn to see Josh poised under the windmill.

Weathered wooden scaffolding centered over his head with the sucker rod running from the hole in the ground. The rod wasn't connected to the blades so the pump ran on electricity. This must be the main water supply for the house. One-inch PVC pipe disappeared into the well.

His gloved hands clamped on the plastic pipe. His face was nearly purple, and veins popped in his neck. He seemed to be in a trap. If he let go of the pipe, it would sink back into the well, but he couldn't get a grip to pull it out farther.

I ran over and grabbed hold of the pipe below Josh's hands. With his injured hand, he probably couldn't get a strong handle on it. My synthetic ski gloves had some texture so I got a better grip, but my sore muscles screamed in pain. The wind blew tiny bits of ice down the back of my neck.

"Ice is collecting on the rod." He strained to pull, and with my help, we managed to drag up the pipe a few more inches. "Not sure why the danged thing quit working, but I suspect it's the old pump."

I'd pulled enough wells in my time. It always seemed the vital wells went out in bad weather. The idea was to pull the pipe from the bottom of the well. In this case, several lengths of PVC were screwed together, so the easiest way to pull it would be to unscrew each length as it came out.

We both grunted with the effort, and I figured my face turned as many bright shades as did Josh's. Even my Thinsulate gloves couldn't keep my fingers from growing numb. Trey was nowhere in sight. He must be getting a good look around.

I braced while Josh unscrewed the top length of PVC. We yanked again until we'd pulled enough pipe from the well he could unscrew another twenty-foot section. We finally succeeded in pulling the submersible pump above the well. It was not much wider than the PVC, a stainless steel bit of metal about two and a half feet long. We laid it out on the ground. Breathless, we stepped back. A gust sent the blades of the windmill clanking overhead.

"Looks like this would be easier if you'd use a block and tackle." I slapped my hands on my thighs to get some blood into them.

"Can't find the pulley, but I didn't think I'd have much trouble pulling this. It's only fifty feet." He set to work disconnecting black, white, and red wires from the old pump.

My mind flashed to the pulley attached to the railroad tie. It hadn't looked like a new piece of equipment. Had it come from Josh's barn?

Josh grabbed the new pump lying on the ground and stopped. He grinned up at me, a boyish expression that made it nearly impossible to think of him harming anyone. "Thanks. I wouldn't have been able to get that by myself."

Trey spoke from the corner of the barn where he stood with arms folded. He didn't seem all that pleased. "You two looked like you've been working together for years. Like an old married couple."

Being married didn't guarantee a peaceful working relationship. Ted and I never would have been able to pull a well together without him losing his temper at some point, sending pliers sailing through the air in frustration, or without one of us walking away. I preferred working alone, but Trey was right. Josh and I had been a pretty good team.

I watched Josh reconnect the wires. "It's hard to work a place alone. I came up with a lot of ways to manage without help, but some things require an extra pair of hands."

Still grinning, Josh said, "Well, thank God for yours."

"Joshua!" The commanding male voice carried reprimand. "What have I said about taking the Lord's name in vain?"

The smile drained from Josh's face. Trey and I both whirled around.

A wiry wrinkle of a man, once tall but now bent at the waist with a caved-in chest, stood with wispy white hair floating around his head like fluff from a cottonwood tree. It seemed unlikely the roar of authority issued from him, but he opened his mouth and proved it to be true.

"You will milk all the cows alone for the next three days to remind you to respect your Creator." The old man didn't seem to notice me or Trey. He threw Josh a curt nod and spun away. With halting movements, he marched back around the barn.

Josh watched him go, sadness settling on his face. "That's my father."

Trey put on his cop face. "He's got dementia?"

Josh watched his father like a blue heeler tracking a calf. "Most of the time he gets along fine. But once in a while his mind slips."

I traced Josh's gaze, squinting into the ice pellets.

"Today is not one of his good days. Excuse me." Josh strode away, but before he disappeared around the barn, he hurried back. "Thank you so much for your help. I'll be able to put the pump back together soon's I get Dad situated."

Trey and I didn't move for a moment, then Trey said, "We need to talk to you."

We followed and caught up with them in front of Josh's pickup. Josh spoke to his father with a cheerful note, like a regular afternoon. "Let's have a cup of coffee."

The old man glowered at him. "If we don't get those bulls out of the pasture, we'll have calves in September, and they won't survive the winter snow."

Josh nodded and without touching or coaxing, managed to direct his father to the side yard. A wood door with a window on the top half opened into the house, probably the kitchen.

Trey and I followed across the yard and into a neat house. Josh and his father dropped their coats on hooks that lined the wall next to the door. We closed the door while Josh's father settled at a chrome-rimmed gray Formica table. Trey focused on the bruise-blackened fingernails of Josh's right hand.

The old man seemed to notice us for the first time. "Who are you?"

Josh stepped between the table and us, as you might put yourself between two dogs to keep them from attacking. "Dad, this is Kate Fox. You remember the Foxes from Hodgekiss." Josh looked at me. "Kate, this is my father, Enoch."

I offered my most polite smile. "My father is Hank. He says he knows you."

Enoch eyed me from my head to my boots. "Why are you dressed like that?"

"I'm Grand County sheriff."

He threw his head back and guffawed. "A girl? Good gravy. What's next?"

Trey grew impatient and addressed Josh. "I'd like to take a look around. Ask you a few questions."

Josh scowled at Trey. "I'd say you got a good enough look already."

Trey unzipped his coat and pulled out his notebook. "Okay. Let's start with you and Chad Mills. You weren't exactly friends, were you?"

Enoch's fist hitting the Formica table made us all jump. "You are not to be around that boy. I told you to stay away from him and that Saunders kid."

The heat from Josh's gaze could have given Trey third-degree burns. He softened when he turned to Enoch. "It's okay, Dad. I haven't been around either of them."

Enoch folded his arms and clamped his mouth.

"I'll make some coffee in a minute, Dad." Josh indicated for us to follow him out of the kitchen into a small living room. The couch looked lumpy and was draped with a chenille bedspread. An ancient brown recliner with lace doilies on the arms crowded into a corner. Several books and reading glasses, old mugs and tissues cluttered TV trays set up as end tables. There was no television. Large windows looked out onto a front porch and the gray afternoon. I stood close to the kitchen, keeping my mouth shut.

Josh stopped and towered over Trey. "Chad and I have been friends from when we were kids. But yeah, we had a disagreement. It wasn't that big of a deal, but I imagine gossips at the railroad would tell you we were sworn enemies."

Trey scribbled in his notebook and waited.

Josh pointed to the kitchen. "You see him? If Chad got the pool changed like he was pushing for, we couldn't stay here. I can leave Dad for a while, but he can't live alone. What would I do? Quit my job? Then how'm I going to pay my bills? Move? That would flat-out kill him."

"So getting rid of Chad was your solution?" Trey said matter-of-factly.

Josh sneered at him. "You have no idea what's going on."

"Why don't you tell me?"

I faced the kitchen and noticed Enoch fidgeted and stood up, going to the wood cookstove.

Josh's gaze slid to me then back to Trey. If I were a betting woman, I'd bet he had a secret he'd like to spill.

Trey looked like he wanted to punch Josh, but he wrote in his book. "What's your relationship with Meredith Mills?"

Enoch reached to a wooden fruit box on the floor next to the stove. He picked up some kindling and threw it into the firebox. He grabbed some newspapers and twisted them, then lit a match and held it to the papers.

Threat dug deep in Josh's throat. "Leave Meredith out of this. She didn't have anything to do with Chad's death."

I didn't see what happened next, but the papers in Enoch's hand were a mass of flames. He waved them and whimpered but didn't throw them in the firebox with the kindling.

I lunged into the kitchen and in less than a heartbeat, grabbed Enoch's arm and shoved it toward the stove and into the firebox. I didn't need to tell him to let go, and when I jerked his hand back, it was empty, the flames already crackling on the kindling.

He glared at me, and I stood silent, panting in post-panic mode.

Dad's uncle Chester and aunt Hester had a stove like this. Chester and Hester, a constant source of giggles for us kids, lived in an old soddy well past the Choker county line. Nowadays, we call them "living off the grid," and they'd be cutting-edge cool. Back then, they were old and eccentric and just a little bit creepy.

With calm that had returned, I said, "Would you like me to make coffee?" No canisters rested on the narrow counter, so coffee was probably stored in one of the clean white cupboards.

Enoch scraped a chair across the linoleum and planted himself. "Now that's what you should be doing. Cooking, making coffee. You've got no business running around being the law in Grand County. You should be raising kids."

Josh hurried back into the kitchen, Trey in tow. "What's going on?"

"Enoch wanted some coffee." And to tell me how I ought to live my life.

Josh's face looked tight as a new boot as he turned his back on Enoch and lowered his voice. "I'm sorry about Dad. He kind of lost his manners."

Enoch's arthritic finger drummed on the table and eyes narrowed. "You Foxes all have the same look. Got to say though, you're better looking than the other one that was here a while back." He turned to Josh. "What was her name?"

Josh spun from me and wrenched open a cabinet. "It'll take a minute to get the coffee going."

Enoch sat back and tapped his scruffy chin. "Linda. Lou. Lou. Louise. That's it. Now that girl knows how to keep her groceries."

Louise? When was she out here? Before I could get the question out, Josh slammed the cabinet and plunked a five-pound can of Folgers on the counter. "A day this cold, nothing to help it but hot coffee, huh Dad?"

Trey stood in the living room doorway and zipped his coat. "Thanks for your time." He sounded anything but grateful. "We'll be in touch."

Josh's expression gave nothing away.

Enoch's chair squeaked as he sat back. He took in Trey's uniform with contempt. "Why is the state patrol and the sheriff here? We've got no business with either of you."

Enoch might have lost our whole previous conversation.

Josh answered his father but kept his eyes on Trey. "They're leaving now."

I produced a Dad-approved polite smile. "It's been good talking to you, Enoch."

He stiffened. "Mr. Stevens."

"Of course."

Trey reached into his breast pocket and pulled out a card. He handed it to Josh.

Josh didn't take it. Trey dropped it on the kitchen table.

Josh opened the kitchen door and stood, not looking at us. The ice storm had stopped. Trey walked out into damp gloom. I stopped in front of Josh. "Why was Louise out here?"

His face clouded over. "I'm not going to tell you that."

Josh had too many secrets. Maybe it was time I quit giving him the benefit of my doubt.

25

I was still wondering about Josh and Louise when we climbed back into Trey's car and headed toward town. What was going on?

We headed down the country road to the highway, but before turning, Trey picked up his phone and eased to the side of the road. "I've got to check in with my sergeant."

While he launched into a discussion, I pulled out my phone and punched speed dial. Louise didn't hesitate when she picked it up. "This better not be an excuse for not going to Mose and Zeke's game."

Dang. I'd forgotten. "Sorry. I've got to work."

Her sigh of irritation was designed to germinate guilt. "Fine. But you'll have to apologize to them because I'm not going to."

Mose and Zeke didn't care whether I showed up or not. "Okay." I hesitated, not sure how to corral her. "I'm going to ask you something I normally wouldn't, but I need you to give me an answer because . . ." Should I tell her why? I had to. "Because it's looking like Josh Stevens is a strong suspect in Chad Mills's murder, and I . . ."

I didn't finish because her gasp was so loud. "Murder? I thought it was an accident. Oh my God."

I gave her a moment to process what I'd been living with, and eventually she circled back to me. "Josh? They think. *You* think he did it?"

"I don't know. But it isn't looking great for him. I know something went on between you two. I need you to tell me what it is." After the ice pellets earlier, the late afternoon sun cast some welcome warmth through the windshield.

"Oh." There was silence long enough for me to hear Trey tell his sergeant that Josh was his prime suspect. "Nothing. I don't know what you're talking about."

I pinched the bridge of my nose and forced a calm tone. "Dad knows but he won't talk about it. Josh's keeping his mouth shut."

"Because there's nothing to tell."

"But Enoch Stevens said you were out to their ranch. Why? Is there reason for me to think Josh might have killed Chad?"

She squeaked. A sound I'd never heard from her. I waited. Trey answered questions about lack of evidence and trying to figure out our next move.

"Okay." Louise sounded like a ten-year-old. "But you have to swear never to say anything to anyone. Anyone. Never."

I was so curious I'd have promised anything. "I won't."

All my brothers and sisters know if I say I won't tell, I won't. Louise hesitated then started in with a weak voice. I plugged a finger in my ear to hear her better.

"This was last fall. Things were not going well. Remember the furnace went out and Ruthie wanted to go to that horse clinic in Fort Collins that cost a fortune? Mose and Zeke had been suspended for that whole pantsing incident. The gas station told Norm they might have to let him go. And Doc Kennedy found a lump in my breast."

This was all news to me. Poor Louise. "I'm so sorry. I didn't know."

She sniffed. "No one knew. Honestly, you were in the middle of your divorce, and Diane had that merger. Mom, of course, she was down in her basement creating. Who was I going to tell?"

"You can always come to me. You know that."

Tears twined in her words. "You don't know how much I wish I would have."

I forgot all about Josh now, just wanting to lend my obnoxious, overly involved older sister some support. "What happened?"

She snuffled again. "I don't know. I suppose in the old days they'd have called it a nervous breakdown. What I did was run away. I drove to Broken Butte and ended up at Froggie's Lounge."

"Oh no." If she didn't sound so awful I might have cracked up. Froggie's was the sleaziest dive in Broken Butte. I assumed the Long Branch was the closest Louise ever got to a bar.

Her tears continued. "I don't know what happened. I really don't. But I've pieced together that I was about to go home with several men when Josh Stevens showed up. He got me out of there and took me to his house. I slept on his couch until about three in the morning. Then he took me home. He and Dad went back to Broken Butte for my car."

"How are you now?"

Her voice turned sour. "Now? After finding out I'm as emotionally unstable as our mother? Coming to the realization I'm an unfit parent?"

This sounded more like the Louise I knew. "You had a bad spell. It doesn't mean you're a flake."

Tears gone. "It means I have flake potential. I've prayed on it, and Norm and I have discussed it. With the good Lord's help, I'll never get to that dark place again."

"I don't think it's about never going dark, I think it's about learning to spot the signs and getting help before it's black."

"You have an undergrad psychology degree. I've had over three decades of a personal relationship with Jesus. I think I can handle my own life."

I grinned. Of course. She was an expert, and that's why she always wanted to run my life. "Thanks for telling me."

"You swore you'd never tell anyone else," she reminded me in her big-sister tone.

"I won't. You've given me some good background on Josh's character."

I hung up to Trey's scrutiny. "Do you have anything to tell me about Josh Stevens?"

I chose my words as he put the car in gear and pulled onto the highway. "His pattern is to help people."

Trey gave me a skeptical frown.

"He helped me out at the Long Branch the night Ted and Roxy were there."

"How?"

I didn't need to tell Trey all about that. "He's done other stuff."

"What?"

"Not going to tell you." Good thing I had Bill Hardy's offer to fall back on, because I might be tanking my career as sheriff on my gut feeling about Josh's character. "I believe he was at Meredith's the night of Chad's murder doing exactly what he said. Helping her out."

"So naive."

Instead of throwing a punch to his jaw, I stared out the window at the winter prairie. We pulled behind the courthouse, and ten minutes later my phone rang again.

"Where the hell are you?" May Keller's raspy yell came through so loudly Trey raised his eyebrows.

Yikes. "I'm sorry. I forgot. I'm not going to make it."

"Why the hell not? I'm not coming to town again for God knows how long. Get your butt out here."

Trey put the car in reverse and backed out. "Where are we going?"

I shook my head. "Honestly, May. I'm in the middle—"

"Bullshit. I heard some man ask you where to. Get your clothes on and get out here. You can finish up your fun later." She hung up before I could argue.

Trey slapped his leg, laughing. "What's that about?"

"Never mind. Go back to the courthouse."

He gave me an insistent look.

"It's May Keller, and she wants me to buy her house."

"Which way?" he asked. I pointed and he turned onto the highway. "We can talk about this case while we're driving."

But we didn't. Both of us retreated into our own thoughts.

The dirt road was frozen so no pings and pocks hit the underside of the car. The sky remained that milky color of unadulterated cold. I directed Trey to a two-track dirt road on the east side of Stryker Lake.

The lake couldn't be more than twenty feet deep dead center. It was barely long enough for a motorboat to get a head of steam to jerk a skier out of the water before swinging a tight turn and racing to the other end. Of course skiing was prohibited at Stryker Lake. Depending on who lived in May Keller's house, the restriction mattered or not. When the fun-loving first-year teacher who wanted to be everyone's best friend lived there, we skied all summer long. My freshman year in high school, Bernard Smith, the bank president, separated from his wife and moved out there. The first time we tried skiing, my sister Diane ended up getting escorted home in the back of the sheriff's car.

Skiing or no skiing, Stryker Lake was the perennial party spot for teens. I couldn't help my grin at the scramble they'd have to find a new place. That is, if I stayed sheriff and if I bought the house. Neither of which seemed likely.

The isolation at Bill Hardy's ranch teased me. No curtains, no neighbors, mornings so quiet you could hear the beating of robins' wings in flight. No emergency phone calls or citizens bugging me for gossip in the name of information. Heaven.

We rounded the east side, still following the least possible excuse for a road, and stopped in front of an old bent wire fence. The house sat at the end of a narrow cement walk. Three wide concrete steps led to a twelve-by-six front porch. The dull pink stucco house hunched in the cold. For some reason the outside walls of the porch were covered in aluminum siding, the mismatched pink paint scratched and gouged, showing the silver aluminum underneath.

May's old turquoise Chevy S-10 pickup was parked outside the fence. Overgrown brown grass covered the yard, making the walk look like a yellow cake layer in between plops of frosting.

Trey shut the engine off and surveyed the house. "Not bad."

The fence needed repair, if not completely replaced. "It's quite a ways from town."

Trey gave me a questioning look. "Really? It's closer to the courthouse than my house is to the station."

I didn't want to debate this with him. I stepped out. Quiet. Deep still silence. The view of the lake peeked through four old cottonwoods at the southern edge of the yard. "Those trees need to be trimmed, or even taken down before they fall."

Trey didn't offer an opinion. Maybe he was learning.

The BNSF whistle sliced through the frigid air. "That's sure loud."

If Trey was aware, he showed wisdom in not pointing out that my parents' house sat forty yards from the tracks in town.

To the left of the house, dead tomato plants and withered pole beans filled a fenced garden along with piles of frozen black squash vines and decomposing pumpkins. That would take a lot of work to clean up.

We clumped up the steps. Dirt, leaves, spiderwebs, and even a crumpled Cheez-It bag littered the front porch. Yuck. It felt neglected and unloved.

A slight breeze ruffled my hair and bit at my ears. My hands immediately tingled. Forget about a three-dog night, you could have a whole sled team and they'd still freeze. I gave consideration to pulling out my cap, but decided against it.

Colorless spongy paint chipped the ancient front door, and chunks of caulking fell from the panes of glass. No screen. That had to be a problem in the summer this close to the lake. No drapes to mask the view inside. I turned the old brass knob and shoved the sticking door. "May?"

Her croak came from the back of the small house, from what must be the kitchen. "It's not in too bad shape."

With a big window to the front porch and three windows along the south wall, the front room was well lit despite the heavy afternoon sky. A scuffed wood floor ran through to the kitchen, and two doors opened to the left. Those would be the bedrooms.

Trey closed the door behind us and surveyed the room, even through to the kitchen sink and the window above it. "This is great. Look at all the natural light. And that archway." He pointed to a curved room divider midway through the front room.

I dismissed it. "They probably meant this to be a living room and dining room. But separating them makes both spaces too small to be much good."

He considered it. "Not really. A table with leaves for when you have company would work here." He eased past me under the arch. "That leaves room for a loveseat and a chair or two."

Great. The artist in him was shining through. I stepped into the front bedroom. Two windows kept the bright sunlight theme alive.

Trey poked his head in behind me. He shoved into the room, his eyes lighting up. "This would be great for a studio or office." He was way too excited.

"It needs new paint and the floor is gouged." I exited, my boots thudding on the worn wood floor.

He followed me into the second bedroom.

"I don't think I could get a queen-size bed in here, let alone a dresser." I moved into the room toward a door.

Trey stood in the center of the room. "The bed is no problem. You could put a chest of drawers in the other bedroom or even in the dining room."

What a problem solver. I peered around the door to see a pocket-sized bathroom. Guess a hundred years ago there wasn't much need for expansive counters and Jacuzzi tubs. The antique pedestal sink didn't allow much storage space, either. I backed out, right into Trey's rock-hard chest.

He looked over my head into the bathroom. "This could use some work. There's enough room here for a bank of shelves. That sink is great, though."

I spared a look of irritation for him and continued into the kitchen, where May waited.

At least she hadn't lit up a smoke. "The appliances all work. I bought a new fridge and gas stove before Bernard Smith moved out, so they're practically new. And last year I put in a dishwasher. Don't know why. It takes nothing to wash up dishes, and then they're done. But Bernard rode me until I gave in just to shut him up. So there you go."

Appliances. Dear God, a black refrigerator with a separate freezer compartment, not one snugged inside the fridge that frosted over so it held only one ice cube tray.

I nearly fainted to see a water and ice dispenser in the door. With, help me Lord, the option for crushed or cubed. I put a hand on the appliance to make sure it wasn't a mirage.

Trey bounded in. "This has some real potential." His eyes swept the room, noting another window along the west and the one over the sink. "Not much counter space, but you could put a butcher block here, you know, the kind with a breakfast bar."

May nodded. "The whole place could be fixed up real cute. Just right for a single gal. Private." She winked at me and her gaze popped to Trey. "You could entertain and no one would be the wiser."

Trey turned crimson by degrees until he glowed. He pointed to the door. "There's a basement?"

May gurgle/coughed. " 'Course. Washer and dryer down there, lots of storage space." She opened the door to show a small back porch with a few hooks and shelves. "Garden out here."

Trey leaned out to look out to the side yard, but I'd already seen the frozen plants.

"I'd go outside and show you the garage, but the cold is hard on my lungs. Doc says I'm allergic to oxygen." She coughed a little to emphasize her condition.

Trey chuckled, as if he thought she joked.

She shot him a questioning look. She probably wondered what kind of jerk laughed about an old lady's allergy. She turned back to me. "So when can you move in?"

I hedged. I could wrestle a two-hundred-pound calf, dig twenty post holes before breakfast, wrangle the last donut at a Fox family breakfast, but May had me cornered. "I don't know."

My phone vibrated, and instead of ignoring it, I pulled it out with an apology to May and a blessing for whoever interrupted me at the perfect time.

Vicki Snyder's harsh voice attacked. "What have you got for me now?"

I'd rejoiced too soon. "Sorry, Vicki, I've—" May wrenched the phone from my ear. "She's busy. You get your gossip someplace else, you old biddy."

May handed the phone back, and I punched it off, hoping Vicki thought it had been May hanging up.

Trey shifted the conversation. "You've lived in Grand County a long time, haven't you?"

This might be fun to watch.

May narrowed her eyes. "What kind of cock-and-bull question is that? My granddad was the first to own land out here. I've been here the longest of anybody."

"Right." Trey looked properly respectful. "So you know Josh Stevens."

She put her hands on her hips, plainly annoyed with this outsider's queries. "Goddamned right I know Joshua and his dad and mom. Black Socks, they were. Not Joshua."

I hurried to explain to Trey. "It's sort of like Amish. Not as strict. They have electricity and tractors. But they're pretty rigid when it comes to religion."

His nod seemed impatient. "I know."

"Joshua's not a bad sort. But he's no Black Socks, if you know what I mean." She winked again. With all the wrinkles around her eyes, it might have been a tic.

Trey waited, and when I didn't answer, he did. "No, I don't know what you mean."

May drew in a gurgling breath and gave him a disgusted look. "He's been playing footsie with someone else's wife, that's what I mean."

We both leaned in. "Who?"

She burst out laughing and ended with a cough I thought might be her last. "You both are like two old hens. But you might find this interesting, being as you're looking for Chad Mills's killer."

"What makes you think Chad was murdered?" Trey asked.

Again, she gave him a look like he was brainless. "I ain't a dummy."

"What do you want to tell us?" I asked May.

The look on her face brought cats and canaries to mind. "Joshua Stevens is having an affair with Meredith Mills."

I didn't want to analyze why hearing May say that felt like a slap. "What makes you think they were having an affair?" I ought to at least get her source.

She reached up to the breast pocket of her pearl button cowboy shirt and fingered the pack of cigarettes there. "You got your daddy's 'show me' attitude. But I seen it. I share a fence with Stevenses. You know, my Frye pasture butts up agin' theirs."

I hadn't known that and gave it some thought. May's headquarters was north of Hodgekiss. The Stevenses' place was north on County Road 67. It would make sense they shared fences.

She pulled the cigarette pack from her pocket. "That last blizzard we had broke posts and the wires all to bits. I stopped by to see if they'd go half to get Tuff Hendricks to fix it. I'm too damned old to be out there fixing fence, and Joshua don't have the time."

Trey's impatience beat in his eyes. If he was going to spend much time up here, he'd be ahead to learn to let folks talk.

"I pulled into the yard and saw that sparkly rig Meredith Mills drives. You know that brand new foreign-made one?"

I did know the Volvo she talked about.

May raised her eyebrows and gave me that sly grin. "She and Josh come hurtling out of the barn like as if I caught 'em smoking." She caressed her cigarette pack.

Trey shot me a look that shouted, *I told you!*

"Okay." I glanced around the kitchen. "We'd better get back to town."

May nearly galloped ahead of me. "I'm good with you renting it for a few months until you decide to buy it."

I gave one last look at the fridge. My better judgment couldn't be swayed by fancy appliances. "It's a great place. You shouldn't have any trouble renting it."

May spun around and stared me down. "That don't sound like a yes."

Trey seemed surprised, but he didn't comment.

I shoved my hands into my coat pocket. "It's too far out of town." My phone vibrated against my fingers, startling me. I pulled it out.

Diane. I didn't really want to talk to my sister, but she seemed the better alternative. I held up a finger to May. "I've got to take this."

She glowered at me. But the urge for her smoke was stronger than her fight with me, and she waved her arm in disgusted dismissal and rushed out.

Trey said, "I'll wait in the car."

I punched the phone on.

"So, how's the house?" A low sound of static told me she was probably on her Bluetooth in Denver traffic.

"Hi, Diane. No, I'm not busy. The weather is cold here, how about there?"

She exhaled, something she probably didn't do enough of. "Look, I'm taking Kimmy to dance and Karl to karate. I don't have time for chitchat."

I walked through the empty room to stare out the living room window at the frozen lake. "Then thank you for sharing your spare time with me."

"Can the sarcasm. I call because I love you. So how's the house?"

I opened my mouth but closed it when I heard her speaking again. "Two naked burritos, one with chicken, one vegetarian, both gluten free."

I waited while a tinny voice responded something. The ice on Stryker Lake stretched smooth, just right for skating.

"Right," Diane said.

Were my ice skates in a box of my things from Frog Creek, or were they at Mom and Dad's?

"Two waters and one extra-large Diet Coke."

Her voice came back strong. "Okay, house."

"It's really small."

"You're only one person."

"It's rundown."

"You need a project to occupy yourself."

"I don't think it's right for me."

She stopped the rapid fire and hardened her voice. "Because it's not Frog Creek? Because Ted doesn't live there?"

My dander rose. "Ted has nothing to do with this. I've moved on."

Her laugh was like a bullet in my ear. "Right."

"So what if I'm not totally over Ted? He was my whole world for eight years. It takes time to get over a divorce."

The rattle of a faraway voice and Diane saying a brisk "Thanks." Then, "Don't spill that in the car. Eat fast."

To me: "That is bullshit. He wasn't your whole world. You had Frog Creek and Carly. Ted was just one part. Frankly, the weakest part."

"Okay, maybe. But I lost them all."

"I suppose you've gone into mourning now that Roxy and Sarah are pregnant and you're not."

Huh? Shock faded to understanding. No wonder Sarah looked so washed out and had been so pissy. Sure, it hurt, since Sarah and I had both been trying to get pregnant. But how could I not feel joy for Sarah and Robert and excitement to be an aunt again? I didn't try to explain to Diane. "Oh."

She paused. "You didn't know. Sorry." And we were back on today's agenda. "So, listen, get the house."

"I'm fine at Mom and Dad's."

"You're not fine."

"Okay, maybe not. But I don't want to commit to a house now."

"Why?"

"Because I may not stay in Hodgekiss long. I don't want to be sheriff forever, and maybe something else will come along." Like welcome isolation on Bill Hardy's place.

"For fuck's sake." A couple of little voices chimed about the fine jar. Diane spoke away from the phone. "I could fund your college education if I kept up with the fine jar. Eat your burritos and let me talk to Aunt Kate." To me: "You're not holding out for some kind of ranch job, are you?"

Bill Hardy. All I had to do is say yes. "Oh, hey, look at that! I've got to go." I hung up. Enough of that.

Dust from May's turquoise pickup swirled in the icy wind. I shut the front door of the house and hurried to Trey's car.

"What's next on the Hodgekiss hit parade?" Trey asked.

"So far, we don't have a lot to go on. Clete says everyone loved Chad. Terminator and Lawn Dart don't agree. Clete says Chad and Josh were best buddies, again, not everyone signs on with that."

Trey nodded. "The railroad guys say Meredith and Chad were crazy in love. May says Josh and Meredith were having an affair."

I waved off the last bit. "May Keller has oxygen deprivation, and you can only trust half of what she says. It's a shame we don't know which half."

"Josh Stevens did it." Not a shred of doubt colored his words. "We need proof."

He retreated down the two-track and out on the highway to Hodgekiss. He glanced at me. "What?"

"I don't think so."

Darkness gathered in Trey's face. "You have a thing for him?"

Was this jealousy coming from Trey? "No. It goes to character and what a person would and wouldn't do."

"You said you don't know Josh."

Might as well lay it out and let Trey decide whether he'd trust me on instinct. "It's the look in his eye more than anything. Some people will kick a dog or tease a child for fun. Not Josh. He has secrets, I can almost guarantee that. But murder? No. There has to be someone else."

The sour set of Trey's mouth showed me what he thought of instinct.

26

"We need to talk to my aunt Twyla."

Trey pulled in front of the Long Branch and shut the engine off. He reached for the key but didn't take it out. "I doubt it will do any good. I already questioned her."

I grabbed the keys from the ignition. "You questioned her, fine. Now I'll talk to her."

He rolled his eyes and took the keys I dangled in front of him. "Good point."

I stepped out of his car, and a biting gust clobbered me, sucking at my breath. Well now, that was a fine reminder of how glad I was to have the sheriff job instead of feeding hay on this frozen afternoon.

Trey came around the front of his cruiser, and we waited for a pickup to pass on the highway, then we hurried into the Long Branch. I pushed open the glass door leading to the restaurant side, windows lining the highway side let in the gathering gloom. Even the sky looked like ice. Except for the smell of grease so strong it practically had a real body, no one occupied the restaurant side.

Trey poked his head into the bar side and drew it out. "She's in here."

I backed out of the restaurant and into the dim bar. Twyla sucked an unlit cigarette and wiped down bottles on the shelf under the mirror. She glanced over her shoulder at me and Trey. "Hey there, Katie." She did a double take and slapped the bar. "Now, sister, that face rearranging ain't looking a whole lot better."

I landed on my barstool, making my back complain with the jarring. "Did you think it would heal up already?"

Twyla pulled the soggy cig from her mouth and set it next to the cash register. She picked up a rocks glass with a splash of whiskey. "Gonna leave a Frankenstein scar."

It's great when your family makes you feel pretty.

Trey settled himself on the barstool next to me. "Can we ask you a few questions?"

Twyla lifted her glass toward him and gave me an *is he for real?* look. She knocked back the whiskey.

I leaned on the bar. "Are Josh Stevens and Meredith Mills having an affair?"

Trey kept from choking but his eyes widened.

Twyla cackled. "That's one I hadn't heard. I can't give credence to it, though."

She finger-combed her hair and caught it into a ponytail. She lifted it and let it fall. "I can tell you Chad and Meredith were hitting a rough patch."

Trey pulled his head back and clamped his mouth shut.

I stood and draped myself over the bar, grabbed a glass and the soda spray nozzle. A *swhooze* filled the glass with Diet Coke. I offered it to Trey. He declined. "Why do you say that?"

"Bits and pieces of this and that." Twyla bent over to pull a Jack Daniel's bottle from the bar well.

"Unbelievable." Trey let the word slip under his breath.

I winked at him while Twyla poured another generous two fingers of bourbon. "Did they have a fight in here or something?"

Twyla swirled the whiskey. "Not so much. It's sort of the body language. The way they looked at each other lately."

I sipped my Diet Coke and waited. Beside me, Trey's leg jiggled with impatience. No wonder he hadn't gotten much out of Twyla earlier.

Twyla walked to the end of the bar and pulled a pencil and order pad from a mess of papers and pens beside the cash register.

I placed a hand on Trey's leg to stop his escaping impatience. He sucked in a shocked breath, and I turned eight shades of crimson in the nanosecond it took for me to withdraw my hand.

Twyla looked up to the bottles on the shelf and muttered to herself, jotted a few words and dropped the pad back in the piles and thrust the pencil behind her ear. She sauntered back to us, took a sip of whiskey and set her glass down. She pointed at me. "You wait. It'll sneak up on you. All the sudden, you can't remember for shit. Distributor comes tomorrow, and I got to make my order."

Trey straightened and took a breath, ready to direct Twyla back to our question, but I shot him a silencing glance.

Twyla picked up her unlit cigarette and held it between her first two fingers. "Those two, they used to be all about each other. You know, Chad went to college and found her, and we all could of told him she didn't belong out here."

One, two, three. Bingo.

"I've seen it happen before when a man brings in a girl from some big city and they never quite fit in. Like they're better than the rest of us."

I gave Trey an aside so Twyla would know I hadn't missed her point. "My mother was raised in Chicago."

Just the mention of my mother made his eyes light up. He kept his mouth shut and nodded.

Twyla swirled her drink. "They don't talk, just sit at the table together and eat their food. Which is not that big of a deal, that seven-year-itch thing. And I think they've been married about that long. Happens more than you'd think."

If I heard that phrase one more time, I might lose the thin grip that held my temper.

She stopped and eyed me. "You and Ted?"

I hated being a cliché. "Eight years."

Twyla sipped her whiskey. "He probably started in with Roxy about the seven mark."

Thanks, Aunt Twyla.

She must have read my reluctance to wander down that path. "So, they stop having dinner and drinks, like an evening out." She pointed the unlit cig at Trey. "This ain't the big city here. Date nights might mean a steak and drinks at the Long Branch because we don't have a Red Lobster or Olive Garden or anything fancy like that." Having defended her establishment, she talked to me again. "They got so they'd just drop in to eat, like on the way home from town or something. Then, it's just Chad coming in. I figure Miss Meredith got enough of country living and couldn't dig Chad's roots out of here."

Trey cleared his throat. "So you think Meredith and Chad weren't getting along?"

Twyla didn't hide her contempt for Trey and shifted back to me. "Isn't that what I just said?"

I buried my grin in my glass, took a sip, and swallowed. I jumped up from the stool. "Thanks for the 411."

Twyla laughed. "Look at you using cop talk and all."

I didn't correct her. "I'd ask Dad about this. You know he's got the scoop on everyone at the railroad."

Twyla rolled her eyes and nodded. "But he won't cough up a single word. He's been like that all his life. The secrets that man knows."

Some folks, like my nosy sister Louise, would love nothing better than to have all those secrets scroll out of Dad's head like documents from a fax machine. I'd rather not know too much about my neighbors and family. Although, now that I was smack in the middle of a murder investigation, selected knowledge, such as whether anyone hated Chad enough to rig up a railroad tie to smash in his head, would be good to know.

Twyla stepped back and turned to the bottles again. I barely heard her. "I'll bet he's got something on every one of you kids. And I'll bet you're all glad he keeps his mouth shut."

A tangled blob of camo filled the vestibule, and the glass bar door swung open, spilling the mess inside. Bringing along a rush of winter cold.

"Sad excuse for skin," Earl Johnson growled at his brother.

Newt's top lip curled back like a little dog on the fight. "It wasn't me what lost that block and tackle getup."

They made inroads toward the bar and stopped midway. Earl pulled a plastic chair out from a four-top and Newt glared, backed two paces and took a two-person table next to a window. He pointed at Earl and raised his voice across the vacant space. "There's you and me, numb nuts. I didn't lose it. That leaves you."

It started small, a tickle in the nose hairs, but quickly grew to an all-out assault on the sinuses. From Trey's shocked expression and the hand he pulled up to his face, I guess it hit him first.

"Holy mother!" Twyla shouted. "What the hell have you been doing?"

Surprised, Earl and Newt stared at her.

She made a shooing motion. "Out. Both of you."

Neither of them moved or even seemed to understand her. They looked at each other and shrugged in unison. Earl questioned Twyla from the far table. "Are you talking to us?"

Trey and I had backed toward the door, desperate to make a

quick getaway. Twyla had her hand under her nose. "You smell like crap deep fried in rancid guts."

Newt raised his arm and sniffed his camo. "Huh?"

Earl hunched his shoulders. "Been skinning 'yotes and muskrats. We're supposed to meet Cam Shifford this afternoon. He's taking the hides to Broken Butte."

That's exactly what they smelled like. Two aging bachelors who hadn't showered since Aerosmith's last hit, rolled in month-old muskrat carcasses. All of a sudden, the dolmades in my stomach considered jumping ship.

Newt gave Twyla the innocent expression of a kindergarten boy who'd accidentally wet his pants. "We just wanted a sandwich before Shifford gets here."

Earl dropped his chin in the most pathetic face I'd seen outside of Facebook baby animal pictures. "We're terrible hungry."

How could anyone have that smell in their nose and feel hungry?

Twyla shooed them. "Get. You wait outside and I'll bring you some burgers."

They didn't move. Then Earl said, "It's fifteen degrees outside."

Newt added, "Wind chill of maybe a hunnert below."

"Christ," Twyla said. She hurried behind the bar toward the kitchen. "Bud, get two burgers and fries going this very second."

Newt turned to me and grinned. "That Twyla is sweet on Earl. She always does him favors."

Self-satisfaction at being such a ladies' man glowed in Earl's smug expression. With effort, I resisted jumping his bones. "You boys had some boxes in your back seat when I pulled you over yesterday."

Newt got a panicky look to his eyes. "We found them boxes."

Earl frowned at Newt. "They was given to us."

A gas mask would come in handy about now. "Who gave them to you?"

Newt hoisted an ankle to rest on his knee, and I was surprised I didn't hear bones scraping on each other. "Gave in the sense that we cleaned out junk."

Earl banged his fist on his table, his face a gathering storm. "We had them boxes a long time."

Newt seemed oblivious to Earl's discomfort. In fact, by the way he sat up straighter and his smile grew, I thought he might be flirting with me. "That was that day you saw we done all that work."

Earl shoved his chair back and stood. "Newt's got diarrhea of the mouth here. I suppose you all need to get going."

Newt stood and edged in front of Earl, thrusting out his chest and giving me some kind of spastic fling of his chin that he possibly meant to look dashing. "You'd be surprised at what we find in other folks' junk."

Earl whacked Newt on the back of the head.

Newt grabbed his noggin. "Hey!"

Earl threw back his shoulders, and it seemed to make him smell even worse. "It's a secret thing between us and the ones we work for. Like a doctor or lawyer thing. We ain't got to tell you about other people's trash."

Trey put a big dose of mean dog in his attitude. "Where'd you get the boxes?"

Earl and Newt passed a look between them, and they retreated to their respective tables, faces neutral. I kept from growling at Trey. He'd just made my job way more unpleasant since now I had to take myself and my nose closer. I chose Newt and sat at his table. "You're not in any trouble."

Newt pursed his lips like a miffed old lady. "I should say not."

Mouth breathing kept me from throwing up but didn't eliminate the stench. "You boys have a real knack for salvage. If it weren't for you, perfectly good things would go to waste. I know you didn't steal those computers. But I'd be grateful if you'd tell me where you got them."

Earl scrunched up his face as if he were sending Newt telepathic signals and his thoughts got tongue tied.

Newt eyed me and tilted his head in the same prissy little-old-lady way.

I rested my elbow on the table and planted my face in my palm, partially pinching my nose. "You've been a good friend, being on my side with my divorce." I hoped it didn't matter that I'd never had a decent conversation with him. "And I helped you out by not issuing a speeding ticket yesterday."

He bounced his crossed leg and flicked his head back and forth like an agitated robin. "I ain't never."

"Come on, Newt. I need you to help me out again."

His glance flicked to Earl, and he leaned toward me.

Earl eyed Trey and then me. "I swear to God, Newt. You keep your mouth shut."

Newt swung his chair so his back was to Earl. "I'm talking with my friend. You just mind your own business."

I tried to give Newt a best-friend grin.

Newt leaned close and I fought my gag reflex. "You know that the Millses have that Dumpster? Out behind their pole barn? County only picks it up every four weeks. Them Millses, they got lots of money, and they get rid of good stuff. We got milk that's barely past the date, and one time we got a whole bunch of cheese we only had to cut the outside off of. Every now and then, they throw away some primo stuff. Got a bunch of telephones a while back."

I whispered to make him feel we had a special bond. "And that's where you got the computers?"

He sat back, a cagey smile on his crusty face. Louder than necessary, he said, "I'm not telling."

"You better not, you igit." Earl spat a triumphant sneer Trey's way.

I pushed back and stood, trying to be discreet in turning my head for a breath. "You're too tricky for me, Newt. Still friends?"

Newt made sure Earl was watching and answered with a swagger, like a high school football star might talk to a star-struck freshman. "I guess."

Twyla rushed out of the kitchen with a brown bag of food, grease stain already spreading. She shoved it at Earl. "Get the hell out of here."

Computers in Meredith's trash. A rock hit the floor of my stomach.

27

I joined Trey at the bar. He'd taken my favorite barstool, and I tried not to notice. Behind me, the door opened, and a group of cowboys entered. They found a table.

"What did the handsome Newt Johnson have to say?" Trey asked.

I walked around the back of the bar and refilled my Diet Coke to delay having to cough up the information. "They found the computers in the Dumpster at the Millses' house."

He mulled that over. "It's got to be Meredith and Josh."

I plopped back on the barstool that wasn't mine. "Don't you think it's too easy? Like someone is trying to set Josh up."

His jaw twitched. "That's stuff for TV drama. The evidence points to Josh because he did it."

More people came in and a few of the tables filled up. Trey glanced in the mirror at the new arrivals, always keeping track of his surroundings. "I need to get back to Ogallala soon. We'll go out to Meredith's and Josh's tomorrow first thing."

I sipped my soda, inhaling the carbonation to try to rid my nostrils of the Johnson brothers. “I’ll check it out now.”

He frowned. “Wait for me. We’ll go together.”

I set my glass down, feeling my spine stiffen. “It will be better if we don’t put it off.”

He pulled out his phone. “Then let me cancel my plans.”

I held my palm up. “I can do it without you holding my hand.”

He pointed at my stitches. “Like when you checked out the railroad car?”

I wrapped my hand around my sweating soda glass and looked directly into Trey’s angry eyes. “I don’t want to hear this.”

He fired back at me. “I get it. But you’re a woman, and the reality is that you aren’t as big or tough as most men.”

Twyla cackled. She was halfway down the bar, and I didn’t know she’d been listening. She might have thought Trey’s comment was funny, but it didn’t tickle me. At all.

He shifted toward the mirror above the bar, and my eyes caught his, mine still shooting ice crystals.

“Look, I want you to be safe.” His voice was so soft I strained to hear.

“Do you try to protect all the sheriffs or only the girls?” I struggled to keep my temper from drowning me.

His index finger rubbed at some ancient carved initials on the mahogany bar. “I’m sorry. That was out of line.”

“If we’re going to work together, you have to trust me.”

My phone vibrated and I pulled it out. Glad to see Shorty Cally getting back to me, I answered and asked him about Josh working for him the day before. “He’s got a banged-up hand,” I said. “How did that happen?”

Trey’s eyes bored into mine.

Shorty paused. “Injured hand? I don’t know. I had to leave before they finished up so I guess it might have happened then. But nobody said anything to me about it."

After a brief exchange about the cold weather and the prospects for the Hodgekiss basketball team, I signed off.

Trey vibrated with tension. "What about the hand?"

I shrugged. "Shorty didn't know about it, but he wasn't there the whole time."

Unexpected anger spewed from Trey. "You're being stupid."

And that's all I was going to listen to. I slammed my glass on the bar and stood.

He swiveled toward me. "You're in denial. You need to arrest Josh Stevens for a murder. But you won't because you've got a crush on him."

Looking in the mirror above the bar, I saw the gash on my forehead fire up like Harry Potter's lightning scar. Or if it didn't, I was certainly mad enough it should have.

"If you don't look at the facts and admit Josh is the murderer, with Meredith as accomplice, you're going to get yourself hurt." He gave a pointed look at my stitches. "Or worse."

I prayed he wasn't right. In my calmest voice I said, "Go to hell."

I spun around as the outside door opened and Josh Stevens walked in.

Trey stiffened. He jumped off his barstool and strode over to Josh, a mask of thinly controlled fury on his face. "You injured your hand working cattle, huh?"

Josh pulled his head back in surprise. "Thought we'd already been over that."

Quick as a rattlesnake strike, Trey latched onto Josh's arm and twisted it behind Josh's back. He reached for his handcuffs so fast the motion seemed to blur. He shoved Josh against the doorjamb.

In an instant, the chatter of the happy hour bar dropped to

silence. The two tables of patrons jumped up and backed away, eyes wide. They acted like a herd of cattle when a coyote trots into the corral. Keeping a distance but not wanting to miss the action.

I threw myself across the room. "Hey! What . . . ?"

Trey leaned against Josh, whose face smashed into the metal door frame. "Thought you got away with it, huh?"

Josh didn't struggle. "What the hell is wrong with you?"

I tried to tug Trey away from Josh. "Wait a minute."

Trey shrugged me off. "Tell her, Josh. You were at the railroad car last night. It was you, wasn't it?"

Josh clenched his jaw and glared at Trey. "Yes. That was me."

I lost my breath for a second. I'd been wrong. Again. Josh had knocked me from the railroad car onto the frozen ground, but this betrayal hurt way worse.

I'd felt this before, when I'd been stupid enough to trust another man who'd let me down. I pulled my hand off Trey.

Josh tried to twist his head to me. "I was trying to figure it out!"

I heard myself speak, but my mind didn't seem to be participating. "Figure what out?"

"Who is framing me. Who threw the computers in Meredith's trash."

Trey growled. "Keep up the lies, cowboy."

I couldn't get my breath. Could only watch as Trey jerked Josh from the door frame.

God help me, he sounded sincere when he said, "I didn't mean to hurt you. I'm sorry."

Trey wrenched Josh backward. "You mean you're sorry you got caught. You probably don't know anything about searching a wheel report or checking the BNSF lineups. We know you spent three and a half years in college studying mechanical engineering, but I'll bet you don't know the first thing about rigging a railroad tie to the underside of a bridge, either, do you?"

Josh didn't struggle against Trey. "I'm telling you, someone is planting . . ."

With a fist full of Josh's collar and a grip on Josh's handcuffed hands, Trey rattled him twice, a growl slipping from his clenched teeth.

Unlike Trey's rage that boiled over, making his face bloom with bright splotches on his cheeks and flashing eyes, Josh smoldered. His dark eyes hooded when his eyebrows drew together, as if fighting to keep his emotions cool. The only sure sign of anger was his jaw clamped so tight it seemed more like granite than flesh and bone.

Trey jerked him, as if resisting the urge to shake him again. "Why did you kill him? Did he find out about your stealing? Or was it to have his wife to yourself? Huh?"

Josh turned his lowered face toward me, his gaze pulling me in, as if no other person mattered. I felt my skin being peeled away so he could stare at my thoughts.

Trey pushed Josh toward the door. "Got nothing to say? Of course you don't, you scumbag."

Josh couldn't have been the one to shove me from the rail car. He didn't kill Chad. I didn't even buy into him having an affair with Meredith.

But I couldn't hide from the truth.

Trusting my instincts had been foolish. I needed to lump all the clues together: the smashed hand, the computers found in Meredith's Dumpster, engineering degree, history with Meredith. Still, I fought against it.

I glanced at Twyla.

She stood behind the bar with a black look trained on Trey. She shifted her attention to me. "What's wrong with that boy?"

Did she mean Trey or Josh? I couldn't answer either way.

The folks in the bar stood like tin soldiers with shock pasted on their faces. This scene would be all over the county before Twyla could serve another round.

Trey shoved Josh toward the door. "Taking you to Ogallala and booking you."

Josh allowed Trey to push him a few steps, always keeping eye contact with me. Trey removed a hand from Josh's collar and planted it on the glass to open the door, and Josh squinted at me with intensity. "Is this what you think? You believe I killed Chad?"

His words were a serrated knife shoved deep and twisted to shred my flesh. No. I didn't think so. Yes, I did. Who else but him? And Meredith?

How many times would I allow my gut to deceive me? And yet, my throat wouldn't cough up the simple yes to Josh's question.

Trey didn't wait. He threw his weight against the door, and together he and Josh tumbled outside. Like a dummy, I trailed them, stepping into the freezing night, and stood as the door bumped closed behind me. A light dusting of snow had fallen while we'd been inside.

Hand now back on Josh's collar, Trey manhandled him across the street and into the back seat of his cruiser, leaving the cuffs on.

It would be a long, uncomfortable ride for Josh.

I found myself outside the door, watching Josh tumble into the back. Trey straightened. "Goddamned piece of shit. I told you he was the one. Why didn't you let me arrest him earlier?"

Josh paid no attention to Trey. He kept watching me. Trey grabbed the car door to swing it closed, and Josh finally opened his mouth. He leaned forward. "You've got to protect Meredith."

Protect Meredith. He was going to jail, and that's all he could think of? "From what?"

Josh shook his head. "We don't know. Whoever killed Chad."

Trey forced a mean laugh. "You killed Chad, asshole."

Josh ignored Trey and pleaded with me. "I was set up. You know that. But Meredith is in danger."

Trey rolled his eyes. "Only from you, cupcake."

Trey took hold of the door, and Josh pleaded with me. "Dad's alone. Take care of him, please."

Trey growled and slammed the door. Josh flung himself back to keep from being hit.

Trey opened his door and panted from the exertion. "Get in. I can bring you back after we interrogate him."

I wrapped my arms around myself to ward off the cold. "I need to make sure Enoch is okay."

Trey opened his mouth as if ready to bellow an order.

I jumped in. "Safety of the citizens comes first, and Enoch might hurt himself if he's left alone too long. Then I'll pick up Meredith."

Trey's grip on the door frame whitened. "Wait until I get back. Meredith might be desperate, especially if she finds out we've arrested Josh."

Resisting the urge to clock Trey, I pointed to myself. "Sheriff, remember?"

With one last frown, Trey threw himself into his car and slammed the door.

28

Before I turned off County Road 67 toward Meredith's house, I shut off my headlights and navigated by the quarter moon. Meredith's yard light tossed a bright glow. I crept toward the house, nearly idling the cruiser in an effort to sneak by without her spotting my car. Like me, though, she rumbled instead of purred. It. Not she.

I worried Meredith would hear us. Meredith's Volvo was parked out front, the hatchback open.

Meredith hadn't pulled the shades, and soft light fell on the skiffs of snow outside her windows. She flitted from the kitchen to the living room with movements quick as a sparrow. If I didn't know she was a recent widow, maybe a cheating wife, and possibly a murderer—and frankly, I'm not sure which of those counted worse for me—it would all look cozy and sweet.

As soon as I rounded the curve west of her house, I turned on my lights and sped up. I didn't have a solid plan, but I hoped to convince Enoch to leave with me. After that, I'd stop at Meredith's and surprise her. I felt confident I could slip some cuffs on her and toss her into the back seat.

Earl and Newt's computer collection from her Dumpster would be enough evidence to pull her in. Add to that the incentive of Daddy's inheritance, the draw of true love, and the fact she seemed ready to quit Grand County, and I figured I had good reason to detain her.

That's where the sketchy details became even more blurry. Grand County's one holding cell was currently storage. Maybe I could secure Meredith there while I figured out what to do with Enoch. I hated to haul him all the way to Ogallala while I booked Meredith and untangled the murder.

The lights of Josh's house grew brighter as I approached.

I pulled up in front and hurried to the kitchen door, thumping on the window. I'd give Enoch twenty seconds to answer before I burst inside. Not because he might be in some kind of danger, but because I wanted to keep my ears from freezing off.

Enoch rounded the corner from the living room at a brisk, if wobbly, pace. He wore a heavy flannel coat, faded from many washings, and black rubber covers snapped tight on his cowboys boots. He reached beside the door and his hand came back holding a grease-stained buff cowboy hat that he rammed onto his head. He opened the door and shoved me back as he flipped off the kitchen light and slammed the door. "Let's go."

I stumbled and got my balance before toppling down the porch. "Where?" Were we heading down to Ogallala to stage a jail break?

He hobbled toward my car. "We can't tarry."

Tarry? I hurried after him. "Enoch? What's going on?"

He wrenched open the passenger side. "I don't suppose she's intending to hang around long. Not with the way she spun her tires getting out of here."

I slid behind the wheel, welcoming the warmth of the car. "She?"

He scowled at me. "You're the sheriff? Seems like you ought to be brighter than this."

There was a reason Enoch Stevens wasn't a popular guy.

He banged on the dash. "She. Meredith. That harlot."

I started the engine and backed out.

"You might think about using more gas, girly. We don't have much time."

I gunned it across the yard and over the AutoGate. "What happened?"

He leaned forward and stared out the windshield into the headlights like a border collie. "If you don't know anything, why were you out at the ranch?"

Not the time to tell him Josh had been arrested. "I wanted to check on you."

He frowned at that but didn't take his eyes from the road. He probably thought I needed the help. "I'm not senile. I have bad days, but I get along fine. Me and Joshua."

Right. "Tell me about Meredith."

"She was just out to my place."

"Why?"

He let out a huff of irritation. "I don't suppose the voters of Grand County realize the feeble mind they voted in."

I ground my teeth.

He continued, "I heard someone pull up and thought it might be Joshua. I figured to surprise him and see what mischief he'd been into, smell his breath for alcohol or maybe signs of perfume. Joshua has been known to find trouble."

Not for a decade or so, I'd bet.

"But when I got downstairs, I see it was that woman. She's out to the barn, got her fancy rig backed up."

We sped around a curve, and the back wheels slipped on the loose gravel.

He gripped the dash and leaned closer as if his laser eyes could stabilize us. "I seen her dragging those boxes from the barn."

I maneuvered down the gravel road as quickly as possible. "Trey searched the barn this afternoon. He didn't see any boxes."

Enoch let out a snort of derision. "Probably didn't check the cellar."

"You have a cellar in your barn?"

He snorted again. "For the end times. Joshua doesn't believe in that, and I'm too old to care about living through it so we don't keep it stocked anymore. Joshua and that woman loaded them boxes down there a couple of weeks ago. He didn't think I knew about it. But nothing goes on out there what I don't know."

"What kind of boxes?"

"They'd be about four or five feet. But not deep."

Boom. My breath caught. In the *Saunders v. BNSF* case they'd stolen flat screen TVs about that size.

Enoch tapped his fingers on his knees. "She worked on that for a spell. Had a devil of a time fighting with them. Then she loaded herself up and drove off."

"Did she know you were watching?"

His lip turned up in a sneer. "I'm not quite as dim as you. Of course she didn't know. I waited until she was gone."

"So you could chase her?" This didn't make sense.

His features became brittle and sharp. "She's on the run and thieving what belongs to Joshua. If you don't want to stop her, then let me out. I'll go myself."

"You'll stay in the car." I gave him that tone Louise often used with me.

It was as effective for me as it usually was for Louise. "The heck you say." That would be as close to cursing as Enoch got.

"I can't predict how Meredith will react. You stay put." I parked on the road with the house in sight so I could sneak up on Meredith.

Enoch grabbed for the latch. "You're all women's lib, but that's foolishness. If you would understand God's natural law and be wives and mothers, we wouldn't be in this mess to begin with."

Great. I needed another macho man like I needed a frozen daiquiri in a snowstorm. I checked to make sure the Smith and Wesson nested in my holster, as if I hadn't felt it there every moment. "Listen, Enoch—"

"Mr. Stevens."

Okay. "I'm an elected and trained officer of the law. I'll take care of this and you will," I leaned toward him and cut each word with a blade, "Stay. In. The. Car."

His bony, long-fingered hands trembled on the door latch. He might have an iron will, but his aging body had limits. "This is what happens when youngsters aren't raised with the rod of Christ."

Yeah? And this is what happens when boys are taught their divine right is to rule the roost. I debated cuffing him to the steering wheel. Instead, I quit the fight. If he wanted to totter after me on this frigid night, I didn't have time for the skirmish.

I bolted from the car, slipped through the two top wires of the barbed wire fence and trotted toward Meredith's house. The windows on the south side showed an empty house until Meredith pitched down the stairs carrying a box. She dropped it on the floor next to the door. I hurried to the front and up the porch steps. Without hesitating, I banged on the door.

"Sheriff. Open up." It's what every American had seen during prime time their whole lives, except maybe Enoch, who didn't own a TV.

Through the living room window I watched Meredith react like the bad guys do on TV. She spun around and ran away.

I crashed through the front door. Meredith had turned into a good Sandhiller, no blinds on her windows, no locks on her doors. She was already beyond the breakfast bar heading for the back door. Her hand slipped on the knob, giving me time to close the gap between us. But she wrenched the door open and sped into the night.

I flew from the kitchen across the patio, crisscrossed with shadows from the moon winking through the pergola. She bounded along the side of the house, her feet crunching on the thick lawn and snow, making her way to her Volvo.

Even with my heavy boots versus her running shoes, I gained on her. I'd catch her before she had time to climb into the car. She slowed and reached for the door latch. Before she grabbed it, the door swung open, catching her in the chin and knocking her backward. She slipped on the loose gravel of the drive and fell, clutching her nose. "Ah!"

What the . . .

Enoch slid out of the driver's seat, aiming a satisfied smirk my way.

Meredith struggled on her back, both hands clutching her face, blood squeezing through her fingers. "My nose. Oh God, I think it's broken."

I knelt over her. "Let me look at it."

I pulled her forearm to help her sit up and peeled her hand away. "Yep." I placed her hand back so she could keep pressure on it. "Looks broken to me."

Enoch stood over us. "You're lucky. That will help you look tough in jail."

With both hands on her nose she shook her head, her whole upper body moving along for the ride. "No. You can't."

Again, I latched onto her forearm and hauled her to stand. "I can and so can you."

Enoch leaned in. "Whatever one sows, that will he also reap."

"I didn't. I swear. I didn't do it." Meredith broke down in desperate sobs.

I directed her toward the cruiser still parked on the road. “Let's go.” That sounded so damned tough. All *CSI*.

“What about my nose?” Sniffing, sobbing, and a nasal wail. “There's so much blood.”

“I've got a first aid kit in the car.” Not that you can do much for a broken nose. Maybe Daddy knew a good plastic surgeon who made house calls to the state pen. “And towels.”

Enoch followed us to the cruiser, his steps slow. His shoulders bent in, and he dropped his head. Probably worn to stubs from his big adventure.

After depositing Meredith into the back seat, I scrounged in the trunk for a towel. The ice pack chilled immediately when I cracked it. I opened the back door and handed the first aid to her.

Enoch eased into the front seat and huddled into himself.

Meredith snuffled and mewled, but other than that, we rode in silence for a while. My phone rang, and I fumbled to unzip my coat and reach into my pocket. Enoch cocked his head but didn't turn toward me.

I pulled onto the highway and answered. “Sheriff.”

Trey didn't hesitate. The concern in his voice annoying. “Where are you? What's going on?”

“Heading into the courthouse.”

Meredith reached for the Plexiglas between the front and back seats, smearing the surface with her bloody fingers. “No.”

Enoch didn't move.

Trey's angst surged through the phone. “Did you see Meredith? What happened?”

More to prove my point than anything, I gave a robotic response. “I apprehended the suspect and am en route to temporary restraint at the Grand County courthouse.”

Meredith banged on the gate. “You can't take me there.”

Enoch joined in the protest as if everyone got a vote. "You get that real officer here. Let him do what needs doing."

Driving and talking on the phone didn't leave me a hand with which to swat Enoch. With Trey talking and Meredith protesting, Enoch's opinion came at me, and I responded without thought. "Trey's busy booking Josh in Ogallala."

Enoch's noodled bones turned to steel, and he popped forward. "Joshua? My Joshua?"

Meredith didn't let up. "Take me there. Down to Ogallala. Take me to Josh."

I held the phone to my ear and spoke to everyone at once. "There is a holding cell at the courthouse. Meredith is going there until I can get Mr. Stevens settled someplace safe. After that, I'll transport the suspect to Ogallala."

Everyone rattled at once, and I didn't listen to any of them. I punched the phone off, stuffed it back in my pocket, and gripped the wheel, letting Meredith and Enoch tell me all the wonderful things they thought about my brains and personality. I think Meredith had a word or two about my looks, as well. We pulled up to the rear of the courthouse, and I shut off the engine.

"Please." Meredith's nose had stopped bleeding, but she still sounded like she needed a good antihistamine. She started to cry. "You don't understand. You can't take me in there."

I swiveled around. "Why not?"

Her eyes had already started to swell. "You c-c-can't."

I drew in a long breath. "Guess I can."

"No. Not here. Anywhere else." She smacked the Plexiglas. "Please."

"You don't get to choose your jail based on being close to your boyfriend."

Enoch jabbed at my arm with his bony finger. "Do a smart thing for once and take us to Ogallala where the real cops are."

I pointed my finger back at him. “Stay here. I’ll get Meredith locked in the cell and be right back.”

“I don’t need some girl telling me what to do. I’m going to Ogallala and get my boy whether you take me there or not.”

I stared at him for a moment. “Tell you what, come on in, and we’ll call Josh.”

Meredith sniffed and wiped her hand under her nose. “Good. That’s good. Josh will tell you I didn’t kill Chad.”

I turned to her. “You sit tight for a second.” I couldn’t leave her there long with the icy temperatures, especially since she wasn’t wearing a coat.

Enoch shuffled to the back door of the courthouse, and I hurried to unlock it and let us in. He lumbered up the stairs, using the handrail to pull his tired legs. He turned and started toward the sheriff’s office. I stopped at the commissioner’s room. “We can use the phone in there.” A more worldly guy might have questioned why I didn’t use my cell phone.

Enoch strode in front of me, his gait tipping from side to side, shoulders hunched. I directed him to the sturdy desk in the corner. Without questioning me, he sat in the hard chair.

He looked around at the old phone books and maps littering the desk. “Where’s the phone?”

With speed born from roping and tying calves, I whipped my cuffs from my pocket, grasped one of his thin wrists, and snapped the other end of the cuffs onto a desk drawer. Since this desk was one of those government-issue metal jobs with drawers that don’t slide all the way out, Enoch would be caught for a spell. He could eventually work his way out, but I’d have Meredith in the luxury accommodations of the cell by then.

Someone as ornery as Enoch would probably be fine on his own.

“You. You, you.” He sputtered and his face turned red. “This is not right. You should not. You are not.” He couldn’t find the words.

I'll bet he never lost them when Josh was young. There would be plenty of *stupids, sinfuls, wickeds,* and *ungratefuls* to toss at a son.

Why was I feeling sorry for Josh? Maybe his upbringing lacked the affection that surrounded me, but that didn't mean it was okay to steal and kill and sleep with your best friend's wife.

"I'll be back for you soon, and we'll get you someplace safe to spend the night."

"I will spend the night in my own home. After I get Joshua out of that jail where he doesn't belong."

I walked away, letting his wrath wrap around itself.

When I hurried out to the cruiser, tears streaked through the blood smeared on Meredith's face, but there didn't seem to be much more damage. I reached for her and she scooted away from me. "I can't go in there."

She was gnawing on my last niblet of patience. "Either tell me what all this hoopla is about, or you're going in."

She shook her head, eyes brimming with fear. "I can't."

I reached for her and after a tussle, got a grip on her wrist, and yanked her from the back seat.

She fought and bucked me all the way up the stairs and into the building, kicking at the door and causing a ruckus. Enoch's bellows only added to the whole crazy symphony.

Meredith pulled against me like an unbroken filly. She kicked and wriggled, nearly sending us tumbling down three stairs for every one we climbed. All the while her sobs growing more hysterical.

I wrestled with her in the hallway, dragging her past the commissioner's room where Enoch ranted and banged on the desk.

It took quite a juggle to unlock my office door while not allowing Meredith to escape. I finally pushed her into the cell, slamming the door closed and locking it.

"Don't! Please. You can't lock me up." Meredith couldn't fake the panic that had her weeping and screaming and gripping the bars of the cell.

I needed to unlock Enoch and get him someplace safe, but I couldn't be sure Meredith wouldn't find something to use as a weapon in the boxes or piles of supplies junking up the cell. "Why are you so scared to be here?"

Her bright eyes focused behind me, as if waiting for a monster to burst in. "I didn't kill Chad."

"But you helped Josh do it." I hated saying that. Couldn't really believe it even now.

Purple bags decorated her face under her eyes, and blood smeared her cheeks. "You don't understand. Josh was helping me. We were trying to find out who killed Chad."

I nodded with false sincerity. "I see. Someone else was stealing from the railroad and hiding big screen TVs in Josh's barn."

She shook her head. "We were hiding them. Hoping that Chad's partner would show himself. But he killed Chad." A sob rattled through her.

"Good one," I said.

Tears streaked down her face. "I know you don't believe me. But you know Josh. He'd never do something like that."

Damn. Her words pierced me like a poisoned arrow. "So why were you running away?"

Her lips looked pale without that lovely lipstick Mrs. Sterling insisted upon. "Because whoever killed Chad will kill me, too."

This was interesting. "Right. And who is that?"

She banged her palm on a bar. "If we knew that we'd have turned them in."

"Then how do you know they're after you?"

"Because I stole their stuff, and they're going to want it back."

"So you didn't steal from BNSF; you stole from your husband and his partner, who is the one who killed Chad. But you don't know who that partner is. You didn't tell me or the state trooper. Why?"

"Because we knew you wouldn't believe us. Like this. And you'd waste time arresting us, and the real killer would get away."

Damn if she didn't sound convincing. Probably too convincing. "So you and Josh are playing detective."

She wiped a hand under her nose and swiped the snot on her jeans. "Ask Clete Rasmussen. He was helping us. He knows."

"Why would Clete be helping you?"

She sobbed before she got herself under control. "His stepson. Ron and Chad were good friends, and Clete always felt Chad was the son he never had. He wanted to keep Chad from trouble. If we could figure out what was going on, we could get Chad to stop, and he wouldn't have to go to jail."

While I tried to process that, she hiccupped and sniffled. Through her swelling nose, she continued, "But when we confronted Chad he said he'd quit. His partner killed him, I know it. And now he'll come after me and Josh."

A bump drew my attention. Was Enoch tugging the desk? I needed to deal with him, but leaving Meredith alone didn't seem like a great idea. What if she was telling the truth and someone wanted to silence her?

The office door banged open and Meredith screamed. That was good because it covered my startled gasp.

Clete strode in with Enoch in tow. "What the hell is Enoch Stevens doing handcuffed to the commissioner's desk?"

I glared at the cuffs in Clete's hand then back at him. "How and why did you unlock him?"

Clete winced as if a burning gas bubble exploded in his gullet. "I used a paper clip. Cuffs aren't Fort Knox. I unlocked him because, for the love of God, it's Enoch Stevens, and I've known him all my life. He's no criminal."

Enoch's contempt for me billowed from him. "This is the kind of foolishness you get when women are in charge."

Clete's mouth popped open when he spotted Meredith in the cell. "Oh, good Lord." He hurried to the cell. "Are you okay?"

Meredith started to cry again. "You've got to help me. She thinks I killed Chad. Tell her. I loved Chad. I wouldn't."

He turned to me. "What have you done?"

"I'm arresting Meredith for the murder of Chad Mills and for theft from BNSF."

Clete blinked. "Meredith? That can't be right."

Enoch sniffed. "It sure as heck is right. Like Delilah. She somehow drug my boy into it, but I'll get to the bottom of that."

Clete digested the scene along with Enoch's words. "Meredith and Josh. Yes. It makes sense now." He dropped onto a metal folding chair in front of my desk. "I should have seen it before."

Meredith clutched the bars. "No. It's not like that. We came to you for help."

Clete massaged his forehead, as if whatever ailed his digestive system migrated north. "You wanted an ally. Someone to stand up for you and Josh. But now I see how you set this up from the beginning."

Enoch twitched his head toward Meredith. "Joshua is not involved with that Jezebel. I may not know everything, but I know that much."

Meredith implored Clete, "I loved Chad. You can't believe I'd hurt him."

Sorrow steeped into the wrinkles on Clete's face. "He deserved better."

Meredith slid to the floor. "You have to believe me."

Clete stood with arms akimbo and studied her, amid the boxes and crap strewn around the cell. "You can't hold her in there."

I figured out a temporary place for Enoch. "She only has to stay here long enough for me to settle Enoch at Louise's house."

Enoch gave me the brick wall stare. "I don't need a babysitter, especially that beefy woman."

I tossed Enoch back the same expression. "You can't stay at your ranch alone, and there's no telling when Josh will be back. You'll stay with Louise until I get back from Ogallala. After that, we'll figure something else."

Clete threw a chin in Meredith's direction. "What about her?"

Meredith watched me. She all but begged me not to leave her alone in the cell, an easy target for the alleged bad guy.

I turned to Clete. "Can you stay here for just a few minutes and watch her?"

Clete's lips clamped down so tight they disappeared. Even so, he managed to mumble, "Ted never needed me to do sheriff work for him."

I didn't recall Ted ever facing this kind of situation. "Come on, Enoch." I put a hand on his shoulder and ushered him into the hall.

He jerked away from my touch.

Dim light cast the basement stairs in deep shadow as we clumped down and to the back door. For the first time in a few days, I didn't gasp at the cold. Maybe that warm front really would make an appearance. I held out about as much hope for that as I did for a peaceful Fox family gathering.

Enoch lost his starch as we trudged to the car, and he slid into the passenger side without a word. Louise and Norm lived three miles west of town, one mile down an oil strip, and a half mile more on gravel behind a hill. Of all my brothers and sisters, they were the closest to town, not counting Jeremy, who bounced from place to place and on any given night might be occupying someone's bed in town.

Enoch didn't talk on the drive out, something I appreciated since my thoughts whirled like tumbleweeds in a tornado. As we turned off the oil onto the gravel road, he flipped his face toward me and scowled. "You youngsters. The good Lord has plans, but young ones rebel and turn sour. Sometimes they come back to their raisin' but not always. Take that woman back there. Pretty as a picture. They think I don't remember when she belonged to Joshua, but I do. Then she up and left him for the Mills boy."

This talkative turn was a whole new side to Enoch. "Chad Mills. He was never any good. When they were young that Mills boy and the Saunders kid tried to get Joshua in trouble. 'Course that Mills boy had no upbringing. His folks didn't hold to any church, and that's the downfall with the whole clan."

I murmured something that might have sounded commiserating.

He snapped his attention to me. "You Foxes are lacking there, too. It would have been good for you, all those children running wild. Parents that don't train their children up in the ways of the Lord end up with heartache."

The biggest heartache Mom and Dad had to weather didn't come from poorly raised kids but from a kamikaze cancer aimed at Glenda's stomach.

Enoch seemed to have run out of steam again. We trundled on the gravel when Enoch surprised me with another barrage.

"Not my Joshua, though. Proverbs 22:6 says it true: 'Train up a child in the way he should go; even when he is old he will not depart from it.' "

The words struck me like bullets in my chest. I'd heard that Scripture recently. Enoch mentioned the name Saunders and then he quoted Scripture. Why did they seem connected? The two pieces intersected in my mind.

Oh. No.

My phone rang at the same time I slammed on the brakes and

Enoch strained against his seat belt like a crash test dummy. I slapped the lever into reverse and executed a three-point turn before my phone rang a third time.

I punched it on, and Trey shouted at me while I brought the phone to my face. ". . . on my way. Don't do anything."

"What?" I yelled back, then realized adrenaline cranked up my voice.

Enoch braced himself with one hand on the dash and the other on the door. He stared out the windshield, helping me drive with the force of his will.

I needed all the help I could get as I buried the gas pedal and we fishtailed on the gravel.

Trey wasn't doing any better in the adrenaline department and kept hollering, "He got away. Took my car."

"Who? Josh?"

An engine roared. "I'm on my way. He'll be after Meredith so get her out of the courthouse. Bring her down here."

I suspected it was already too late for that. "Where are you?"

"I've got a patrol car and I'll be there in a half hour." If he drove more than a hundred miles an hour. Which he would do.

We reached the oil strip, and I pulled my foot off the gas but didn't brake. We slid, and I tossed the phone to use both hands. I didn't have time to explain to Trey, but Meredith was in a lot of trouble.

And I'd put her there.

29

Keeping my eyes on the road, both hands on the wheel, and the gas pedal down, we sliced through the night. I spoke in the most serious voice I could conjure.

"You've got to stay in the car. Don't try to help me out because you think I can't handle this. This is more serious than smashing Meredith's nose."

Still braced, Enoch didn't answer.

No vehicles were in sight on the highway so I didn't turn on my flashers. I used my stern Diane voice. "Do you understand?"

He kept still as a stone. "I understand Joshua is coming. I will not allow you to hurt him."

My voice rose too loud for the car. "I don't want to hurt anyone! But if you interfere, it makes everything more difficult."

Silence.

"Damn it, Enoch! Don't make me cuff you again." I needed his agreement because I didn't have any more cuffs on me and I didn't have time to argue.

Enoch drew in a shocked breath. I was sure he'd take exception to a woman cursing.

I raced up Main Street and slid into the slot behind the courthouse. I was too late.

But I had to know for sure. I sprinted for the door, fumbled with the key, and took the stairs two at a time. I dashed to my office. I crashed through the door and lurched across the room to yank on the heavy metal door to the cell.

I'd braced myself for blood. A body ripped up, the stench of death. I slumped against the concrete wall and stared at the empty cell.

Five seconds for relief and a plan. Out of the office, down the stairs, I threw myself into the cruiser.

Thankfully, Enoch hadn't jumped the fence. "They'll go to the ranch."

"Who?"

He put the stink of a cesspool in his voice. "That girl and Clete Rasmussen."

I careened back onto the highway, heading to Meredith's place. "Why do you think that?"

"You want to be sheriff but can't put two thoughts together."

I had put it together, just not soon enough. Clete's stepson, Ron. College buddies with Chad and Josh, probably Meredith. Ron Saunders. As in *Saunders v. BNSF.*

Scenarios played out in my mind involving Meredith, Josh, Chad, and Clete. Clete and Ron had an operation going on with Chad. Josh or Meredith discovered Chad was involved and went to Clete. Scared Chad would finger him, Clete killed Chad and pinned it on Josh.

Or Josh and Meredith were in the operation with Ron. When Chad ferreted out the truth, Josh killed him to shut him up. Now Clete learned about the thefts and wanted to hurt Meredith for getting his stepson in trouble.

What tipped me more to the first scenario was my suspicion that Clete was taking Meredith to the ranch to find the TVs she stole from him. Then there was the black ladder Newt and Earl had lashed to their Monte Carlo. They said they got it from Clete's dump. Whether Clete murdered Chad or not, he couldn't mean anything but trouble for Meredith.

I jerked the car from the highway and sped down County Road 67. My tires squealed when I yanked the car onto the gravel road. I radioed to Ogallala since I couldn't take the time to find my phone. Her Volvo was parked in the ranch yard so we streaked past Meredith's house. Right before the last curve to Josh's ranch, I slid to a stop and cut the lights. "I'm going to sneak up on them. At least I'll have surprise on my side."

Enoch put his hand on the door, ready to push it open. "You're going to get yourself killed."

That might be true, but I still had to try. "You stay here."

I didn't wait to see what he'd do. Even if he refused to wait, it'd take him some time to hobble to the house. Maybe by then Josh would be here, and he'd take care of Enoch.

I'd need to do something about Josh, too, but I had to deal with the devil at hand first.

The moon hovered above, casting its blue glow over the winter prairie. Slight wind didn't mask the crunch of my boots on the dirt road as I trotted around the bend, my gun in the holster feeling like a sandbag of dread. In a few minutes I slowed, the house in sight. My breath puffed in moist clouds, and sweat cooled on my face. I pulled my gun as I hurried toward the kitchen door.

Clete's rage vibrated through the walls. I crept up the steps and inched to the window, staying low, keeping my breath as shallow as possible. I raised my face to the glass and peered through the ruffled curtains.

Meredith sat in a kitchen chair pulled from the table. Her arms wrenched back, probably tied. Her legs were lashed to the chair. I couldn't be sure, but I thought a few more bruises colored her face. She wheezed through her sobs.

"Tell me what you know." The normal discomfort and annoyance rumbling through Clete had magnified a hundred times.

Meredith squeaked, "I don't know anything."

Clete whacked the back of Meredith's head and her neck snapped forward and bounced back. She cried out.

I closed my hand on the cold doorknob, my other hand gripping my Smith and Wesson.

Clete paced in front of her. "You and Josh. You couldn't leave it alone, could you?"

He pulled his hand back, ready to let it fly at her again. I executed a Kate Beckett move and burst into the room. "Freeze!"

I don't know if I thought it would do any good to act like a cop on a Monday night TV series, and if Clete would really give up that easily. But I was surprised he reacted as quickly as he did.

A gun appeared in his hand. From his back pocket? I hadn't seen it earlier. He raised it and fired three shots. Bam, bam, bam.

Meredith screamed. And screamed some more.

I dove and rolled, improbably imitating a ninja. I popped back to my feet and brought my arm up to aim, but in the small kitchen Clete loomed in front of me. He might be old but his mighty frame wasn't frail. He slammed a massive hand on my gun and snatched it from me before I could bring myself to pull the trigger. The first rule of law enforcement: Don't draw your gun unless you intend to use it. But I'd hesitated because it was Clete. The county commissioner since before I even knew there was a Grand County. With his self-importance and booming voice, the butt of so many Fox family jokes.

My hesitation had probably doomed me and Meredith.

But I wasn't the only one with a slow trigger finger. Clete's pained expression showed a moment of indecision as he shoved my gun into his belt. And in that split second, the sudden flash of red and blue lights flared across the window over the sink.

He tensed and raised his gun hand, the barrel pointed at my chest. The roar of Trey's engine grew. Clete's eyes narrowed and his jaw clenched. He was bracing to send a bullet into my heart, to rip the flesh and stop its beating. Meredith kept screaming.

Trey must have flown to get here so quickly. But his arrival only fueled Clete's determination to shoot.

I held Clete's gaze, not necessarily daring him to fire but not backing down from him. If he was going to kill me, he'd have to look me in the eye while he pulled the trigger. Small justice for someone who'd murdered before, but the only hand I had left to play.

We both held our breath in that instant that seemed like a lifetime. And then the window above the sink shattered. The explosion ripped through the kitchen, and Clete flung himself to the floor. Plaster rattled on the linoleum, and a bullet hole sheared through the wall just inches above where Clete's head had been. It couldn't have been Trey. His car was still roaring toward the house.

Josh. Or Enoch. Neither one made me feel any better. Not only was Meredith sitting in the open with bullets flying; an old man and a potential murderer ran around in the dark. At least one of them armed.

Another shot zinged through the window, breaking more glass and putting another gaping hole in the plaster. I must have hit the floor, though I don't recall doing so, and was surprised to find myself with my hands covering my head.

Meredith's hysterics ratcheted up a few levels. Part of me wanted to join in, just scream my head off until it all went away.

Clete commando-crawled out the kitchen into the living room, probably making for the front door. I imitated the crawl and took off after him, keeping my head low. With his long legs and powerful build he lengthened the distance between us and made it to the front door well before me.

The moment he opened the front door, a shot ricocheted off the doorjamb with a burst of splinters. Clete jumped to his feet and sprinted out the door while the shooter cocked the rifle for another round. His heavy footsteps thudded across the porch while I lunged toward the door. I hit the ground just shy of the doorway and wondered about the shooter and whether I could avoid death tonight. Mine, certainly, but everyone else's, too. I didn't have a gun but I was determined to go after Clete to keep tabs on him.

Trey's car skidded to a halt, the lights berserk in red and blue. Meredith's screams tapered off to sobs. Her chair scooted and thumped.

"Get down!" I shouted, still on the living room floor. The chair kept thudding.

"Freeze!" Trey's voice sounded sure and strong. But ineffective, as another blast came from the rifle. This time, not in my direction.

I jumped to my feet and ran out the door. Clete could be anywhere by now, but I'd heard him take off to the west, and I headed that way. I jettisoned from the porch and didn't even land before strong arms circled me and I collided with a brick wall. I landed on the frozen ground with an *ooof,* sucking freezing air down my throat and coughing it back out.

Trey rolled off me, grabbed me by the shoulders and scanned me up and down in the blue moonlight, broken by the garish disco of his light bar. "Are you okay?"

I shoved him away and scrambled to my feet.

Trey grabbed my arm and threw me back to the ground. "Stay down."

I wrenched my arm free. "Clete is getting away."

"What about Meredith?" Trey asked, still looking me over for injuries.

I crouched on the balls of my feet, ready to spring after Clete. "She's in the kitchen. Tied up."

"Josh is out here. My stolen car is parked by yours."

I thought as much. Fueled by adrenaline, I panted. "I think Enoch is the shooter. He's probably confused. We can't trust him to know who or why he's shooting."

Trey looked into the darkness for a second. "Go back and protect Meredith."

"I'm going after Clete." I readied for a sprint toward the barn. "Josh won't hurt Meredith."

"You aren't trained for this kind of situation. Please. Go back inside, protect the victim."

He was sending me out of harm's way, protecting me like some macho asshole. I wanted to fight, but he was right. One of us had to take care of Meredith, though I'm not sure I thought of her as a victim. Trey had more experience, plain and simple. Fighting him wouldn't make me a feminist standing up for women's rights; it would make me a rookie jerk ready to prove myself and hinder the situation.

I switched course and bounded for the house. Another gunshot decimated the top porch step. If Enoch was the shooter, he'd definitely forgotten I wasn't the enemy. I blessed his shaky hands that lessened the sure aim of his younger days.

I dove through the front door and skittered through the living room into the kitchen. Meredith still sat upright, tears streaking through the dried and smeared blood on her face. She screamed again when she saw me.

"Stop it," I commanded. Crouched, I grabbed the back of the

chair and wedged my foot against a leg and tugged. She toppled over and screamed again.

This time I grabbed her chin. "Be quiet."

She whimpered and I worked on the knots at her hands. The rope was soft, probably an old piggin' string. Clete had trussed her like a cowboy would a calf at a rodeo, and her struggling had tightened the hold. I worked at the knot to haunting silence outside.

Maybe Enoch kept a rifle in the barn, a leftover from his survivalist stash. Assuming Enoch had the gun, and that only one guy out there was shooting, that left Trey, Clete, and Josh in the darkness. Who was stalking whom?

Was Josh out to kill Clete before Clete could turn him in? Was Josh on his way into the kitchen to end Meredith and me? Was Clete circling back to do the same? Was Trey after Clete or Josh?

It'd be nice to have my Smith and Wesson. I freed Meredith's hands, and she lay on her side, rubbing her wrists. "Untie your feet." Obviously she needed survival tips.

Reaching up and groping along the counter, I found the knife block. It didn't take a lot of thought to grab the sturdiest handle. I hoped Enoch and Josh kept their kitchen knives sharp.

I realized I hadn't heard any shots for several minutes. Meredith huddled in a corner under the sink. Her sobs might camouflage the sound of someone sneaking through the living room. I regretted not slamming the front door behind me.

I scooted to her and put my head close. She shrank from me, as if I intended to use the knife on her. I put my finger to my lips and breathed a *shhhh*.

She hiccupped and brought the volume down to a whimper every now and then. She shivered, her arms wrapped tightly around herself. In shirt sleeves, with the window shot out and front door wide, she must be freezing. I had enough adrenaline zipping through my veins I was in no danger of hypothermia. I unzipped my coat and shrugged out of it. I dropped it on her. She didn't move, and again I tempered my irritation at her stupidity.

"Put it on." She was probably in shock. She wasn't used to gunfights, kidnapping, having her life threatened. But then, neither was I.

30

I eased up and strained to see through the shattered pane. The moon didn't give off much light, and even that bloomed in and out with clouds overhead. A movement near the barn caught my focus. Definitely a man, he crouched and ran along the side of the building.

Meredith tucked herself into the corner of the kitchen and whimpered.

The wind had picked up and whistled through the bare trees. Another man waited in the shadows at the front of the barn. The two would collide. The waiting figure had the advantage. He'd know the other was approaching. I couldn't identify him. Should I shout a warning?

In the second it took to decide, footsteps dashed across the living room. I swung around, jumped in front of Meredith, who shrank even farther into the corner. I crouched and held the knife in front of me, ready to attack.

Josh's lanky figure shot into the kitchen, his head sweeping back and forth, trying to see in the shadows cast by weak moonlight. He gave an anguished cry, "Meredith!"

She lunged forward on her hands and knees, knocking into me. "Josh!"

Now everyone had a name. I grasped the knife. "Back away."

I must have sounded menacing because he froze. He held his hands up. "Wait. I'm not going to hurt her."

"It's not Meredith I'm worried about. Why would you hurt your girlfriend?"

He lowered his hands, his face twisted in confusion. "Is that what you think? That we're having an affair?"

"I think maybe you're together, and you killed Chad because he found out you're robbing freight cars."

He nearly shouted in frustration. "How do you explain Clete?"

"He's your partner. You needed him to set up the trains. He knew what each car carried and found a reason to set them out on the siding. But you and Meredith got greedy and took his share of the loot."

Josh actually smiled. "Loot?"

I felt ridiculous holding the knife in front of me. I didn't see a gun, but Josh probably had one ready.

Josh grew serious. "Dad is out there with his gun, terrified. You got Deputy Dawg on the hunt, and that in itself is dangerous. Then you got Clete, who's desperate. You're the only sane one in the bunch. You need to quit messing around in here and get this situation under control."

"And leave you and Meredith to escape?"

"We're not going anywhere. Would you get it through your head I'm not with Meredith? We didn't kill Chad."

"Then why do you have the stolen TVs? Why is Meredith running away?"

"We don't have time for storytelling."

A cloud skittered away from the moon, and it shone through the open window.

"Once upon a time." I stared at him.

His face outlined by the moon, he snarled, "It was Chad. He got himself involved in this thing. At first Meredith liked the expensive art and that Volvo. But he wouldn't tell her where he got the money."

Meredith scooted away from the corner and rolled to her hands and knees to crawl toward Josh.

He squatted down and pulled her to him. She trembled violently enough I saw it from where I crouched. Josh put his arms around her and kept his attention on me. "She asked me to help her. We figured out about the stealing but not who his partners were."

Meredith pulled her head up and in a quavering voice said, "Chad did it to make me happy. He thought I wanted all that expensive stuff. But not like that."

"Why didn't you tell me?"

"At first, I didn't trust you," Josh said.

"But you trusted Clete?" I couldn't hide the incredulous tone of my voice.

He closed his eyes and rubbed his forehead as if a great pain jabbed his brain. "That was a mistake."

Meredith managed to choke out words between sobs. "That was me. I thought Clete cared about Chad and he'd h-h-help us."

Josh patted Meredith's back. "I still don't trust Deputy Dawg. But then, we were getting close and I . . ."

I had no reason to believe him. But I did. "You what?"

He wouldn't look me in the eye. "I didn't want to put you in danger."

I let loose and yelled, "Damn it to hell!"

A crack of a rifle and a whizz of a bullet too close to my cheek sent me diving. I slid into Josh, who flattened himself partially on top of Meredith.

Shit, shit, shit. I was honest to God being shot at. Every nerve sizzled and I wanted to dive into a hole.

Meredith started screaming again—just what I didn't need. Josh patted her and soothed, "It's okay."

"Is that your father?" As if it was all Josh's fault.

He shook his head. "It was earlier but this isn't Dad's 12 gauge."

"Clete," I said.

"How do you know it's not Deputy Dawg? He's dumb enough to shoot at whatever moves."

I glared at him. "It came from the direction of the barn."

Something crashed on the steps of the back porch, and Trey yelled, "Kate."

Damn it. I hollered, "Get down."

The doorknob rattled. "I saw Clete shoot in here. Are you okay?" He'd called me stupid, but risking himself to check on me trumped every dumb thing I'd ever done.

The rifle cracked again and Trey yelped, "Ah!" The door trembled as if he fell against it.

I sprang up, keeping my head down and scuttled to the door. I reached for the knob and pulled it open. "What the hell are you thinking?"

Trey fell into the kitchen with a grunt of pain. He panted and lay back, and in a whisper said, "Kate. Thank God you're okay."

"Dumbass." If I could punch him or Josh or any other damned man who thought he needed to protect me, I would have. In the nose, to hear the cartilage crunch and see the blood spurt. I had half a mind to let Trey bleed out.

Josh crawled to me and tugged Trey into the kitchen, and I

slammed the door. I slid back and bent over Trey. Meredith curled into a ball in the middle of the kitchen and resorted to hysterics.

Trey groaned and clutched his knee to his chest. I peeled his hands away. "Where are you hit?"

He licked his lips and whispered, "You're not hurt? Stay down. I called for backup."

Backup meant Milo, fifty miles away, or the state troopers from North Platte or Broken Butte. We couldn't hole up against Clete that long.

I found the source of Trey's bleeding. The bullet hit a fleshy part of his left calf. I surged across the kitchen and whipped a kitchen towel from the handle of the stove. Meredith lay in a fetal position in the middle of the kitchen floor, her hands over her head, gurbling and sobbing. Josh eased up to look out the shattered glass of the kitchen door.

I wound the towel around Trey's calf. "Josh. I need you to hold pressure here."

He kept his focus out the window. "I think Clete is going into the barn. There's an old pickup in there."

"Does it run?"

Josh nodded. "Probably has quarter tank of gas. He can damned sure get down the road."

"Where's Enoch?"

Trey moaned. "The old man."

Josh flung himself to the ground. "What?"

Trey winced. "He's down."

Josh's words were strangled. "Did you shoot him?"

Trey shook his head, his forehead wrinkled in pain. "No. He collapsed by the windmill."

Josh started for the door.

"Stop," I ordered. "Stay here. Meredith will freak out if you leave, and I need you to put pressure on this."

Meredith forced herself to sit. "Josh? Josh. Don't leave me. Please. Please." She scurried across the floor and wrapped her arms around his legs. "No. Don't go."

I had to agree with her sister, Emily. Meredith had a knack for drama.

Josh knelt down and pried her free.

I grabbed Trey's gun from his hand. "I've got this." Done talking, I ran in a crouch across the living room and out the front door. I continued across the front porch and tumbled down the stairs. No shots.

Clete was in the barn. Clouds now shrouded the moon, sinking the prairie in darkness. I ran from the house across the open ranch yard and sprinted along the side to the back of the barn. I hopped the wood fence and landed on the frozen sand of the corral, running for the windmill before I hit the ground. In the darkness, Enoch looked like an unstuffed scarecrow. Even without bright moonlight, his face looked pale as flour. I leaned close and detected a hint of breath. The heartbeat in his throat jittered.

I shoved the gun in my holster and gathered him in a fireman's carry, his feeble protests not slowing me. "Shh. Enoch. You need to be quiet," I whispered. I thought about taking him back to the house, but we'd be an open target. Our best shot was the barn. I could hide Enoch in a stall and stop Clete from escaping. If I were Wonder Woman. Or really lucky.

On a normal day, flinging the extra 120 pounds over my shoulders might have seemed difficult. Tonight, he felt like little more than a sack of potatoes, and I humped to the barn door at the back. The metal latch froze my hand when I eased the door open.

Luck played fast and loose with us, and the clouds cleared the moon, flashing a slit of light into the black interior. I managed to get us inside and kick the door closed. The wind died out, and the only sound was my heavy breathing.

A shot exploded and wood splintered on the door behind us.

Enoch and I hit the dirt of the barn alley in a puff of dust. The door of a stall was open an inch. I jumped up. The combination of near-total darkness, Clete's probable panic, and maybe poor aim evened out the bad trick the moon had played by lighting us up.

Huffing and scruffing along the hay-strewn floor, I managed to drag Enoch. I pushed the stall door open and yanked Enoch inside and piled hay on top of him. Maybe the insulation of the barn and straw would keep him from freezing to death. It was all I could do for him until I dealt with the shooter. Dust and hay scratched my nose, smelling musty and green.

"Clete," I called out. He didn't answer, but straw stirred so I knew he was moving.

"Backup is on the way."

"Liar," he hollered at me, and I placed him close to the front of the barn.

I pulled Trey's gun and eased from the stall, slowing my breathing and not making a sound. A gust of wind rattled against the barn walls, and Enoch let out a slight moan. I strained to hear Clete, but there was only silence. Where was he? "If you give up now, it will be better for you."

Pop. Zwing. Thunk. A bullet lodged somewhere in the barn wall behind me. My heart clogged my throat, and I clenched my teeth to keep from screaming.

He'd given up the rifle for my Smith and Wesson. "Let me go. Don't make me kill you." His craggy voice had an edge of fear.

I stared into darkness as thick as a stack of black cats. "That's not going to happen. Even if you get away, we're going to catch you."

He laughed, the sound of the last clutch at hope. "I know these hills. I can hide."

He was moving closer to the stall where Enoch lay. I backtracked to stay between them. "I know the hills better. I'll find you."

Pop. Hay ruffled and whispered. My senses shouted, and I fought to keep from turning tail.

He wasn't aiming so much as guessing, but that might kill me just as true. "It's your son, isn't it?"

"Stepson!" He sounded like Meredith with his high-pitched wail. "He's not my blood."

"But you raised him. You taught him right from wrong." I lunged, then tucked and rolled.

He didn't shoot again. "If I didn't help him, my wife said she'd leave. She'd take half my retirement."

I tried to lead him away from Enoch by tossing a shovel across the alley.

Clete was willing to kill for a $4,000-a-month pension? I couldn't understand that. "You've paved the way for him all his life."

Clete seemed to be circling, maybe trying to get a bead on me. "Not me. His mother babied him."

"But Chad, he was the son you never had, huh?" I took a few quick steps to the right as silently as possible.

Clete wasn't masking his movements. "Chad had something on the ball. He was smart and didn't mind a little hard work."

"So you recruited him."

"No. Ron moved out to Needles because it was an easy job. Then he got involved in this gang. He tried to get Chad to move out there, but Chad figured out stealing would be easier here. And it was. They drew me into it, and for a while, we were in high cotton. But then Ron got caught."

I kept my silence and tried to close in on Clete.

Clete sounded teary. "I didn't want to kill Chad. I don't want to kill anyone. But he was going to quit. How long would it take Josh and Meredith to convince Chad to turn us in?"

I had to be within a couple of yards from Clete. I calculated whether I should jump at him and take him down or shoot. The academy told us our goal is to stop the threat. Could I do that without killing Clete?

Clete's heavy breathing moved toward the pickup.

I crept a few steps.

Clete's voice sounded farther toward the front of the barn than where I thought the pickup was parked. "Leave it alone, Katie. No one expects you to solve a murder."

I tiptoed forward, frustrated at my slow progress but needing to stay silent.

I shouldn't have bothered. I expected Clete to fling open the pickup door, throw himself inside, crank the engine and barrel through the barn door, giving me ample time to shoot the tires, or in the worst case, shoot Clete. He had other ideas.

The creak of the back barn door made me jerk my head around. I changed directions and lunged after Clete. I stumbled in the hay and whacked my elbow on the pickup, but lurched through the darkness toward the sliver of light left by the open door.

By the time I flew into the barnyard, Clete was halfway to Trey's cruiser. I sped after him then pulled up short and spun around. Enoch might be freezing in the barn. I couldn't chase Clete and leave Enoch to die.

I sprinted back, burst into the silent barn, and flung myself into the stall.

"Enoch!" I felt in the hay until my hand hit against his still form. A thin moan escaped from him when I hefted him to a fireman's carry. "You're alive. Good. That's good." I breathed hard and uttered the words to give us both courage.

Back out the door, moving much more slowly than previously, I murmured to Enoch, "Gonna get you some help. Josh's here."

The door to Trey's cruiser gaped, and the car light reflected on emptiness. I prayed Clete had fled and wasn't aiming his gun on us now. Enoch might be little more than porous bones, but I struggled under his awkward weight. My boots thudded like a rockslide up the step and I hurled us into the kitchen.

Meredith screamed, of course. Josh knelt on the floor next to Trey, and both of them stared at me when I stumbled in. Josh jumped to his feet and grabbed hold of Enoch before I cleared the threshold.

"Dad!" Josh held the old man.

"Get him in there." I pointed to the living room. I yelled at Meredith, "Gather blankets." I ran after Josh. "Backup is on the way and they'll have an ambulance. For now, try to warm him up."

Meredith still huddled in the corner of the kitchen. "Now!" I grabbed her arm and jerked her to her feet. "Clete is on the run. You're safe."

Trey winced in pain and spoke around clenched teeth. "Are you okay?"

Instead of shouting at him to shut up, I bent over. "Give me your keys."

He hesitated and I didn't wait. "Keys! Clete is probably going to find my car down the road, and I left my keys in it."

Trey still didn't reach into any pockets. "Let him go. Wait for backup."

I threw myself to my knees and thrust a hand in his jacket pocket. He struggled, but I had the advantage of not being wounded. When that search came up empty I dove my hand into his other pocket. Bingo.

With a pasty face and a quarter his normal strength and fight, he said, "Don't go. Let the troopers—"

I was already out the door, leaving my words to fall on his head. "It's my job."

31

I took off for Trey's cruiser. I didn't have a coat, gloves, or a cap. It had started snowing, and the wind whipped shards of snow through the air, but the blood pulsing through my veins kept me plenty warm. My hands automatically did what they were supposed to, shutting the door, inserting the key, cranking the engine, backing out, and taking off down the gravel road.

I rounded the corner, not gratified I'd been right that Clete would take my car. It was gone, but Trey's car, the one Josh stole, sat in the dark. Without thinking about the action, I grabbed the radio and keyed the mic. Just before I spoke I threw it aside like it was an angry rattler. Clete would be able to hear anything I said.

I took a hand off of the wheel to search my pocket for my phone. No surprise it wasn't there; probably lying in any number of places on the Stevenses' ranch. I knew backup was on the way, just not how far away.

I headed east, toward Meredith's house and County Road 67. I figured Clete would make a run for the paved road and race away as fast as possible. I scanned the road in front of my headlights but didn't see any tracks in the blowing snow that had barely begun to stick to the road. Nearly to the curve, I glanced in the rearview mirror. Crap. I caught the flash of a brake light. I'd guessed wrong. Clete had taken the gravel road to the west.

The frenzied blue and red lights of Trey's borrowed patrol car beat into the night. Clete thought I was going in the wrong direction. I doused the flashers, headlights included, and jerked the wheel to the right, flying off the road and bouncing along the pasture in my panicked U-turn. I pulled back on the gravel and buried the gas pedal. I had to catch Clete. The backup trooper didn't know what to look for. He would be on his way to Stevens Ranch, via County Road 67. He wouldn't know Clete was traveling in the opposite direction.

I slid on the gravel but kept my grip on the wheel, steering out of the waggle and speeding down the middle of the road, bouncing with the uneven surface. I caught another glimpse of taillights, closer this time. Clete couldn't know I trailed him, and he tapped his brakes. Then he was gone again, and all I had was the faint image of his tracks on the road.

In a few seconds I hit a series of washboards, and the wheel felt like a jackhammer. My fingers clamped down, and my arms clenched in an effort to keep it steady. The back wheels bounced in a staccato, and the rear of the car took off for the left. I pulled my foot from the gas, but refused to apply brakes. This must have been where Clete had slowed.

My brain galloped ahead and jittered with impatience as my body, trapped in the vibrating car, lagged behind. The road evened out, relatively, and I pushed the gas pedal with the weight of my whole body. I pulled Trey's gun from my holster and wedged it between my seat and the console, ready for me to grab if I got the opportunity.

I'd like to take matters into my own hands. I'd been shot at way too many times in one night. An old man had been left for dead. Chad six feet under. That felt like a good enough reason for me to end it here and now. But I couldn't let loose and execute Clete.

I'd still like to grab hold of that jerk and see some justice come his way.

I assumed Clete was heading for the north-south gravel road a mile west of County Road 67. Head north on that for about twenty-five miles, and you'll come across Shorty Cally's summer range, and another forty-five miles emptied you out onto Highway 20 in Choker County. Clete probably thought to head up that isolated road and detour into the hills. A body could hide out quite a while this time of year. Cally used that pasture only in midsummer. But if I kept Clete ignorant of me following him, I'd know where he hid.

I leaned into the windshield trying to make out the road without headlights. I could see only a few feet ahead of my grill, and the skiff of snow obscured the details of the road. If I came across a washout or some other hazard, I would have no time to react.

The engine roared in my ears, and all my focus pinned to the two tracks in front of me. I didn't know if I was closing the gap, but I might lose all my teeth from the bone-rattling jarring of the road. Anything with a smidge of wiggle room rattled and shook.

I should be coming to the intersection of the north-south road. I squinted, fighting to see into the darkness, but I was reduced to trusting in fate, something I hated. The road followed a series of rolling hills, and I felt like a sailor in a gathering storm, rising up, dropping down. On the next rise I thought I made out the intersection. I looked to the north and saw nothing. At the junction ahead, I was surprised to see Clete's tracks take to the south.

This was a whole new problem. If he hit the highway with my cruiser's powerful engine, we'd be in a high-speed chase that could endanger others. It's not like the county highway was as busy as the

D.C. Beltway at rush hour, but if even one car was out there, it would be dangerous.

I flipped on my headlights and flashers as I turned left onto the road and accelerated. I snatched the radio and keyed the mic. It didn't matter if Clete heard me now. I had to do everything I could to stop him. "In pursuit of suspect, heading south on the . . ." damn, what was this road officially called? "Cally's summer camp road."

Marybeth, the dispatcher, might have responded or not. I didn't even think about dropping the mic. It and everything else vanished from my mind as I clutched the wheel and raced toward my cruiser. I didn't expect Clete to pull over at the sight of my lights, raise his hands in the air, and surrender, but it would have helped keep my heart from catapulting from my ribs and lodging in the back of my throat if he did.

This gravel road was even worse than the last. I barely missed dropping a wheel into a crumbling hole that ate half of the left side. And just as I yanked the wheel to the right to avoid it, another washout opened in front of me. I zagged, then zigged, keeping my foot on the gas, gaining on Clete.

The highway couldn't be more than a quarter mile away, but I was closing in. Damn. I came up with only one option. The PIT maneuver. Sure, the conditions weren't right. At the academy, we had an open space of concrete, wide as the Safeway parking lot. Here, we had a gravel road with washouts and ditches on either side. But it was my best shot at stopping Clete before he hit the highway.

I'd match his speed, place the right front panel of my car an inch from Clete's left back panel. With slight pressure, I'd steer into his car and accelerate. If it worked as it was supposed to, his car would collapse in front of me and spin to my left.

If it worked.

Milo had said, "Trust your training."

With this goal in mind, I urged Trey's car faster, even if the gas pedal was already to the floor.

The night lit up with a bloody flashing of warning lights. "NO!" I screamed.

The arms of the BNSF railroad crossing sprang to life, all garish and threatening against the blackness. They began to lower, and the alarm bells jangled. The tracks curved around a tall hill to the west, so visibility was limited at this crossing until the last minute, when a train would shoot around the curve and roar across the road.

The arms flared and flashed. Screeching at us to stop for the train.

I hit my brakes. But Clete had another idea. His brake lights didn't so much as flicker. I guessed he gave my good ol' cruiser all she had and decided to take his chances with the train.

"No!" I shouted again, as if I could stop Clete.

I slammed my foot back onto the gas and the engine roared. My hope hinged on the PIT maneuver. I had to stop Clete from trapping me on one side of the train while he escaped. I was sure the patrol car had more umph than my cruiser.

The steering wheel and gas pedal became extensions of my will, and I focused on Clete's taillights. Closer, closer. I aimed my front bumper for the right edge of his car, hoping a slight tap would cause a skid, spin him around, and stop him from getting to the tracks.

The white-hot dagger of a spotlight burst through my windshield as the train rounded the curve. Too close. We were going to crash. I pulled my foot off the gas. Clete surged ahead of me.

Oh dear God, he was trying to outrun the train. Didn't he know there was no way he could make it?

The godforsaken engineer laid on the train whistle, but a hundred tons of racing steel couldn't stop. Couldn't slow down. He must have put the train into emergency, setting the brakes, because the wheels started a banshee shriek. Like a thousand fingernails on a chalkboard inside my head. I wanted to clap my hands over my ears.

Clete had to know he had no hope of beating the train.

I slammed my brakes, certain that I'd never be able to stop before I ran into the side of the roaring mass of steel. Sound crashed in my ears like ocean waves. My back wheels skidded to the right, and I steered that way, my eyes glued to the disaster playing out in front of me.

Clete didn't slow and the train could not. With my right foot grinding on the brakes and my back slammed into the seat, I braced myself. My countersteering caused me to spin in the opposite direction.

The dinging of the crossing arms and the shattering squeal of the train's brakes screamed along with the squad car's engine. Red lights blinked, and the headlight of the train flared.

Stop. Dear Lord, Clete, stop! I clenched my teeth, my hands, my whole body, willing Clete to stop. Train speeding. Clete racing. No. Oh, no.

He ended in a dead heat with the train.

First the crossing arms flew skyward, and then even the thunder of the train and the blare of the whistle couldn't mask the explosion when the speeding car hit a wall of steel. Fire, dirt, debris, and my screams. I fought my steering wheel, suddenly realizing I was heading for the same end as Clete.

The howling of the train sucked the ground up and down as the wheels raced over the crossing. The couplers clacked and pulled, chirping and squealing, hot steel sending up a smell of burning composite, a bitter electric odor. I was going to collide with the side and be crushed beneath a million tons, shredded like spaghetti. Every bit of me tensed. My eyes squeezed closed and then sprung open. Closer, closer.

I screamed and ducked as the train ripped the side mirror. My arm flung over my head wouldn't stop it from being blended into mush by the steel wheels.

I could reach out and touch it. The monster could rip my arm from my socket. I kept sliding, slower and slower, but too close. One more inch to death.

My car rocked and bounced and something shattered the passenger window. Glass flew and I flung myself into a fetal position, hands over my head. My eardrums felt shredded as the train's wheels dragged against the rails. I would be crushed under those wheels, mangled in the metal, ripped into strips.

The car stopped.

I tried to breathe as the crossing alarm kept dinging, the train roared on, sucking all the air from the car, and the road under my wheels bucked and dipped. Bucked and dipped. Clacking, clacking, each car raging on. *Clang, clang, clang, clang.*

After three decades the train started to slow, the wheels retreating down the tracks with a *tshk-tshk-tshk*. The red lights faded. The rocking of the pavement stopped, and even the bells of the crossing arms ceased. I opened my eyes and unclenched my jaw, daring myself to draw in a breath. Silence dropped, not even a 'yote to interrupt it.

With shaking arms, I pushed myself from the seat, pellets of glass tinkling around me. Cold air blew in from the broken window.

I hated that the moment I spotted the figure standing on the other side of the tracks, outlined by the headlights of his pickup, I burst into tears.

But by the time he'd navigated the tracks with his cane and made it to me, I was able to keep from falling into Ted's arms.

32

I sat behind the wheel of Elvis, letting the midday sun slather February cheer all up and down my face. When I opened the door, the dazzle would be diminished by the temperature hovering at zero, but for now, it felt practically tropical.

I tapped his wheel with an ungloved finger and spoke into my phone. "I already signed the contract. You three can join me or not."

Milo Ferguson sighed all the way through his county and into mine, and I smiled into the phone. "Kyle Red Owl might be qualified for deputy, but he doesn't have any experience."

"Until about a month ago, I was light on that count, too." The two clouds hovering over Stryker Lake in the china blue sky cast shadows on the ice, and I wondered again where my skates were hiding.

The springs of Milo's office chair squeaked through our connection. "Just 'cause the BNSF sent you a nice letter thanking you for your help, don't go gettin' above your raisin'. I'm still not comfortable with a girl in charge down there."

I laughed to let him know I didn't mind his obvious teasing. "I talked to Kyle and am dead certain he'll make a great deputy. I'm willing to give him a shot because . . ." I paused and thought about the unanswered messages on my phone. "I'm a young, sexy woman and I need to have one weekend a month off to pursue my happiness."

I wished I could see Milo blush, as he surely did. "Welp. That's understandable. Glad to hear you're," he cleared his throat, "moving on."

Yeah, he and my entire family. Changing the subject, "The new cruiser will be delivered next week." Guess I wouldn't need to worry about getting the pine deodorizer.

"Gonna remember to take the keys with you from now on?"

I let him get the upper hand just to be a good sport. "Talk to Kyle Red Owl. You'll like him even if he's Lakota."

He coughed. "Well now. You know. Hey. That's not the problem. I don't hold nothing against the Native Americans."

I signed off, pulled on my gloves, and climbed from Elvis. His tailgate stuck, but with some wrenching and a bit of cursing, it pulled free, and I reached for the biggest box. I maneuvered to the front walk, unlatched the dilapidated metal gate, and something on the front step caught my attention. Bright red with swirls of primary colors, the garish Asian-themed vase took shape. When I clambered up the three porch steps, I noticed the gash on the lip of the side next to the house. Balancing the box on my hip, I reached for a torn sheet of notebook paper taped to the vase.

With nearly illegible printing in pencil, the note read, "From Newt and Earl."

This had to be one of their treasures saved from someone's dump. The thoughtful housewarming gift almost made me tear up.

May hadn't given me any keys because there wasn't a lock, so I braced the box on my thigh and pushed open the door, letting myself into my very first home.

You'd think by the time a woman turns thirty-three she'd have acquired some furniture and cookware. I'd gone from living at home, on to college, then to joining Ted at Frog Creek, and back to my parents' house. Ted and I hadn't bought much because we'd never got around to it.

I cringed at the thought of Ted. He might be having even more trouble moving on than I was. That night, and probably every night before and since, he'd been tuned into his police scanner. Whether he'd raced to the scene to rescue me or to help out, he didn't say. Either way, I needed to claim my life and my livelihood.

I'd called Bill Hardy and with only slight regret, turned down the job. Then I'd called May and told her I'd buy the house.

She offered to let me move in before we had the paperwork started. Gotta love living in the Sandhills where a handshake, or even a phone call, is binding.

I set the box on the floor and pushed the door closed, turned around and, "What the . . . ?"

The tiny living room now contained a leather love seat and chair, with a cherrywood coffee table and a plush rocker. A pair of end tables completed the cozy room with just the right amount of comfort and casual. Stupefied, I tromped to the first bedroom. A desk, a filing cabinet, and a floor-to-ceiling bookshelf filled the small space, and I marveled at the luxury of my own office with room for my books.

The bedroom contained a platform bed with a bank of drawers underneath. Someone had added yellow and blue curtains, just right to highlight all the sunshine from the west-facing windows. If I'd have designed it myself, I couldn't have picked the furniture and accessories to better suit my personality. But, of course, I'd never have spent the time or money to create such a clever setting, where everything tied together and complemented everything else.

Only one person could have pulled this off. I took out my phone.

Baxter answered on the first ring, a hint of laughter in his greeting. "All settled in?"

I stared at the TV. A tasteful size attached to the wall, perfectly arranged for me to snuggle on the loveseat. "You know I can't accept this, right?"

He didn't skip a beat. "That's why I didn't ask beforehand. My assistant threw some things together, so you can replace it at your leisure. In the meantime, enjoy it until you can get something to suit your taste."

As easily as I could detect humor in his voice, my baloney meter was just as effective. No assistant could have picked this stuff out to fit me so well. I could fight Baxter on this, but to what end? It made my life more comfortable.

As I intended to do with the vet, Heath Scranton, I'd add another IOU to my list and figure out some way to make good on this kindness. I may not have known him a long time, but I knew he was one person who could out-stubborn me.

For now, I'd say thank you kindly to my friend, the rich guy. The superrich media mogul, tycoon guy. I must have stepped into a universe parallel to Grand County because this friendship was more than unlikely. "You got it all just right." The softness in my voice surprised me.

A moment of silence sealed our connection, then Baxter said with a brisk tone, "Not having much luck on Carly's lead."

I sank into my new rocker, feeling Carly slip further away. "She'll call me again. I'm not giving up."

His good cheer returned. "You're the only person I know who's more stubborn than me."

I grinned at that.

"So," he started down another trail, "you've got new digs, and you've proved you're a good sheriff."

Baxter's praise felt almost as fine as when Dad patted me on the back. Maybe my gut wasn't such a bad judge of character, after all.

Baxter's voice sounded light. "The next thing your brothers and sisters are going to start nagging you about is your personal life."

There were those two messages from Josh Stevens, four from Trey Ridnoir, and one from Heath Scranton on my voice mail.

And that troubling late-night call from Ted. He said he'd called to make sure I was okay after Clete's horrible death. But the silence told me he had more to say, and I hung up before he spit it out.

I put a smile into my voice. "I'll see what I can do to head off that nagging."

Did he hesitate? Naw, that was my imagination. "Good things are in store for you, Kate Fox. Just keep me in the loop."

"You've got it."

I hung up and surveyed my bungalow. Here I was with my few boxes, my sleeping bag and blow-up mattress, my entire divorce settlement sunk into a house.

Guess I'd let go of that root and jumped from the crumbling ledge. I sure as heck hoped there was a net.